## Hadley's Hellions

*Four friends united by power, privilege*
*and the daring pursuit of passion!*

From disreputable rogues at Oxford
to becoming masters of the political game,
Giles Hadley, David Tanner Smith,
Christopher Lattimar and Benedict Tawny
live by their own set of *unconventional* rules.

But as the struggle for power heats up, so, too,
do the lives of these daring friends. They face
unexpected challenges to their long-held beliefs
and rigid self-control when they meet
four gorgeous independent women
with defiant streaks of their own...

Read Giles Hadley's story in
*Forbidden Nights with the Viscount*

Read David Tanner Smith's story in
*Stolen Encounters with the Duchess*

Already available

Read Benedict Tawny's story in
*Convenient Proposal to the Lady*

Available now

And watch for the final Hadley's Hellions story,
coming soon!

## Author Note

For modern women, it's almost impossible to imagine the limited choices faced by women of the past. A well-born girl was expected to marry; ladies did not work, and unlike gentlemen, couldn't indulge in anything as vulgar as earning money. So what did you do if producing art was what you were born for? Lady Alyssa struggles to fit into a world that neither interests her nor appreciates her talent. It will take an uncommon man to see the brilliance in this rough-hewn gem.

It's also hard for a modern world with its acceptance of out-of-wedlock births to imagine the lifelong stigma carried by a Regency-era individual born outside of marriage. Though well-born bastards, if recognized by their noble fathers, often did lead prosperous lives, there must always have been this hunger to understand why, and a struggle to believe themselves equal to their peers. Although Ben Tawny knows what he's worked to achieve makes him exceptional, there are always mockers around to remind him he wasn't born a gentleman. When a quest to save a girl from his mother's fate lands him in a marriage of convenience, he must face all those demons—including a strong aversion to falling in love.

I hope you will enjoy Ben and Alyssa's journey to love and fulfillment.

# JULIA JUSTISS

---

# *Convenient Proposal to the Lady*

Recycling programs for this product may not exist in your area.

ISBN-13: 978-0-373-29921-8

Convenient Proposal to the Lady



This edition published by arrangement with Harlequin Books S.A.

For questions and comments about the quality of this book, please contact us at CustomerService@Harlequin.com.

**Printed in U.S.A.**

**Julia Justiss** wrote her first ideas for Nancy Drew stories in her third-grade notebook and has been writing ever since. After publishing poetry in college, she turned to novels. Her Regency historicals have won or placed in contests by the Romance Writers of America, *RT Book Reviews*, National Readers' Choice and Daphne du Maurier. She lives with her husband in Texas. For news and contests, visit juliajustiss.com.

**Books by Julia Justiss**

**Harlequin Historical**

***Hadley's Hellions***

*Forbidden Nights with the Viscount*
*Stolen Encounters with the Duchess*
*Convenient Proposal to the Lady*

***The Wellingfords***

*The Wedding Gamble*
*The Proper Wife*
*A Most Unconventional Match*
*One Candlelit Christmas*
"Christmas Wedding Wish"
*From Waif to Gentleman's Wife*
*Society's Most Disreputable Gentleman*

***Ransleigh Rogues***

*The Rake to Ruin Her*
*The Rake to Redeem Her*
*The Rake to Rescue Her*
*The Rake to Reveal Her*

***Silk & Scandal***

*The Smuggler and the Society Bride*

Visit the Author Profile page
at Harlequin.com for more titles.

To the Birding Brothertons of Daingerfield, Texas,
whose guide to local birds and enthusiasm
in sharing their expertise on all things avian
are the inspiration for my heroine, Alyssa.

# *Chapter One*

*The things one does to soothe one's conscience.*

With that rueful thought, Benedict Tawny led his horse stealthily along the grassy verge of the drive curving through a pretty wood to Dornton Manor, early-morning October sunlight just beginning to dapple the few leaves overhead. A gust of wind tugged loose his hat and he jumped to catch it.

If his fellow Hellions could see him now! he thought with a grin, jamming the cap back on his head. Not that he was the delight of his tailor, but in his worn jacket, serviceable breeches and scuffed boots, he hardly looked like a respectable Member of Parliament, one of the leaders of the Reform movement and a rising force in government. Surprising how easily he'd fallen back into the role of intelligence-gatherer he'd performed for the army in India.

All to safeguard the virtue of a female he'd never even met.

But with the Parliamentary session over until Grey could convene a new one later in the year and the other Hellions out of London, he had time on his hands.

He might as well use it to perform a good deed.

A flicker of light in the woods up ahead caught his eye. Through the slender tree trunks, he could just make out the figure of a young female. Shifting his position to get a better view, he saw that she was short, her dark hair thrust up under a sadly out-of-date straw bonnet—and that her entire attention was focused on the sketch pad balanced on her knee.

Though the gown was as outdated as the bonnet, the cut and cloth were of good quality—the garment too unfashionable a cast-off to tempt a lady's maid and too fine to be passed on to a housemaid—so she must be Quality. And only a lady of quality passionate about her art would be out sketching this early in the morning.

Petite, unfashionable, avid artist—the description fit to perfection the lady he sought. Delighted to have been handed the solution to the problem of how an unrelated male would find a way to speak alone with a gently bred virgin, Ben approached quietly, not wanting to alarm her.

But even as he reached the clearing where she sat on a felled log, she remained so absorbed in her drawing that she didn't seem to notice him. Finally, clearing his throat loudly, he said, 'Lady Alyssa Lambornne, I presume?'

Gasping, the maiden nearly dropped her sketchbook and the box containing her pastels did go flying. Ben jumped to nip them up before they fell to the forest floor. 'Sorry, I didn't mean to startle you,' he said.

Straightening, he reached out to hand back the box, met the gaze she'd focused on him—and froze. Shock zinged through him, as if he'd walked across the library carpet on a crisp winter day and touched the metal latch.

Her eyes were magnificent—large, fawn-brown, with an intelligence in their golden depths that drew him in and invited him to linger. There was a fierceness and intensity there, too. Not just in her eyes, he thought dazedly, but in the whole set of her body, as if she were poised to flee—or attack.

Indeed, in her drab gown, a wisp of dark hair escaping from under the shabby bonnet, the shawl slipping off her shoulders, she seemed almost…feral, as if she were as untamed as the woodland she sketched.

Something primal and passionate and powerfully female about her called to everything male in him. Desire thickened his tongue, thrummed in his blood, sent arousal rushing to every part of his body.

Drawn to capture those lips, he reached out for her, rattling the pastels in the box he'd been about to return.

That small noise, loud in the stillness, broke the spell. He shook his head, searching for his vanished wits.

*Pull yourself together, Tawny. This is not a passionate Diana, ready for a frolic in the woods, but a modest, virginal girl.*

No matter what his erratic senses were telling him.

The response that so unsettled him seemed to have suspended time, but it must have lasted only an instant, for Lady Alyssa was still studying him, frowning as she evidently struggled to place him.

It was not a *girl* who sat before him, but a woman, he realised as he returned her scrutiny, still fighting the lingering effects of that sensual firestorm. Her face a perfect oval, the cheeks and nose dotted with freckles that were probably the bane of a mama trying to make her fashionably pale, she had a pert little nose shadowing full rose-petal lips.

A 'little dab of a thing' she might be, being of shorter-than-average height, and her hair *was* an unremarkable brown, but that was the only part of the description he'd been given that seemed accurate.

*Drab...long on the shelf...a spinster past her last prayers?* He'd have rather called her a 'pocket Venus.' The unfashionable high-waisted gown emphasised an attractively full bosom and the worn fabric clung in all the right places to some very pleasing curves.

And how could any man meet that fiery gaze and not be swamped with the need to possess her?

Anger stirred anew that Denbry would sacrifice this lovely creature to achieve some petty revenge against her brother.

Since the lady had yet to speak—perhaps she *was* shy—Ben finally mastered himself enough to give her a pleasant smile. 'It being such a lovely day, I was walking my mount—' he gestured towards his horse '—when I saw a female in the woods. Thinking some lady might have got lost, I came to offer assistance. I see now that you were sketching and apologise for interrupting you.'

Leaning over to hand her the box of pastels, he caught a glimpse of the scene on her sketch pad. 'Your drawing is excellent, by the way,' he added in surprise, craning his head to study it. Every young woman sketched; this one was actually skilled. 'How cleverly you've caught the form of the bird, as if he were about to take flight.'

'Thank you,' she said at last. 'But you have the advantage, sir; you know who I am, while I still cannot place you. I am sure we are not acquainted, for had we been introduced, I would certainly have remembered you.' She scanned him again from head to toe, as if noting every detail. 'Are you Lord Fulton's secretary, perhaps?'

She *was* observant! She'd drawn just the conclusion he'd been aiming for when he donned this disguise: his cultivated tone of voice indicating he wasn't a farm worker or a labourer; his clothing well made, but too worn and unremarkable to proclaim him the sort of fashionable peer Lady Fulton would have invited to her house party.

'No.'

'But not a newly arriving guest, either. You're not dressed for it, nor do you carry any baggage. How did you know me, then?'

'I've been staying in the village, where the gossip is all about the assembly at Dornton Manor. One of the attendees, Lady Alyssa Lambornne, was described as petite, dark-haired and very fond of sketching.'

Looking wary now, she said, 'Were you asking about me, particularly, and if so, why? I know we've never met!'

'Let me rectify that. Lady Alyssa, may I present Mr Benedict Tawny, Member of Parliament for Launton.' He swept her a bow.

Her frown deepened. 'Excuse me for acting as witless as my father always claims me to be, but I'm afraid your parliamentary status doesn't enlighten me at all about your purpose for coming here. Are you to consult with Lord Fulton?'

'No, I'm not acquainted with either Lord or Lady Fulton. I came here to find you, Lady Alyssa, and am delighted to have encountered you where we could have a private chat, without my having to figure out how to steal you away.'

'You came here to have a private chat with *me*?' she echoed. 'I can't imagine why! Would you explain, please?'

'Certainly, and I don't wonder at your confusion. *We* have not met before, but I was at Oxford with your brother, Lord Harleton. And I'm afraid I have some rather distressing information to impart to you.'

The woman's puzzled expression cleared. 'Now I remember! You were one of the group Harleton called "Hadley's Hellions",' college mates who intended to go into politics and reform government. Although he usually called you the Chil—' She stopped suddenly, heat suffusing her face. 'A name I shall not repeat.'

*The Chilford Bastard.* Ben clenched his teeth against the automatic wave of anger the epithet evoked.

He knew his own experience made him far more sensitive than the rest of society about the disproportionate amount of shame and blame shouldered by a woman caught up in scandal—while the man's behaviour was passed over. But watching the way his mother, whose only sin had been believing the promise of marriage given her by the man she loved, had been treated after his father's family brought all their weight to bear to prevent their son wedding a woman they didn't find suitable, he couldn't help but be rubbed on the raw by a plan to target an innocent female.

Hence his presence here.

Most women of ruined character had no recourse but the streets, if their families rejected them. His mother had been lucky; though he'd hated his father for years for abandoning her for wealth and a title, the Viscount had made sure they had a place to live and enough to eat. Which hardly compensated for turning his mother into an outcast, and himself into a child who'd grown up taunted by the bully of the moment for being a bastard.

Pulling himself back to the present, he said, 'Thank you for not repeating the name—though I'm distressed your brother would use such language around his maiden sister.'

'If you know Harleton at all, you know he does whatever he feels like, whenever he feels like it, without regard for the wishes—or sensibilities—of anyone else.'

'I'm only too well aware of that,' he said with a grimace. Though he'd made no attempt to hide the fact that he'd been born out of wedlock, most of his Oxford classmates discreetly avoided the topic. Not so Lord Harleton, who'd never missed an opportunity to point him out as 'the Chilford Bastard'.

'So you are not one of his...particular friends?'

'Far from it. Without wishing to give offence, I must confess that, at Oxford and since, I have avoided your brother whenever possible.'

For some reason, that comment made her laugh. 'It seems we have at least one thing in common, then. But why have you discovered so much about me and why would you want to speak with me? Has something happened to Harleton?'

'It does involve your brother, but as far as I know, he is in good health. I'm afraid it's rather complicated.'

'If Harleton is involved, I'm sure it is. And probably disreputable, as well.' Setting down her sketchbook, she patted the log beside her. 'You'd better explain.'

'It's disreputable for certain,' he said as he seated himself rather further away than she'd indicated. Which was only prudent; their exchange of rational conversation might have muted the sensual attraction that had immobilised him upon first seeing her, but nothing save death could eliminate it entirely.

'As I said, I'm a Member of Parliament,' he began. 'Some fellow members and I often gather at a public house near the Houses of Parliament, the Quill and Gavel. Parliament being currently out of session, I was there alone about a week ago when another former Oxford acquaintance noticed me and pulled me into a group of gentlemen who were proposing a wager. Organised by the Earl of Denbry, who is no admirer of your brother.'

'Denbry!' she exclaimed. 'Yes, I've heard Harleton snarling about him. Apparently they've been trying to best each other at various dubious activities since their Oxford days. Was this some challenge, intended to discomfort my brother?'

'It was. But of a particularly venal sort. Your brother recently ran afoul of Denbry by overbidding him for a team of horses he wanted. And then, even worse, by stealing away the...loyalty and affection of a woman.'

'That opera dancer?' At Ben's raised eyebrows, she said, 'My brother's servants love to gossip about his horses, his women and his gambling, and my maid loves to repeat the stories to me. My brother outbid Denbry for her...affections?'

'Apparently. Which so infuriated Denbry that he designed a revenge he intended Harleton to remember for the rest of his life. Much as I hate to even speak of so despicable a wager to a lady, I felt you must be warned. What Denbry proposed was to have one of his group... seduce and abandon you.'

Her eyes widening in surprise, Lady Alyssa gasped—and then burst out laughing.

'What a faraddidle! Surely you can't expect me to believe so preposterous a tale. Was *that* the wager, to get me to believe your outrageous story, so I would go off into hysterics you could report back to my gloating brother?'

'I only wish it were. Preposterous it may be, to say nothing of venal and disgusting, but I assure you, Denbry's plan to seduce you is the absolute truth. The challenge was accepted by this group of men, who all chipped in a stake, the winner to receive it upon the… successful accomplishment of its terms.'

Her mirth fading, she studied him again with that unusual intensity, sending another wave of awareness through him. While he resisted it, she said, 'Unless you are the most convincing actor in the history of dramatic farce, I'm forced to consider that you might be telling the truth. So there really is a wager? In this game of besting one another, Denbry seeks to trump a stolen mistress with a ruined sister?'

'I'm afraid so.' Having voiced the despicable proposition, Ben felt sick—and ashamed. Denbry didn't just give aristocrats a bad name, he tarnished the whole male gender.

'But how could any of them believe they would be able to accomplish it? I'm not such a nodcock that I'd allow myself to be drawn into a compromising position by some sweet-talking gentleman!'

'Denbry somehow obtained a list of the country-house parties you were to attend, to which the competitors could wangle invitations. Imagining themselves to be men of great address with ladies, they intended to… persuade you to an elopement, carry you off to some inn, seduce and then abandon you.'

She raised a sceptical eyebrow. 'If they abandoned me, why couldn't I just quietly return home, with no one the wiser?'

'The seducer was to take your gown. If he were nowhere to be found when you were discovered, you'd not be able to accuse him later. Society always believes the worst of the female; you'd make yourself a laughingstock as well as a byword, if you should name him without proof.'

Anticipating her next question, Ben went on, 'In case you still managed somehow to keep the matter quiet, the perpetrator was to furnish the name of the inn, the landlord, the maidservants, the grooms in the stable, so Denbry might have a scurrilous broadside created, "Foiled Elopement with a Mysterious Gentleman". The more you attempted to deny it, the more it would be believed. Even if you revealed the seducer's name to your family, calling him out would only add more credence to the report. You'd be ruined, your family embarrassed, and in the game of chess between them, your brother's queen taken by Denbry's higher one.'

Her face going pale during this recital, Lady Alyssa remained silent for some time after he finished, as if contemplating all the sordid details. Until, alarm widening her eyes, she looked back at him.

'But...you told me you were *pulled into* the discussion. Not that you merely *overheard* it. So...*you* were invited to take part in this?'

As if suddenly recognising that she was alone in the woods with a man who could easily overpower her, she scooted away from him. Thrusting out her sketchbook, she held it up between them, as if that flimsy bit of paper and cardboard could protect her.

Ben rose and stepped back, giving her more space. 'I assure you, Lady Alyssa, you have nothing to fear from me! Your brother…took such great pleasure in taunting me at Oxford, the other men seemed to think I'd be willing to embrace any scheme, no matter how despicable, to revenge myself upon him. If my character were so deficient that I'd agreed to take part, why would I have come to *warn* you?'

'Perhaps you thought it a clever ploy?' she cried. 'If you were asked to participate, you must also be considered a "man of great address with the ladies"!' Perhaps you thought your news would alarm me enough that I would fall fainting into your arms, whereupon you could steal away with me to that nefarious inn.'

'I would have to believe you dull-witted in truth, to imagine you would faint into the arms of a stranger, rather than run screaming back to Dornton Manor and the protection of your mother,' he countered. 'Nor could I carry you off to the inn against your will, if I wanted us to look like two lovebirds eloping, once we got there.'

'But you would have *me* believe you were dissipated enough to be present at this conference, but possessed of too tender a conscience to want it to go forward? Or was the reward not high enough to tempt you?' she added bitterly.

He stiffened at that insult, more stung than he should be at that assessment. Ben might be a self-confessed rake, but he considered himself a principled one. He never seduced a lady who wasn't willing, always paid his small staff and the merchants he patronised on time and tried as best he could to be a help to his fellow man.

But it wasn't reasonable to expect her to trust him, an almost total stranger, especially as he'd just identified himself as associating with a group of men who must represent the most idle, spendthrift and useless fribbles the aristocracy had the dubious privilege of counting among its members.

'Since you know nothing of me or my character, I cannot prevent you from thinking that. I don't deny I'm claimed to have a certain…reputation with the ladies. But I have never treated any of them with less than courtesy and respect.'

Rather than open himself to more disparagement, he'd convey the rest of the essential information and go. And had to damp down an immediate sense of…disappointment. The unusual Lady Alyssa intrigued him, nor could he remember ever feeling such a powerful initial attraction to any woman.

Both compelling reasons for him to end this little tête-à-tête as quickly as possible.

'Indulge me for one more minute and I will leave you to your sketching. Let me give you the names of the men currently at Lady Fulton's party who *are* participating in this scheme.'

After staring at him, disbelief, wariness and a trace of anger warring in her countenance, she said, 'I still find it hard to imagine even men as venal as my brother could have come up with such a despicable scheme. But if they have, it's not logical you would have come to warn me if you *were* participating in it. And you are right; I know nothing of you save that you belonged to a university group called "the Hellions" and that my brother mocked your heritage. His disdain is hardly a disqualifying factor, since I have very little respect for him or his opinions. Aside from weaving me this fantastical story, you've done nothing to warrant my censure.

If you *are* speaking the truth, you've gone to a good deal of trouble to warn me. I owe you an apology, and my thanks—though I am still not sure I believe you.'

Her abrupt about-face spoke well for her sense of fairness in admitting that she might have been mistaken. More than that, rather than turning missish and going off in fit of weeping at his alarming news, as he suspected many a maid of her sheltered upbringing would have, this fierce warrior princess looked like she'd prefer to face the offending gentlemen and level a sword or pistol at them.

Even more intrigued by those observations, he nodded. 'Apology accepted. I know the tale must seem—fantastic.'

'It does. Though I still find it difficult to believe the wager exists, neither can I explain why you would suddenly appear out of nowhere to convey such a tale.' She shook her head, looking puzzled again as she apparently tried to sort out all he'd told her. 'But—you also said you'd spent a few days in the village? Why, if your purpose in coming to Sussex was to warn me about this nefarious plot?'

'I knew you would be at Dornton Manor, but little else about you. To devise the best way to approach you, I needed to learn more. I also needed to learn who had actually attended the party. While as far as I know, I was the only one to argue against the wager that night, all the participants were rather foxed. Upon sober reflection, others might have decided they wanted no part in it. I didn't want to present you just a list of those present at the Quill and Gavel, lest I malign some gentleman who later chose to repudiate it.'

'Oh, no, we certainly wouldn't want to malign any

*gentlemen*,' she said acidly. 'Though I don't see how lingering in the village helped you. I'm not known there, and while I'm sure there is gossip about the party, how could you be certain who was in attendance, unless you actually came to Dornton?'

'Ah, but I did.'

She blinked at him. 'You visited and were not able to see me?'

'I didn't call at the front door.' At her exasperated raise of eyebrows, he chuckled. 'My time in the army taught me that it's best not to blunder into enemy territory without first doing a thorough reconnaissance. Nor do you want to ride about in full uniform, rattling your sabre, so that every spy and sharpshooter on the enemy side notices you. No, such a delicate mission required...stealth.'

'Stealth?' she repeated. Her lips twitched, as if she were suppressing a smile. 'What sort of "stealth"?'

'I had no possible excuse for calling on you, nor do I move in the social circles that make me the sort of eligible *parti* Lady Fulton would invite to join her party. But, thanks to the army, I know how to mingle almost invisibly among regular folk. Dornton Manor is the largest estate in the area, which means Dornton Village supplies much of the goods consumed here and most of the labour to staff the house. Some rounds of ale at the local tap house, some conversations with the various merchants who provision Dornton Manor, a mention to one of them that, as a returned soldier currently out of work, I wouldn't mind earning a few coins, and I had a commission to deliver food supplies. That fine fish you enjoyed last night and the pineapples for the compote for dessert?' He tapped his chest. 'Brought here from the village by Ben Tawny. Once at Dornton, it was easy enough, over a mug of ale in the servants' hall, to learn who was valet to whom, and to flirt with the ladies' maids and unearth a few details about each of their mistresses. *Voilà*—your size, colouring and love of sketching.'

'In other words, you misrepresented yourself to the staff here and lied to the merchant,' she said, her severe tone at variance with the half-smile curving her lips. 'You are the most complete hand! How can I believe anything you say?'

'I didn't misrepresent!' he protested. 'I merely…created an illusion.'

'You lied.'

He shook his head. 'Not true! I *am* a former soldier; I grew up poor enough to always be in favour of earning a few coins and many believe that being a Member of Parliament means I do no work. The staff here may have assumed I was a deliveryman because I brought out supplies, but I never *told* them I was.'

'I'm sure neither the merchant nor the staff could have imagined you were a Member of Parliament, seeking personal information about Lady Fulton's guests!'

He shrugged. 'If, after I presented "A" and "B", they erroneously arrived at "C", that's not my fault.'

She shook her head. 'You are a dangerous man.'

He grinned. 'I certainly hope so. Are you any closer to believing me now?'

'Yes…no. Oh, I don't know! Your voice and manner are those of a gentleman, but your stories! If I didn't recognise your name and your association with Oxford, I would think you a charlatan, travelling the countryside selling shares in bogus canal projects!'

'The army trained me to gather intelligence; it's surprisingly easy to get even strangers to talk about themselves, with a show of interest and a little prompting. And I did unearth the information I sought. Won't you let me convey it to you?'

'Very well. Although I make no promises about believing it!'

'Denbry arrives today. Quinlen and Rossiter are already here. Even if you can't bring yourself to believe the wager, be very careful around them. Watch how they treat you. I think you'll discover they will be unusually flattering and attentive, quite ignoring the lures cast out by any other females present.'

The mirth fled from her face, replaced by an expression of chagrin.

'They've already begun their campaign to win you over, haven't they?' he guessed.

'Their campaign to sweet-talk me?' she said, recovering her composure enough to scoff. 'I still don't see how they thought they could—'

She broke off abruptly, a flush slowly suffusing her face. 'Ah, now, the rationale behind the wager makes sense,' she said. 'The men believe that, given my advanced age, unmarried state and lack of feminine charms, I would be so thankful for the attentions of an eligible bachelor, and so desperate to attach one, that with a little flattery I'd be willing to do anything they ask?'

While Ben hesitated, loath to confirm that was exactly the description Denbry had given, she nodded. 'Though it was kind of you to try to spare me that humiliating assessment, I would have understood sooner if you hadn't.'

'I couldn't have said such a thing!' he replied, touched as he watched her gather up the shreds of her dignity, and angered on her behalf at the insult. 'For one, I would never tell a lady anything that unchivalrous, and secondly, I've seen with my own eyes it isn't true. You are lovely, quick-witted, independent, and highly talented. If you've remained unmarried, it must have been through your own choice.'

Though he meant every word, tears sheened her eyes. 'I thought it was the other gentlemen who would try to sweet-talk me.'

He shook his head. 'The honest truth, as I see it. At least I know now that, even without my intervention, you wouldn't have been easily duped.'

She swiped the tears away with one impatient hand, that small act of bravery touching his heart. 'Even understanding why they would pick me as the linchpin of the wager, I still have difficulty believing it. And for you to come warn me! I appreciate a sense of honour—but you've expended a great deal of effort on behalf of a woman you've never met, who has no claim to your protection whatsoever. Why would you care so much?'

'I know what it is for a woman to be deceived—and to bear the cost of it for the rest of her life.'

Sudden comprehension lit her eyes. 'The Chilford Bastard,' she said softly.

'Exactly,' he said, struggling to keep the bitterness from his tone.

'If it's true, I owe you an even more sincere apology—and my thanks.'

He waved it away. 'Just remain on your guard and watch the behaviour of the men I've mentioned. I doubt any of them would be lack-witted enough to try to make off with you against your will, for seduction would be necessary to ruin you and win the wager, to say nothing that attempted kidnapping carries severe penalties under law.'

'I will certainly watch all of them.'

Despite that assurance, he couldn't seem to rid himself of a vague uneasiness. Then he hit upon something that would not only help allay that concern—but would give him an excuse him to see this unusual woman again.

'Would you meet me here, about this same time tomorrow? If those gentlemen's behaviour does seem suspiciously beguiling, you'll know I was telling the truth. I can return to London, then, reassured that you believe me and are forewarned. Could you do that?'

He watched her as she weighed his request, almost visibly ticking off the pros and cons in her head. 'I suppose,' she agreed.

'Good. But when we meet tomorrow, bring your maid, even if Molly can't abide accompanying you on your sketching excursions, since you either walk too fast, or dawdle for ever. Don't go wandering by yourself in the gardens, either.' He grinned at her. 'You never know what sort of ruffian you might encounter.'

Relieved, and far more eager to see Lady Alyssa again than he should be, Ben handed her back the box of pastels she'd set on the ground, and strode to the lane to reclaim his horse.

He felt her speculative gaze on him as he rode away.

Lady Alyssa Lambornne certainly wasn't what he'd expected when conscience had compelled him into this mission, he mused as he directed his horse towards the village. From Denbry's description, he'd thought she'd be meek and mousy, the sort of shy, self-effacing creature who would never make a good impression on the Marriage Mart. As each year ticked by and she remained unwed, failing to achieve the only respectable occupation most women could hope for, she'd have become ever more anxious, apt to embrace even an unequal match to attain the respectability of marriage.

Instead, he'd found her uncommonly intelligent, self-possessed and confident, with a truly exceptional talent for drawing. As he'd *not* told her, far from being a mousy, he'd found her alluringly attractive. With a fat dowry and that physical magnetism, how had she managed to remain unmarried?

Perhaps because most men wanted a conventional and biddable wife, and were put off by the untamed aura she radiated?

It certainly appealed to *him*. He let the image of her play across his mind…soft lips, full breasts and deliciously rounded hips. The alertness in her body and the feral intensity of her gaze hinted of a passionate nature, barely covered by a thin veneer of civility…

Desire fired up again and he fought it. Despite her age and that illusion of restrained passion, Lady Alyssa was undoubtedly an innocent. The voice of self-preservation nattered in his ear, warning that he'd never engaged in the dangerous pastime of beguiling innocents and it was no time to start. That way led to the altar and he was neither interested, yet, in confining his interactions with females to a single specimen, nor had he attained the position he felt a woman he'd admire enough to marry would deserve in a husband.

And if he were truly honest, having witnessed the

misery and deprivation a blighted love had caused his mother, he wasn't sure he ever wanted to care that much about anyone.

He should therefore be extremely circumspect in his dealings with Lady Alyssa. Though she herself appeared to have little interest in entangling a suitor, that unusual attitude was almost certainly not shared by her family, who would probably much prefer her to put down her sketch pad and embrace the role of wife and mother. At her age, even the natural son of a viscount, a man who'd not yet achieved a superior position in the world, might be acceptable to them.

He had to laugh. Her family would have to be desperate indeed to consider a bastard son good enough for the daughter of an earl.

But he could risk seeing her one more time, before prudence dictated he distance himself. To make sure she was taking proper steps to protect herself. And, he admitted, for the simple pleasure of talking with this most unusual lady.

Anticipation filling him, he rode back towards the inn on the outskirts of the village where he'd engaged a room. He'd enjoy the fine fare at the Rose and Crown, while away the evening playing cards in the taproom and look forward tomorrow to meeting again the unexpectedly compelling Lady Alyssa Lambornne.

## *Chapter Two*

For a long time after Mr Tawny rode out of sight, Alyssa stared off in his direction, her mind turning over his almost unbelievable story—and marvelling at his potent masculine appeal. The whole episode still seemed incredible, but the evidence he presented was so convincing, she was almost forced to believe him, even if it was dismaying to admit she'd been made the means to exact an unprincipled revenge.

Unless she were to awake and find all of this had been only an incredible dream, there seemed no other explanation but that Mr Tawny was exactly who he said he was and what he'd told her was true. If so, by coming to warn her, he'd committed a selfless act.

Too bad he wasn't one of the 'beguiling suitors'. Since she didn't intend to marry anyway, it might be worth being 'ruined' to be seduced by him.

Desire stirred within her at the thought. She hadn't been so attracted by a man in a very long time. Though she was still a maid, her experience of passion limited, she had no difficulty identifying—and appreciating—

the reason for the heat that had flamed through her body when she'd first looked into his eyes.

A reaction that distracted her from observing him with her normal artist's dispassion while he stood looming over her, his countenance so arresting she couldn't make herself look away.

She recalled the startled moment when she'd first seen him, his broad shoulders blocking the ray of sunshine piercing the forest canopy, haloing his tall, well-muscled form and gilding the edges of his dark brown hair. Handsome, with a look of command about it, his lean face had a sharp nose, prominent cheekbones and the faint trace of a scar running from the left temple down almost to his jaw. Keen eyes the colour of an emerald illumined by sunlight held her gaze captive; his firm mouth looked made for kissing, that impression reinforced by a voice that was deeply pitched, almost—*bedchamber* intimate. When he'd held her gaze without flinching—his unexpected appearance and powerful attraction making her forget to drop her eyes modestly, as Mama kept instructing her—she'd felt so strongly drawn to him, she'd almost gone into his arms.

With his handsome face, virile body and shiver-inducing voice, she had no difficulty at all believing he was 'a man of great address with the ladies'.

Though his sudden appearance had certainly startled her, she'd not felt threatened. Which was a curious response, given the venal character and violent tendencies of the men of her family. She should have felt an immediate wariness; instead, there'd been something about him that *drew* her. Continued to draw her, even after the shock of her first, intensely physical response faded.

Her usual reaction to the arrival of a visitor was to

escape before Mama could call for her, or, if caught, get away as quickly as possible. Ben Tawny had evoked the opposite response; she'd *wanted* him to linger.

As they talked, that strong initial attraction still humming between them, his appeal expanded to include admiration for a man who would take so much trouble to safeguard a woman he didn't even know. A man of intelligence and strong principles, who exuded a sense of purpose and a quiet competence.

A self-confidence, too, as if he felt easy in his own skin. He possessed the same sort of calm self-assurance that Will had, she realised, that conclusion followed with the inevitable pang of grief.

No wonder she'd felt so drawn to him.

It occurred to her that, not only had he learned about her, he knew her maid's name, the fact that Molly didn't like to accompany her on sketching excursions and why. What a clever intelligence-gatherer he was, indeed!

He *ought* to appear competent. Only look what he'd discovered about her and the other members of the house party, and in such an unusual manner! She couldn't think of anyone else who could have managed such a chameleon-like performance.

She could easily believe he'd been an intelligence-gatherer for the army. She knew for certain he'd been to Oxford, joined a group of like-minded reformers who aspired to Parliament and achieved that ambition. What had he done, since joining the Commons? Her family having little interest in politics, she didn't know much about what went on in government, though even she had heard vague rumblings about a new Reform Act. Were he and his group moving that forward?

Was the man who'd accosted her, in fact, Benedict

Tawny? With no acquaintance present to introduce them, she had only his word for it. Though she couldn't think of a good reason why someone else would pose as the man and come to warn her of a pernicious plot.

Was there any way she could make sure he was who he said he was? Asking Mama if she knew anything about a Mr Benedict Tawny would only result in a grilling about why she'd suddenly developed a most unusual interest in a gentleman to whom she'd never been presented. Besides, Mama knew few politicians, and by his own admission, Mr Tawny didn't appear at society functions, which would be the only place her mama would encounter him.

Perhaps she could talk to Lord Fulton. Though he was not, to her knowledge, involved in politics, he'd certainly know more about Parliament and the Reform movement than any of the females present.

At the prospect, she felt a rise of eagerness and anticipation.

Mr Tawny was not only the most attractive gentleman she'd met in a very long time, he was the only one who'd aroused her interest and excited her curiosity. Although she was unlikely to ever see him again after tomorrow, she was suddenly very glad she'd agreed to meet him.

In the interim, she'd attempt a little intelligence-gathering of her own.

Anger stirred out of the ashes of humiliation. While she plumbed Lord Fulton about Mr Tawny, she'd also encourage the attentions of Rossiter and Quinlen and try to work out the dimensions of their plot.

Those dissipated, idle men might think to make her the target of their ploy, but she no intention of playing into their hands. In fact, she thought, their intended manipulation calling up her ever-simmering fury and resentment at her father's strong-armed control over her life, perhaps she could try to turn their stratagems against *them.* If they counted on her being naïve, persuadable and desperate to capture their interest, she could count on them to be arrogant, sure of their superior cleverness and too unobservant to see anything but what they expected to see.

Despite their ill intentions, she wouldn't attempt to ruin *their* lives, even if she could. But she'd have no regrets about exploiting their scheme so they, rather than she, ended up surprised and embarrassed.

The steady burn of anger reinforcing that intent, she gathered up her art supplies and headed back to Dornton.

Alyssa had hoped to return to the manor and change into more presentable clothing while her mother was at breakfast. Unluckily, as she tiptoed back into their bedchamber, she found Lady Aldermont still at her dressing table.

'Sorry I slept so late, darling,' her mother said—before catching a glimpse of her in the dressing table's mirror. 'Merciful Heavens, child!' she said with a gasp. 'Wherever have you been, wearing that hideous old gown?'

'Just sketching, Mama. It was still very wet after yesterday's rain and I didn't wish to soil any of the lovely dresses you brought for me. None of the guests were up, so I got out and back without being seen.'

'Sketching, always sketching,' Lady Aldermont said fretfully. 'If only you'd paid a fraction as much attention to the things that really matter during your London Seasons, we wouldn't be reduced to attending this dreary series of house parties in dismally remote locations!'

'I know you hate being out of London,' Alyssa said, suppressing a guilty pang at the knowledge that it was the chance to sketch in different areas of England that prompted *her* to press for attending the 'dreary series of house parties'.

'At least in town, there's visiting and shopping and a variety of company. Here, we are condemned to see the same faces day after day.'

Putting down her supplies, Alyssa walked over to pat her mother's hand. 'Has Lady Sutherland been plaguing you?'

'Insufferable woman!' Lady Aldermont cried. 'If she's not crowing about the brilliant marriage her eldest made, snagging the Duke of Wessex, she's waxing eloquent about the beauty and accomplishments of Lady Alice. All this said with pitying glances at me.'

Alyssa sighed. 'I know what a disappointment I've been to you, Mama.'

Though that was patently true, her mother seized her hands. 'Of course you haven't, my darling! Well, I do wish some gentleman—some *eligible* gentleman—had caught your eye after your come-out. I still think it most unwise that your Papa refuses you another Season, for I know he wishes you to wed and the selection at these smaller parties is so limited! It just grates on me when I see those empty-headed chits celebrated, when you, who are far more accomplished, are overlooked!'

*Little brown wrens are always overlooked when there are beauteous swans about,* she thought. Her mama had been one of them, the most beautiful, sought-after and well-dowered maiden of her debut Season, thirty years ago. Alas, though she'd inherited her mama's short stature, she'd not received the golden hair, the arresting face or the summer-sky-blue eyes that had inspired suitors to write verses in her honour and propose in droves.

'There's no accounting for the taste of gentlemen,' she said, giving her mama a kiss. 'Why don't you pick out your favourite of my new gowns for me to wear?'

Mentioning fashion was guaranteed to redirect her mama's thinking into more cheerful channels. Brightening, Lady Aldermont said, 'Yes, I will! Several of the gentlemen have been paying you a flattering amount of attention; we must inspire them to continue!'

*And it certainly hasn't been because of my charms,* Alyssa thought, frowning as she remembered Tawny's warning.

'Surely, my dear, out of all the single men about, you might find *one* to your liking. Is it so wrong of me to want to see you wed and settled, with a house of your own and children?'

Alyssa noted her mother wasn't hypocritical enough to add 'happy' to that description—her mama's own marriage having given her little reason to expect wedded bliss for her daughter. 'You never give up hope, do you, Mama?'

'It would be so much better, if you could find a kind man you could tolerate as a husband,' her mother said coaxingly.

'Better than living under Papa's thumb,' she admitted. In the face of her father's stern, tyrannical rule, her mother had always been too timid to please him, she too rebellious. Or rather, she had tried to please him when she was little, before she realised earning his approval was impossible. Since the incident three years ago, they'd regarded each other with active hostility.

'But if I married, my new husband would get control over Aunt Augusta's money, so I still wouldn't be able to use it for what I want.'

*The ability to live independently and pursue her heart's calling.*

'Yes, but you would have friends and society around you—rather than being alone and isolated in that cottage you talk about! And you know Papa will not let you use the funds for that. Only think of the scandal, an earl's unmarried daughter living all on her own!'

Alyssa sighed, unable to dispute the truth of that. With her father named a trustee on the fund, unless she married, she'd need his approval to access the money. As of now, she'd not figured out a way to convince him to allow her to set up a separate household, which is why she had not, yet, approached him with her intention to do so.

'I expect I shall devise some way to bring Papa around. In any event, with luck, he'll predecease me.'

'I don't know,' her mama said. 'The Lambornnes are distressingly long-lived.'

Sadly, Alyssa had to admit the truth of that daunting observation. Would there still be time for her to make a life for herself and accomplish the work that drove her, if she truly couldn't begin until after Papa died?

She must come up with a better alternative than waiting for the Earl of Aldermont to cock up his toes.

First, though, she needed to deal with this despicable wager.

Due to Mr Tawny's unexpected appearance, she'd

not finished her drawing today. Over the summer, she had completed twenty more watercolours and needed only a few more to be able to contact Mr Waterman in London about putting together that colourised book of English birds he'd expressed such enthusiasm about to Will. If she could just get her hands on her money, so she might travel to the more remote regions and finish the final sketches before the deadline he'd given…

With Will gone, she'd need to find someone else to approach the publisher on her behalf, she thought, the familiar, sharp wave of grief sweeping through her.

*I will finish the sketches and get them published, as you would have wanted*, she silently promised him.

Then Molly was back, fitting her into one of the explosions of lace, ribbons and ruffles her mama so adored. Since, in her opinion, the enormous sleeves and ballooning skirts made her look ridiculous—almost as wide as she was tall, she'd overhead one malicious maiden remarking—it was fortunate she had no desire to attract any of the eligible swains gathered for this party.

Tapes and pins secured, she told her mama, 'I'm going to stop by the library. I'll see you in the drawing room.' Giving her mother a kiss, she hurried out before Lady Aldermont could object.

Hoping to catch her host before the party gathered in the parlour, Alyssa slipped down the stairs. As she entered the library, the latest London paper caught her eye. Which, quite fortuitously, carried a lengthy story on the progress of the Reform Bill.

Snatching it up, she scanned the article. It seemed the bill, having passed the Commons in late September, was sent on to the Lords. Contrary to the expectations of its supporters and an agitated populace, instead of winning approval in the upper house, the Lords Spiritual—upper clergy who had votes in that hereditary body—summoned enough members to defeat it. The result had been riots in many areas of the country and Lord Grey pressing the King to prorogue Parliament so a new session could be summoned in December.

Not until the very end did she find what she sought: a list of the most prominent members of the Reform committee. Which included all four of those Oxford friends she remembered her brother calling 'Hadley's Hellions': Giles Hadley, Viscount Lyndlington, David Tanner Smith, Christopher Lattimar—and Benedict Tawny.

She'd just finished the article when her host walked in. 'Lady Alyssa!' he cried, halting in surprise on the threshold.

She rose and curtsied. 'Lord Fulton, I hope you'll forgive my invading your library.'

'Of course, my dear. Can I assist you with something?'

'I was just reading the latest London paper. Have you followed the debate on the Reform Bill? There's quite a lengthy article.'

He gave her an odd look. 'That's not a topic generally of much interest to ladies.'

'Truly? I found the discussion fascinating! Are you acquainted with any of the movement's leaders?' she asked, tapping the list in the paper. 'I find myself wondering what manner of man would support such a… drastic initiative.'

'I've not been much involved, myself,' he admitted,

gazing down at the names she indicated. 'Hmm…all four of them outsiders from society, which might explain their radical views.'

'Outsiders? In what way?'

'Hadley, the son of the Earl of Telbridge, was estranged from his father for years, after his father divorced his mother, but they've recently reconciled. David Tanner Smith…quite the scandal there! A commoner, he recently shocked society by marrying the widowed Duchess of Ashedon, though he is, it must be admitted, a good friend of her family. Lattimar…father is Lord Vraux, although it's well known that's not his real father. Five children and probably only the eldest was sired by the baron! Benedict Tawny…not sure I know that name.'

Before she could suppress her disappointment, he said, 'Now wait, I do remember. Born on the wrong side of the blanket, but his father, Viscount Chilford, later took him up and sponsored him in Parliament.'

'Does he resemble his father in appearance—is that why the Viscount decided to recognise him?' she probed.

'Chilford's a member of my club. Can't say as I've met the son, but I've heard the boy favours him. Tall, dark-haired, green eyes. Quite a magnet for the ladies. A group of rogues, all in all.' Lord Fulton chuckled. 'M'wife would blister my ears for repeating such scandalous gossip to an innocent like you!'

'I'll not mention we spoke of it!' Alyssa promised as she tucked away the details.

*Tall, dark-haired, green-eyed and a magnet for the ladies?*

The description certainly fitted! Desire fluttered

in the pit of her stomach as she recalled the gaze that had held her spellbound. That final bit of evidence was enough to convince her that the gentleman in the woods had in fact been Benedict Tawny.

Pleased to have elicited so much information, she said, 'I've disturbed your peace long enough. Thank you, Lord Fulton!'

Bidding her host good day, Alyssa walked out to join the rest of the party.

The scrutiny of both the ladies and gentlemen who turned to inspect her as she entered immediately made her conscious of her new attire. In comparison, the style Alyssa found so unflattering on her short form only emphasised the tall, elegant figure of the waspish Lady Sunderland's daughter, Lady Alice. With her lovely face, sky-blue eyes and golden curls set under a wide-brimmed hat, she looked like the illustration of perfect maidenly beauty from the latest lady's fashion magazine.

Which made it all the more suspicious that, rather than lingering with the other men beside the Paragon, as soon as she entered, Quinlen and Rossiter hastened over to her.

'Lady Alyssa, at last! The party was dreadfully dull until you appeared,' Quinlen said.

'And what a lovely gown! You look so…fashionable,' Rossiter added.

Normally, Alyssa responded to compliments from a gentleman in monosyllables and evaded his company as soon as possible. This time, she fluttered her lashes at Rossiter and tried to manufacture a blush. 'Oh, do you really think so?'

'Absolutely! The prettiest lady here,' Rossiter said.

Since that was patently untrue, Alyssa had to suppress a strong desire to roll her eyes. Instead, she peeped shyly up at him. 'You are very kind, Mr Rossiter!'

'Merely truthful, Lady Alyssa. Lady Fulton is about to begin a game of charades in the salon. Won't you join me?' He offered his arm.

'She ought to accompany me,' Quinlen said. 'I'm a much cleverer partner.'

'Oh, dear!' Alyssa said, putting her hands to her cheeks in mock distress. 'I shouldn't wish to slight either of you!'

'Give an arm to each, then,' Quinlen said, offering his.

'I'm really not very good at charades,' she added, assuming the role of bashful wallflower they expected. 'You gentlemen would do better partnering another lady.'

'Nonsense, there's no one here I would prefer to you,' Quinlen said.

'Quite true!' Rossiter added.

Embarrassed in truth at all the falsehoods being exchanged, she had no trouble summoning a blush. 'Well, if you are quite sure you want my company...'

As both gentlemen waited expectantly, Alyssa gave a hand to each and allowed them to walk her to the salon. Since they didn't think her witty enough to add much to the conversation, she was able to get by with murmuring a few 'yesses' and 'nos' as they entertained her with London gossip.

She made a great show of refusing to participate in the charades, and when finally 'persuaded' to play, was so hopeless at giving or interpreting clues that her mother, speechless at the abysmal performance of her normally needle-witted daughter, pulled her aside to ask in an undertone whether she felt quite well.

'I'm fine, Mama,' she whispered back. 'I didn't wish to outdo the other participants, especially not when Mr Quinlen and Mr Rossiter are showing me such flattering attention. Haven't you always told me gentlemen don't truly wish for intelligence in a wife?'

'Yes, but you've never before paid me any heed,' Lady Aldermont replied.

The game broke up, and with the day turned warm and fair, plans were being made to walk in the garden when Lady Fulton announced a newcomer was joining them. Striding into the parlour came Lord Denbry, greeting his hostess and apologising for making a tardy arrival at her party. As he bent to whisper something in her ear that made her blush, his gaze roved the room—before finding, and resting on, Alyssa.

She didn't have to feign the heat that touched her cheeks at his blatantly appraising glance. So this was Denbry, her brother's detested competitor for winning women, games of chance and eager acolytes. Though she'd never met him, she'd heard enough about him from her brother to have been on her guard, even without Mr Tawny's warning.

Above medium height, dressed in the vanguard of fashion in a coat flared at the shoulder and nipped in at the waist, he looked wealthy, handsome and arrogant. She already knew that he, like her brother, used those good looks to charm hapless women out of their virtue and induce gentlemen to grant him whatever he desired.

And what he currently desired, apparently, was to see her ruined.

If Mr Tawny hadn't been so persuasive, she'd have found it almost impossible to believe this stranger would casually plan to destroy her. If she could prove to herself that was truly his intent, it might be time he was taught a salutatory lesson.

He wasn't the only one who could plot.

As she watched covertly, he made a circuit of the room, letting each lady bask in his charming smile and tossing greetings to the competing swains that changed their resentful looks to pleasant, if not entirely friendly, nods.

Not until he'd greeted everyone else did he approach Alyssa.

'Quinlen, Rossiter, good to see you,' he said, shaking both gentlemen's hands. 'I've left the best for last. Won't one of you introduce me to this ravishing creature?'

*A good ploy—if she were a woman whose interest he wanted to pique.* A wallflower who'd wistfully watched his progress around the room, knowing she hadn't the wit or beauty to catch his notice, and therefore shocked and thrilled to have attracted it. That unjustified bit of flattery seemed to reinforce that enticing her was exactly what he intended.

'Lady Alyssa Lambornne, may I present the Earl of Denbry?' Rossiter dutifully pronounced.

She dropped a curtsy, ready to resume playing her part. 'I'm so pleased to meet you, Lord Denbry,' she said, trying to imbue her voice with just the right tone of flustered gratification. 'Although you are far too kind! I know I'm not…ravishing.'

She gazed up at him, aiming for the pleading expression of one who knows better, but hopes to be persuaded anyway that the gentleman finds her attractive.

'You are to me,' he murmured, bending to kiss her hand.

Knowing his intentions, at the press of his lips against her fingers she almost jerked away. Catching herself, she uttered instead a little 'ooh' of gratification.

If she hadn't been forewarned, she might have missed the knowing smile that passed between Quinlen and Rossiter.

Were most females so self-deceiving? she wondered with disgust. Or so desperate to marry that they persuaded themselves to believe what common sense argued against?

But she shouldn't judge her sex too harshly. She had resources to support herself, mitigating the need to wed. How desperate might *she* be, if the alternative to marriage were destitution, or a life as an unpaid servant, shunted from family member to family member to assist with children, the ill or the elderly?

'The party is about to walk in the gardens. Won't you let me escort you?' Denbry asked, giving Quinlen and Rossiter a little wave of dismissal.

The speed with which they abandoned the field reinforced Tawny's contention that Denbry was the ringleader of the plot. 'Well, I don't know. My brother has told me a lot about you,' she said, aiming for a tone of both curiosity and reproof.

'Probably none of it good!' Denbry said with a groan. 'As I'm sure you are aware, your brother and I having been friendly competitors for years, so you mustn't believe everything he says! Please allow me to walk with you, that I might have a chance to defend myself.'

He gazed at her with such a look of warm entreaty, she could understand how females unaware of his true character might find themselves beguiled. 'I suppose that is only fair.'

Tucking her hand under his, he walked her from the salon towards the garden. 'Just what has your brother told you about me?'

*Another good ploy,* Alyssa thought. *Find out what you need to explain away.* 'That you've often competed in races with horses or curricles and gambled with each other, sometimes for high stakes. And then, there were…' she dropped her voice, as if embarrassed '…certain, *um*, ladies…'

'All true.' He leaned closer, so that he was almost whispering. 'Though it was very *naughty* of your brother to mention the ladies.'

*A whiff of sin, designed to titillate,* she thought. 'It does make me wonder what you are doing at this gathering of eligible maidens.'

'Perhaps your brother has not reached this point yet, but there comes a time when a man grows tired of pursuing idle pleasures. When he begins to long for a more…settled life and one special lady to share it.'

If it were not for the slight smirk at the end of that speech, she could almost be fooled herself by his apparent sincerity.

'And you have…reached this milestone, Lord Denbry?'

'I believe I have.'

'You are anticipating the next Season, then, so you may seek that…special lady.'

'Not if I am fortunate enough to find her before then.'

'And how will you know when you have found her?'

'One just…knows.' He tipped her chin up with one finger. 'Do you not believe so, my lovely Lady Alyssa?' he murmured, gazing into her eyes.

*How much ardent entreaty he put into those words*, Alyssa thought, gazing back with what she hoped looked like surprise, gratification and attraction. *He really was quite good at this—the blackguard.*

Giving an uncertain laugh, she looked away. 'But you hardly know me, Lord Denbry.'

'But I've heard much about you. Your loveliness. Your purity. Your tender regard for your family.'

'I would hope all unmarried ladies possess such qualities,' Alyssa countered. *Take that, for presenting me with such a list of bland generalities.*

A hint of annoyance briefly crossed his countenance. 'Not to the extent you do, dear Lady Alyssa,' he replied smoothly. 'But I see you are not yet convinced of my regard—or how serious I am about turning my life in a new direction. Won't you get to know me better before you decide?'

She gazed back up, trying for a worshipful look. 'I should like to…get to know you better.'

He pressed another kiss upon her captive hand. Alyssa had to work hard to suppress the strong desire to knee him in the groin. Instead, after suffering him to fondle her hand for several minutes, she pulled away, as if reluctantly. 'Oh, Lord Denbry, you mustn't!'

'You are right, Lady Alyssa. I must control myself—no matter how difficult you make that.'

'We should go back to the house now,' she announced, but with a regretful glance at his lips that said the virtuous maiden was sorely tempted to be less virtuous.

Smiling with satisfaction, he leaned down as if to steal a kiss—before straightening again. 'You tempting creature! Yes, we must return before I forget myself and do something...scandalous. But promise you will let me escort you to dinner, and partner with me for cards afterward.'

She gazed up worshipfully. 'If you truly wish it?'

'With all my heart.'

*Do you even have one?* she wondered as she let him lead her back into the house.

She left him then, pleading the need to change for dinner. She found her mother already in their chamber, her maid helping her into her evening attire.

Once Molly had done the same for her, Lady Aldermont dismissed them both before turning to her. 'May I have a moment, my dear?'

'Of course. What is it, Mama?'

'I appreciate you making an effort to be agreeable to the gentleman. But Denbry...' Her mother's voice trailed off. 'I've...overheard some things about him from your brother and I don't believe he's at all the sort of suitor you wish to encourage. I was quite shocked to see him at this gathering—not that Lady Fulton invited him, for he comes from an excellent family, is quite wealthy and will inherit the marquisate one day. Shocked that, with his...proclivities, he bothered to attend.'

It wouldn't be prudent to confide to her mama any of what Mr Tawny had revealed. A shocked and outraged Lady Aldermont would demand that their hostess be told, so she might send the offending gentlemen away before they could carry out their nefarious plan.

That would put her mama and their hostess in an awkward position—and let Denbry get away without receiving the lesson she had in mind. She was now almost as determined to deliver that as she was to foil his revenge.

'I know Harleton doesn't like him,' Alyssa said. 'I've heard he's a gambler and a womaniser.'

'So I accused him of being. He admitted to it, but said he was ready to change—for the right lady.'

Lady Aldermont shook her head. 'Men don't truly change, my darling. I want you to marry to improve your situation—not become mired for life in a union that would exchange the tyranny of your brother and father for a man who is no better.'

'I have no intention of doing that, either,' she said emphatically.

'As long as you are on your guard against him. There's no man more charming than a selfish rake intent on getting what he wants. I should know.'

Was that how her father had persuaded her mother into marriage? Alyssa had often wondered what had led her sweet-tempered, if shallow, mother to accept the hand of her selfish, arrogant, iron-fisted father.

Yet another reason to avoid wedlock, for how could a girl possessed of a handsome dowry trust any man not to be deceitful about his reasons for wanting to marry her?

Benedict Tawny's face flashed into mind. Perhaps there was one man who seemed to truly care about a woman's welfare.

'Don't worry, Mama. I know what sort of man Denbry is.'

'Very well, my dear. But do be careful.'

'Oh, I intend to be.' *Careful...and cunning.* Tossing the spangled shawl around her shoulders, she followed her mother out.

## Chapter Three

Early the next morning, Ben waited in the woods where he had discovered Lady Alyssa the previous day. As he paced, he had to admit feeling an anticipation a good deal stronger than it ought to be.

All he expected to gain from this meeting was a confirmation that Quinlen, Rossiter and Denbry were in fact trying to attach her, as he predicted. Once assured that she would not be taken in by them, he could return to London and begin preparing for the final battle for the Reform Bill.

Still, he had found Lady Alyssa uncommonly interesting, unusual as it was for him to be drawn to a female he wasn't trying to persuade into his bed. Which, unfortunately, was not possible in this case, despite the promise of passion in that lush body and those mesmerising eyes.

Ah, what delights he could teach her!

Too bad those delights came with wedding lines attached. While acknowledging that, he could still look forward to conversing with a lady whose personality was as intriguing as her physical charms.

What, besides the physical, was it that had so impressed him? he asked himself again.

The independence and sense of purpose that led her to tramp the countryside unescorted to pursue her sketching was part of it. And the fact that, unlike most unmarried females, she seemed driven by something other than a pressing need to find a husband. Or at least, to capture the attention of any gentleman she encountered.

Now that he considered it, he realised she'd made no attempt to attract him at all. A novel experience for a man who normally had all manner of lures cast his way. If he'd not been so distracted by her sketching and pressed to inform her about her threatening situation, he might have felt downright insulted by her apparent lack of interest.

Also exceptional was her ability to discuss in a calm, rational manner a disturbing situation that would have reduced most females to tears. Since when had he met a female who employed *logic* in evaluating a situation? Or who, in distressing circumstances, retained enough presence of mind to admit her conclusions might be in error?

In short, she acted with a deliberate, almost...*masculine* sense of intelligence and self-control. Though, he thought, recalling her lush form, there was nothing at all mannish about her.

Unique and impressive indeed!

He'd like to ask her what she intended to do with those excellent sketches. Ladies did not produce items for sale, but he could try persuading her into gifting him one. He'd give it pride of place on his library wall—a memento of a most unusual lady.

Then he spied her hurrying across the meadow—and felt again that rise of anticipation.

Spotting him, she made her way over, sketchbook and pastel box in hand. There was not, he noted with a frown, any maid trailing in her wake.

'Sorry to be late, Mr Tawny,' she said as she reached the shelter of the trees. 'I almost couldn't get away.'

He gave her a severe look. 'Where is Molly?'

'Just gone down for breakfast. I couldn't be cruel enough to drag her away from that, especially since, as you've discovered, she hates accompanying me to sketch. Besides, I was coming to meet you, so I knew I'd be in no danger.'

'You might meet someone else coming or going. I trust you now believe there might be danger in that?'

Her expression turned exasperated. 'It was just as you predicted. Not only did Quinlen and Rossiter continue their attentions, Lord Denbry made straight for me when he arrived, despite the fact that there were several more beautiful ladies in the room. Just in case any of the three had suddenly developed some malady affecting their vision, I conducted myself through charades and the evening activities as the most shy, backward ingénue on the face of the planet! In spite of that, their attentions continued unabated.' She paused, chuckling. 'They must have been praying for the evening to end. I know I was; trying to act like a bashful ninny is far more exhausting than I anticipated.'

'Did none of the other guests notice the marked change in your behaviour?'

'Since I generally participate as little as possible in these gatherings, they don't know how I normally behave. Though initially, my mother was alarmed! But after I assured her I was only trying to follow her advice, deferring to the gentlemen, she couldn't really protest the behaviour,' she ended with another chuckle.

How those gold-flecked eyes mesmerised when she was amused, Ben thought, once again fighting the urge to take her in his arms. 'A case of being careful what you wish for.'

'Perhaps.' Her amusement fading, she said, 'In particular, I watched Denbry, for the others deferred to him. I even told him at the outset that I had not received a good account of his character from my brother.'

Surprised that she would almost…bait the man, Ben said, 'To which he replied?'

'He protested that, as he and my brother had always been rivals, Harleton was unlikely to give him the best report. Then added a great deal of claptrap about how he'd outgrown his misspent youth and now was ready to settle down—with the right lady, of course. That bit of rubbish accompanied by ardent looks and much flattery.' She twisted her lip in disgust. 'A great rake, suddenly reforming his womanising ways? Are there truly any females who would believe such nonsense?'

'That the love of one special lady might convince a man to change his character? It is a romantic notion, you must allow. It would depend, I think, on how persuasive the gentleman was.'

'And how naïve and sheltered—or desperate, the female?' she said, her bitter tone making him wonder about her own experiences. Had some rake led her on, then betrayed her, when she was young and naïve?

'So you do believe now that they are trying to entice you.'

A flush heated her face. 'Humiliating as it is to acknowledge, I'm forced to admit it must be true.'

Angered again on her behalf, he said, 'Fortunately, they have no idea they are dealing with a lady far different than the slighting description they received. Now that you know what they are about, you can simply ignore them.'

Her expression hardened, something—indignation?—sparking in her eyes. 'Yes, they *are* dealing with a female far different than what they expected—not that my performance last night gave any indication of it. But I don't intend to ignore them; I intend to continue giving Denbry all the encouragement he needs to believe his scheme will succeed.'

'You're going to *encourage* him?' Ben asked, frowning. 'Why in the world would you do that?'

'What if I *had* been the sort of anxious, desperate-to-marry female they envisioned? Why should Lord Denbry be able to target the virtue of some innocent maid, callously ruin her life—and walk away, completely untouched? Knowing what he intended, I can't just...let him go and do nothing!'

Beguiling as it was to fantasise about a warrior princess, it was disturbing in the extreme to consider she might actually act like one. Alarmed, Ben said, 'I strongly advise you to do just that! Were he to discover that you'd been playing him for a fool, he'd be furious. You know what sort of man he is! Regrettable it might be, and certainly unfair, but gentlemen hold most of the cards in this game; there are any number of retaliatory actions he could take to besmirch your character. All he need do upon his return to London is put it about—very discreetly, of course—that you'd allowed him to take liberties with your person as you walked alone in the garden and your reputation would be in shreds. It wouldn't be as dramatic as the ruination he planned—but it would limit your ability to secure a suitable marriage almost as effectively.'

'Perhaps—but don't I invite that sort of retaliation, regardless of what I do next?' she argued back. 'If I were suddenly to shun him, he would be forced to admit he'd miscalculated my character—or his own attractiveness to females. Either result would show him up in front of his friends, who have all witnessed the marked attention he paid me. Wouldn't that outcome be just as likely to spur him to some retaliation?'

Swallowing the oath that observation prompted, Ben paused, irritated that he'd hadn't foreseen that possibility himself. She truly was needle-witted! Much as he'd like to dismiss her concern, the damnable fact was, she was right.

Before he could devise a safer way to counter that threat, she said, 'Since there's a good chance he's going to make a run at ruining me in any event, instead of retreating in submissive, helpless fashion, why shouldn't I at least take advantage of the opportunity to administer a lesson of my own?'

'Administer a lesson?' Ben echoed, truly aghast now. 'Dam—Heaven forfend! What crack-brained notion have you taken into your head?'

'Well, I *would* very much like to shoot him—if I were a man and he had impugned my honour, I'd be able call him out, wouldn't I? I am an excellent shot, by the way. But since, regrettably, he'd only laugh at a challenge issued by a female, I shall have to take a different path. I intend to seem to go along with his plan, letting him "entice" me to the point of an elopement. I shall insist I dare not leave Dornton Manor with him, but will slip away after dark and meet him instead at some inn. I'll beg him to hire the horses and a coach for a dash to the border—or wherever it is he plans to carry me off—and wait for me there. Only instead of a silly, eager female running into his arms, he'll receive a message, reproving him for his dishonourable intentions and expressing the hope that he will not, in future, try to lead some other unfortunate young woman to her ruin.'

'Don't do it,' Ben said flatly.

'Why not? How does it put me in any more danger than I stand in now? I've already walked in the garden with him, alone, so he'd easily be able to return to London and impugn my reputation in the manner you described. No matter how angry he might be, he wouldn't go as far as to try to make off with me by force—there's that law against kidnapping you mentioned. Nor would he try to physically assault me—there are statutes against that, too. He may be venal, but I do not think he is stupid.'

Though Ben wasn't as confident as she seemed about that, to his relief, a better solution came to mind. 'No, confide in your mother instead. Have her invent some sudden illness and carry you back home. There'd be no insult, no blame. If he were to believe his design had been succeeding and someone who suspected the truth spoiled the plan, he would hold your mother at fault. There's nothing he could do to injure her.'

'Maybe. But there's still the possibility someone could titter behind his back that my mama thought him so deficient in character, she felt compelled to remove her innocent daughter from his presence. He'd still be free to make allegations about my virtue—and get away with it.'

Looking furious, she stamped her foot. 'When I think of that smug, conceited face, I'd like to plant him a facer! It's not as if I want to pay him back in a manner as damaging as what he intended for me. But how can I slink away and do…*nothing*?'

She gazed up at him, her outrage so justifiable, he couldn't help but sympathise. Even so, it would still be most ill advised for her to try to retaliate. Warrior princess or not, she was still a female living in a society entirely unforgiving of any woman whose behaviour violated its rules. Somehow, he needed to convince her of that.

'He's despicable, I agree. But in the case of something as precious as your reputation, discretion would be the better part of valour.'

'Would *you* just meekly walk away and do nothing? If he'd tried to impugn *your* honour and ruin *your* good name?'

She had him there. 'It's not the same,' he protested. 'I'm a man and there's only so much he could—'

'Why is it, just because I'm female, I'm supposed to let this…this reprobate threaten me and look the other way?'

'You know why!' he shot back in exasperation. 'Don't engage him in a battle it would be far too easy for him to win and you to lose! Once destroyed, your reputation is gone for ever.'

'You'll say I'm naïve, or I haven't considered the matter rationally, but I assure you, I don't *care* if my reputation is ruined. It might even be helpful. I can afford to engage in a battle most females, whose futures *do* depend upon possessing a spotless character, could not.'

He stared at her, perplexed. Had she really been so traumatised by some previous heartbreak that she was reckless enough to throw away her future? 'No woman—or man, for that matter—can do without a reputation. What do you possibly hope to achieve without it? Surely, in spite of whatever—unhappy experience you may have had earlier, you can't be that opposed to eventually marrying.'

'No, I'm not—or I wasn't—opposed to marriage.' She looked up, sighing, and for an instant he caught a glimpse in her eyes of an anguish so great, he felt the shock of its reverberation like a blow to his chest.

Then, the fire seeming to leave her, she said quietly, 'I suppose I shall have to explain, lest you lapse into superior masculine manner and think me mentally deficient, like all of my sex. Very well.'

With a distracted air, she paced deeper into the woods, motioning him to follow. 'I've always had a passion for sketching,' she said as they walked, 'and during my second Season, one swain who became aware of that obsession brought me to see one of the folios of Mr Audubon's *Birds of America*, for which his cousin, the Duke of Northumberland, was a subscriber. How transported I was by the marvellous detail, the wonderful colours! I began a conversation about them with the Duke's secretary, William McCalister, which led to my meeting Will again later and showing him some of my own watercolours. He thought them excellent and that, with the great success of Mr Aubudon's engravings, some publisher might be interested in bringing out a similar work for British birds, as Mr Bewick's otherwise very comprehensive guide is illustrated only by black-and-white woodcuts. With my permission, he approached a publisher, who was not only interested, he wrote out a contract on the spot, giving the artist—he had no idea it was a female, of course—until the end of this winter to finish the drawings.'

By this time, they'd reached the clearing. Absently, she took a seat on the log, Ben sitting beside her. 'Harleton learned of my meetings with Will and reported them to my father, who forbade me to see him again; the son of a younger son of minor gentry wasn't a fitting companion for an earl's daughter. Yet, how could I help loving Will? The only person I'd ever met who not only showed an interest in my drawing, but understood how much it means to me and encouraged me to use my talents for something more useful than decorating china plates. When I continued to sneak out to see him, fearing I might make a misalliance that would embarrass the family, my father arranged to have him offered a position with a colonial official in Barbados. A clever man, my father—seeing this as a way to earn the wealth and advancement that would make him "worthy" of me, Will accepted the position. My father locked me in my room until Will's ship sailed for the Indies, to make sure I could not elope with him. Six months after his arrival, Will contracted some tropic disease, and died.'

Ben had never been in love, fully and completely. But he knew how much his mother had dared in order to be with the man she'd loved and he knew how much the support and friendship of the Hellions had meant to him at Oxford, an outcast with aspirations no one else understood. To have all that wrapped up in one person and lose it… 'I'm so sorry,' he murmured.

'No man of good birth would allow his wife to work as an artist, for payment. Nor could I tolerate being a useless society wife. I have money enough that I don't need to marry to be able to set up an establishment of my own. Except that,' she added with another sigh, 'despite being of age, I cannot access the funds from my great-aunt's trust without my father's approval. Which he is unlikely to give, an earl's daughter living on her own being almost as scandalous as her running away to marry a nobody. But if I were *ruined,* with no hope of marriage, an embarrassment for him to have under his roof, he might wash his hands of me and let me live the life I want. The sooner, the better, since if I do not submit the portfolio by the end of the year, I will likely lose the opportunity to publish altogether. If confronting Denbry risks ruination, I'm ready. And if I'm right and implementing my plan only delivers a smack to the nose of his disreputable intentions, at least I'll have been able to strike a small blow for a woman's right to respect. One most females couldn't risk delivering.'

Ben stared at her, his mind in turmoil. She was of age and entitled to decide on her own actions. He was barely more than a stranger, with no connection of blood or friendship that gave him the right to dictate her behaviour. But every instinct argued against allowing her to launch a plan that, to his mind, had so many chances of ending badly.

'I don't have any standing to keep you from attempting this. I even concede that ruination might—*might*—prove useful, if the scenario played out as you envision it. But my time in the army taught me that if you're heading into an ambush, you should always plan several alterative counter-strikes to every conceivable attack your enemy might deliver. Never walk into a fight with only one defence in mind.'

'What other outcome could there be, besides a chastened—or at least stymied—gentleman, or the ruin of my reputation?'

'I don't know. But I don't like being boxed into a corner.'

'Mr Tawny, I appreciate your taking the time and trouble to warn me about Lord Denbry's scheme. You could have had no idea, before meeting me, how unlikely I was to be taken in by it and can justly commend yourself for preventing what could have been some poor female's ruination. But having delivered that warning, you really bear no further responsibility for what happens next.'

He studied her for a moment. 'You're going to do this anyway, regardless of my advice.'

'I really think I must. I'd feel such a…coward, backing down now.'

'Prudence is not the same as cowardice. Do you really think showing up Denbry will teach him a lesson?'

'Probably not,' she conceded. 'But *I* will feel better, having made the attempt. As I'm sure you do, having put forth the effort to stop his scheme.'

'I've not really stopped it, if you allow it to continue.'

'Surely whether or not it continues is now my decision. Or do you, like my father and brother, feel that because I'm a female, I am not fit to choose my own future?'

'If you were a friend and a man, I would still advise you to avoid a confrontation. Please, Lady Alyssa! I can understand why, after your father stole from you the life and the love you wanted, you would resist a man's guidance. But don't let your anger over that previous injury propel you into a situation that could end up much worse.'

He watched her, hoping his appeal would persuade. He had to find some way to put a stop to this before her plan progressed any further. Even if it meant doing what he'd hoped to avoid—confronting Denbry himself.

'Will you promise me not to intervene?' she asked. 'That's what you're considering now, isn't it? Riding up to Dornton Manor, seeking out Lord Denbry and telling him you've warned me of his intentions, so he might as well take himself off?'

Sometimes she was *too* needle-witted. 'Would that be so bad? He'd be furious, of course, but hardly surprised; I told him the night he proposed the wager that I found the scheme disgraceful. He'd get over his anger—and if he didn't, there's not much he could do to injure me. Having me intervene would preserve all your alternatives. You could still argue your father into releasing your great-aunt's funds. But, if you were not living in exiled disgrace, you would safeguard your opportunities to meet, and marry, a respectable gentleman. Like your Will.'

'That's a generous offer. But you can't be eager to insert yourself into this tawdry affair, else you would have confronted Denbry at once, rather than warning me.'

'I hadn't intended to confront him,' Ben admitted. 'But I'm certainly prepared to do so, if that will prevent him causing you harm.'

'But this is personal now—don't you see? Not just a threat to some poor nameless female, *he* has threatened *me*. I want to see it through myself—not hand it over to a male champion. Will you give me your promise not to interfere?'

Ben hesitated, trying to think of a pledge that he could, in good conscience, manage to keep. 'How about this?' he said, improvising as he went along. 'I promise not to come to Dornton Manor and confront Denbry, if you promise to meet me here each morning and report your progress. In the interim, I'll remain in the village, where I can keep an eye on the posting inns, in case… further assistance should be needed.'

While she paused, considering his suggestion, he ran the plan through his head again. It wasn't perfect by any means, but it was the best guarantee of safety he could come up with on the spur of the moment. Denbry would have to hire a carriage; he wouldn't risk trying to abduct an unwilling female on horseback, her struggles clearly visible for any passer-by to notice. If Lady Alyssa insisted in holding her ground, there was nothing he could do to minimise the risk that the Earl might later try to spread rumours about her, but he could at least make sure the man couldn't make off with her.

'Do you really feel so strongly that, despite having delivered your warning, you cannot just return to London?'

'Not now—when it's the warning I gave which has prompted you to take further action. Not until Denbry, Rossiter and Quinlen leave and the danger of any confrontation is over. It's hard enough to accept that I can't do anything more to prevent them whispering about you later.'

She sighed. 'You really do have the deepest sense of responsibility I've ever encountered in a man.'

'From what you've told me of the men of your family, that wouldn't be difficult.'

'Very well. Though I hate to further delay your return to London, I agree to meet you here each morning—as long as *you* promise not to come to Dornton Manor. I don't believe it will take much longer for Denbry to suggest an elopement. First, because spending time in my company must be wearisome for him, and second, because he can't be sure my brother won't unexpectedly show up and he knows Harleton would never believe he harbours "honourable intentions" towards me. Speaking of being found out, how have you managed to lurk about Dornton Village? Hasn't the merchant who engaged you begun to wonder why a poor, unemployed former soldier remains in town, freely spending his blunt at an inn?'

'I told him there was a possibility of getting some work at Dornton later—which is true!' he added, holding up a hand to forestall her protest. 'I didn't specify *when* such employment might become available. Sooner or later, a large country house like Dornton will find itself in need of another gardener or groom or footman. And I've funded my food and lodging by engaging the locals in a few rounds of cards every evening. One couldn't leave the army in India without becoming an expert at every known game of chance.'

She shook her head at him. 'You *are* the most complete hand! I only hope you didn't fleece the poor villagers out of too much blunt.'

'Just enough to pay my shot,' Ben assured her with a grin.

She glanced up, studying the slant of sunlight through the trees. 'It's getting late. I must go.'

They both stood and he bowed to her. 'I cannot wish you good luck with your plan, Lady Alyssa, but I do wish it swiftly completed.'

'Fair enough.' She offered her hand and, bemused at that conspiratorial touch, he shook it. A startlingly intense sensual connection rocketed from her fingers to his, firing the smoking attraction between them back to flame.

For a moment, they stood that hand-clasp apart, gazes riveting, the desire he recognised in her eyes making it even more difficult for Ben to fight off the urgent need to kiss her.

Before he lost the battle, she dropped her gaze and pulled her hand free. 'No one has ever volunteered to be my champion,' she said, her voice gruff. 'I'm very touched by your offer—even though I can't accept it. Until tomorrow, Mr Tawny.'

'Until tomorrow, Lady Alyssa.'

Absently rubbing his fingers, where her touch still seemed to tingle on his skin, he watched her walk away, battling the urge to follow and intervene, despite her express wish. He hated having his hands tied, even though he'd devised a plan that stood a reasonable chance of protecting her.

Concentrating on how best to guarantee her safety might help him fight off the desire that simple handshake had just fired in him. He should also remind himself that a gently bred virgin was off limits, no matter that it seemed she wanted him as much as he wanted her.

Although he disagreed with almost every other particular, he thought she was correct in assuming Denbry would push to complete his plan in the shortest possible time. He certainly hoped so.

Then he could get himself back to his work in London and bury any lingering regret at bidding farewell to the dangerously alluring Lady Alyssa Lambornne.

# *Chapter Four*

Three days later, Alyssa walked in the early morning sunlight towards the clearing where, as promised, she'd been meeting Mr Tawny. She'd begun looking forward to those encounters far more than she should—the novelty of conversing with an intelligent man who listened to her opinions and observations as she reported on the progress of Denbry's wooing; the delight of making him laugh as she described the timid, yet increasingly adoring behaviour that must be exasperating the Earl almost beyond bearing.

And then there was that sensual awareness in his eyes as he watched her; the zing of attraction that made her pulses leap when she saw him and kept her awake at night, wondering what it would be like to kiss him. Be possessed by him.

In turning her back on marriage, she was likely shutting away passion as well—before she'd ever had a chance to fully taste its pleasures. Pleasures that what he'd admitted about himself, and what she sensed every time she was near him, said he'd be able to deliver in full measure.

Sadly, their meetings would end before she had a chance to decide if it was worth the risk of pursuing that attraction. Yesterday, Lord Denbry had finally revealed his plan for the elopement he'd several times hinted at and last night was to have been the rendezvous.

With a smile, she wondered how he had reacted when, instead of her ardent self, he received at the inn the note she'd had delivered.

She doubted he'd return today to confront her—what could he possibly say, in front of her mother and the assembled guests? And she'd certainly not agree to any more cosy walks alone in the garden! Most likely, after cursing her soundly, he'd availed himself of the horses and carriage and set off—wherever it was dissolute young men like him set off to assuage their frustrations.

Intent on watching the drive for signs of Mr Tawny, she didn't hear the footsteps behind her until a branch snapped close by. Alarmed, she whirled around—but it was only Mr Rossiter, who'd ceased approaching her, once his charismatic friend had begun monopolising her time—though his hopeful gaze still followed her.

Relieved that she wasn't facing a potentially nasty interview with a furious Lord Denbry, she said, 'Mr Rossiter! What brings you out so early?'

'You do,' he replied, giving her a shy smile. If she hadn't known he'd been involved in the wager, she might almost have been charmed by it. 'Your maid, Molly, told me you liked to come out early to sketch.'

'I don't wish to be uncivil, but she should also have told you I prefer to sketch alone.'

'Oh, sorry—I didn't intend to bother you. I—I

guess Denbry did enough of that. Quite a joke you played on him.'

'He told you about it?' she asked, surprised that the Earl had confessed his come-uppance to anyone.

'Yes. He was furious when he arrived back last night, but after telling Quinlen and me about it, realised that remaining so could only make him look ridiculous. We had a great good laugh. You needn't worry that he intends to confront you; he decided it would be better to pen you a note of apology and take himself off quietly.'

The gaze he fixed on her seemed so open and genuine. But she mustn't forget he was one of Denbry's friends. She would be foolish to relax her guard.

She'd feel a lot better if she could induce him to return to the house before Mr Tawny arrived. This would probably be her last meeting with that fascinating gentleman; she didn't want an uninvited intruder watching, imposing restraints over what should be their private victory celebration.

Then a far more unpleasant realisation struck her. At present, Denbry had no reason not to believe she'd foiled the elopement all on her own. But if Rossiter were still lingering when Mr Tawny arrived, he would almost certainly conclude that Tawny had warned her about the plot—and inform Denbry. Which might well cause Tawny problems with the disgruntled conspirators.

She didn't want to repay his generosity by making him some rather nasty enemies.

'I hope, now he's gone, I might claim more of your time?' Rossiter was saying, giving her that tentative smile. 'I would like to get to know you better.'

'That's kind of you—but later, please? This morning

light will be gone soon. Again, at the risk of seeming impolite, I work better alone.'

'Of course. Before I go, won't you have some of this?' From a bag slung over his shoulder, he produced a jar. 'The morning being chilly, I got the kitchen to make up some coffee for us. Surely you can spare the time to have a cup.'

'Very well.' Eager to get rid of him, she waited impatiently as he poured out some coffee, then drank hers quickly down, despite it being cloyingly sweet. 'Very warming, thank you,' she said, offering back the cup.

'Another one?'

'No, that was quite enough. I'm anxious to begin,' she reminded pointedly.

'I'll just gather these up and be on my way, then. Until later, Lady Alyssa.'

Quickly she handed over the cup, gathered her supplies and made a show of walking from the glen, intending to return once Rossiter was out of sight.

As she stepped down the pathway, she stumbled over the uneven ground and had more difficulty than she should righting herself. Her hands felt unusually warm, her tongue thick, her head woozy.

And then Rossiter was behind her. 'Is something amiss, Lady Alyssa?'

'I—I feel suddenly so…strange.'

'Let me help you,' he said and reached out to steady her.

An instant later, he pulled her into his arms and slapped a rag over her nose and mouth. For a moment, she flailed against him, but her arms and legs seemed clumsy, unable to obey her commands. And then her head started to whirl and dizziness claimed her.

A few moments later, Alyssa's vision cleared, but the weakness in her limbs continued, while her tongue seemed too thick for speech. With the rag wrapped around her mouth and nose, she had to take quick, shallow breaths to keep the blackness from overwhelming her again.

Her feeble efforts at resistance did not prevent Rossiter from carrying her down the lane, where around the next bend a coach waited. So it was to be forced elopement after all, she thought, still too weak for the ripple of anger running through her to give her the strength to prevent it.

*Rest now and marshal your resources for later.* She sank back limply against the seat, pretending to faint again. She was too angry to bandy words with Rossiter and, knowing how carefully schemed this was, there was little chance she'd be able to talk him out of it anyway.

She dozed off in truth, not waking until the jolting coach halted. They must have reached the inn, she thought muzzily. Now would be the time to make her escape. But a tentative moving of her limbs showed her she was still too impaired to fight off her abductor.

'End this now…let me go…and I will…say nothing,' she gasped under the confining cloth.

'Rest easy, Lady Alyssa, I mean you no harm,' Rossiter assured her. 'Can't have you sticking a spoke in the wheel now, though.'

Before she could respond, he tightened the cloth until she could barely breathe. He wrapped her tightly in a long cloak before extracting her from the coach, carrying her into the inn and immediately up the stairs.

'…sister…overcome on the road…'

She heard Denbry's voice in the background. A moment later, Rossiter carried her into a large room, shouldering the door closed behind him, and deposited her on the bed, her head reclining against the pillows.

'Sorry for this, Lady Alyssa, but couldn't have you shouting down the innkeeper,' he said as he pulled off the rag. 'No need for tears, though. As I said, I mean you no harm.'

She took a deep gulp, the influx of fresh air helping to clear her muzzy head. 'Just what do you think you are about?'

He gave her a jaunty grin. 'We're eloping! Denbry promised once his "seduction" was complete, I could have you. That didn't work out so well for him, but he's kept his word on the other, so you will end up respectably married after all.'

He had the gall to smile at her, as if his condescending to wed her excused everything.

'Can you truly believe, after you drugged me and carried me off against my will, I would consent to marry you?' she asked incredulously.

He patted her hand, as if she were a dim-witted child. 'You're ruined now, so you'll have to wed me. Won't be so bad, really. You'll be mistress of your own house in the country and I'll be in London. I'm not adverse to children; if you want them, I can nip back now and then to do the deed.'

'While my dowry funds your London activities, I suppose? I can't imagine any other reason you would want to run off with me.'

'Couldn't marry a pauper. You've got the funds, the

proper pedigree and, at your age, should consider yourself lucky to end up respectably wed.'

Though her head was almost clear now, she still lacked the strength to give him the slap she would have liked to deliver. 'I'm *vastly* sorry to spoil your dream of getting your hands on my dowry, but I have no intention of marrying you. That trick with the laudanum won't work for a wedding; the church requires willing consent and that I will never give. Instead, I mean to lodge charges of assault and kidnapping against you with the first magistrate I can find!'

His cheerful expression fading, he drew away, for the first time looking less than confident. 'There, now, no need for anything like that! Made you a respectable offer of marriage, I did!'

'You drugged my coffee, carried me off against my will and forced me into this inn. I don't believe any of that qualifies as a "respectable"!'

'But you have to marry me! An elopement is bad enough; when it gets out that you've come to the inn with me, your reputation will be ruined! No one in society would ever receive you again, nor would you ever have a chance to marry.'

She nodded, pleased to find the motion did not bring a return of the dizziness. If she could keep him talking long enough for her to fully recover, she should be able to get away before he could bundle her back into the coach.

'That may be true. But I would rather live in isolation with a ruined reputation than marry you. And since my reputation will already be destroyed, why should I be bothered by the additional scandal of bringing you up on charges of assault and kidnapping?'

He blinked at her, obviously having never anticipated any reaction but tearful acquiescence. 'You can't really intend to bring charges against me.'

'Unless you release me this minute, I intend to do exactly that.'

He stared at her, a worried frown creasing his forehead. When she stared back, unmoving, he backed to the door and opened it a fraction. 'Denbry! She says she won't come with me. What do I do now?'

So the Earl was still the puppet master. A moment later, the man himself walked into the chamber. 'Lady Alyssa, you are making yourself quite a nuisance.'

'Because I haven't gone into weeping hysterics and gratefully embraced your scheme?'

'You may not be weeping, but you must be hysterical,' he said with a patronising smile. 'Come now! What other reasonable option do you have, but to marry Rossiter? At least he's *willing* to marry you! Surely you're not stupid enough to imagine any other respectable man would offer for you, once word of this fiasco gets out—and it will, you know. Scandal this delicious can't be hushed up.'

'You'd be sure to see to that, wouldn't you?' she flashed back.

Exasperation wiped the kindly expression from his face. 'Listen, you contrary little…! I've got no more patience with your doubts and complaints. You're going to accompany us downstairs and into the carriage with every evidence of cheerful compliance. If I hear any more about charges or protests, I'll ruin you myself and leave you here. With no reputation, no wedding and perhaps a bastard brat to look forward to!'

'Ah, fine, I can add attempted rape to the charges.

And I'd rather bear a bastard brat than marry either of you.'

'Attempted—wait, now!' Rossiter cried, holding up a hand. Looking back at Denbry accusingly, he said, 'You told me it would be simple! Just get her to the inn, she'd make a few token protests and then we'd be off to the border and I'd have a rich, compliant wife. I don't want any part of rape, or assault, or charges! I'm finished here.'

With that, Rossiter hurried from the room.

Denbry looked back at her. 'Stupid girl! You just lost your last bid for respectability. Rossiter would at least have married you. Whereas I have no such intention. But after all the trouble you've caused, I think I'll have a little fun before I leave you to your fate.'

The longer the conversation lasted, the more recovered Alyssa felt from the weakening effects of the drug. She probably still couldn't fight off a Denbry intent on raping her—but she could shout the house down. It was still early morning, with an inn full of guests and maids bustling about. Someone was bound to hear her.

An angry glitter in his eye, Denbry advanced on her. But before he reached the bed, the chamber door flew open—and Benedict Tawny strode in.

Closing the door behind him, he halted, his rapid gaze taking in Alyssa stretched out on the bed—and Denbry rounding on her. With a furious oath, he launched himself at the Earl, delivering a roundhouse punch to the jaw that sent the man reeling backwards.

'Lady Alyssa, are you all right?' Tawny cried. 'When I found your sketchbook in the woods, I thought—'

'I'm fine. Rossiter drugged my coffee so he could carry me off, but I'm almost over that now. And he—'

she motioned towards Denbry, who was staggering to his feet '—hasn't touched me—yet.'

'If he tries to touch you, it will be the last time he ever uses that hand,' Tawny said furiously. Turning to the man, he said, 'Get up. And get out, before I forget that I, at least, am a gentleman and pound the life out of you, you miserable cur.'

'Tawny,' Denbry said as he rubbed his jaw. 'Should have known the wench couldn't have figured this out on her own. How long have you been coaching her?'

'You knew I didn't approve of this…wager of yours. I thought it only right to warn her. Though I'd advised her to simply leave Dornton Park, rather than risk having things escalate to—*this*.' He gestured around the room.

'But it can still end well,' Tawny said, turning back to Alyssa. 'The innkeeper told me the gentleman's "sister" found herself too unwell to embark on her journey, so as far as anyone knows, your reason for being in this room is entirely respectable. Once Denbry departs, I'll await you downstairs, telling the innkeeper that though you've somewhat better, you've decided to return to Dornton Park.'

After reassuring her, he turned to the Earl. Despicable Denbry might be, and obviously no match for Tawny's pugilistic prowess, for he'd made no move to try to return the punch, but Alyssa had to allow he was no coward. Knowing his adversary could best him if he chose, he stood his ground, rather than trying to flee.

'As for you,' Tawny said, 'if even a whisper of scandal about this emerges, I'll know who's responsible. And when I track you down, I will have forgotten I'm a gentleman who only fights fair.'

'Given your breeding, you could have no idea what it means to be a gentleman.'

'If it is breeding that tells, you'd better question your mother about her activities nine months before your birth,' Tawny shot back.

'Enjoyable as it would be to stand here, trading insults, I believe I will depart.' Straightening his cravat and using a handkerchief to mop at the cut on his chin, he said, 'How fitting that you felt such concern about safeguarding Lady Alyssa's reputation. Since you're now going to have an opportunity to do so in truth.' With that parting shot, Denbry strolled out of the room.

A moment later, they heard the click of a key turning in the lock.

Tawny walked over to try the door, finding it had indeed been locked from the outside.

'What does he hope to achieve by that?' Alyssa asked. 'Unless he means to tell the innkeeper that his "sister" feigned an illness to sneak away to an assignation.'

'If he does, we'll say your cousin has a warped sense of humour. You just need to look suitably ill when I escort you back down the stairs.'

'How do we get back down the stairs? Pound on the door, until someone comes to release us?'

Tawny went to look out the window. 'This room overlooks the fields, rather than the main road or stable yard. It would probably be better if I climbed down and came up to fetch you, then went back to report that you'd somehow locked yourself in.'

'Yes, that would probably be wiser.'

The full significance of what Mr Tawny had done for her was just beginning to register in her still-sluggish brain. 'It appears you've prevented ruination after all, Mr Tawny. I'm not so sure I want to thank you for that, but I do very much appreciate the sense of honour that led you to continue watching out for me, no matter how much you disapproved of my scheme.'

'Denbry will take himself off now, his acolytes in tow, so I don't think you'll have any further trouble with them. Though I'm certainly not sorry to have prevented your ruin, perhaps I can make up for my unwelcome intervention by helping you think of a way to convince your father to release your funds.'

Her relief, now that Denbry had departed, the charming smile that accompanied Tawny's remark and the sudden realisation that they were alone in a bedchamber, with her still reclining on the bed and him a few steps away, prompted a resurgence of the simmering desire he triggered in her whenever he came near. A desire that urged her to invite him down into her arms.

She struggled to banish it. If Tawny, rather than Denbry, had been the one to propose the ravishing, she would have been tempted to acquiesce. Will had been torn from her before she'd had to the chance to sample more than a few torrid kisses. Once she obtained her aunt's funds and withdrew from society, it was unlikely she'd ever have another chance to seduce—or be seduced by—a gentleman whose intelligence, honour and kindness she admired as much as did Ben Tawny's.

Inviting him on to the bed would be too dangerous—she didn't want to risk conceiving a bastard. But surely she could invite a kiss.

'My rescuer deserves my thanks, whether or not I wanted to be rescued.' Rising, she started to walk towards him, then swayed, as dizziness suddenly returned. 'Sorry,' she said, clutching the side of the bed. 'It seems I'm not fully recovered yet.'

Tawny came over to steady her. His warm hands on her shoulders instantly catapulted desire from languor to urgent need, her already swimming senses engulfed by the power of his nearness. She leaned into him, all her being focused on one aim.

She'd have that parting kiss—if he wanted it as much as she did. Willing him to act on the sensual connection between them, she angled her face up—and waited.

'This makes it all worthwhile,' he murmured. And leaned down to claim her mouth.

His lips were gentle, tender. A wave of grief and regret for all she'd lost was soon swamped by an overwhelming need that had her moaning deep in her throat as she clutched his shoulders and pressed closer.

She'd just opened her lips to the tentative probing of his tongue when, with a fierce oath, he thrust her away.

With an incoherent protest, she opened her eyes—to find him gazing at the door, his expression grim. Before she could ask what was wrong, a strident female voice cried, 'Lady Alyssa! What is the meaning of this?'

## *Chapter Five*

Dismay extinguishing ardour, Ben watched the two ladies rush into the room with a sense of detachment, as if this farce were being played out on a London theatre—not on the stage of his life, where the curtain had just rung down on the current act. When it rose again, he was going to be forced to play a very different part from the one he'd envisioned.

And there was absolutely nothing he could do to prevent it.

*So that was what Denbry had meant with his parting remark about safeguarding Lady Alyssa's reputation.* Before he left Dornton Manor, the Earl must have tipped off the ladies to the impending elopement, knowing once the 'lovers' were discovered, Lady Alyssa's family would insist the shame of her seduction be concealed by marriage.

'My darling child, what have you done?' cried the female who must be her mother. 'What are you doing at this inn—and who is that *man*?'

'I think it's rather obvious what she—and he—were doing, as we interrupted them in mid-embrace!' the other lady proclaimed. 'Shocking behaviour! If I hadn't seen it with my own eyes, I would never have believed it of you!'

Her eyes reflecting consternation as profound as his, after whispering 'I'm sorry!,' Lady Alyssa turned to face the women. 'Mama, Lady Fulton, you must let me explain. Things are not as they appear.'

'Before you explain anything, we must get you out of this common inn, before the world and all his brother sees you—and your reputation is shredded beyond mending!' Lady Fulton exclaimed. Confirming Ben's suspicions, she added, 'Thank heavens, having spent so much time in your company, Lord Denbry suspected something was afoot and warned us in time!'

'Did he really?' Lady Alyssa said drily.

'Come along this instant. And *you*, whoever you are,' Lady Fulton said, glaring at him, 'had better present yourself at Dornton Manor immediately!'

'Benedict Tawny,' he said with a bow. 'There will be time for explanations later, but first, let me inform you quickly that the innkeeper was told Lady Alyssa was the sister of the gentleman who brought her here and had been taken ill on the road after leaving Dornton. If you ladies support that story, explaining that you've come to escort her back to the manor, she should be able to leave here with no aspersions cast on her honour.'

'As long as neither of you came rushing in, claiming elopement,' Lady Alyssa added.

'Of course we wouldn't be so foolish,' Lady Aldermont said. 'We hoped to arrive in time to prevent one!'

'Then, Lady Alyssa, if you would play the invalid, I suggest all of you return to Dornton,' Ben said. 'I'll pay the shot and join you shortly.'

'Thank heavens you can do *something* useful,' Lady Fulton said acidly, giving him a glance that informed him she still viewed him as a vile seducer. 'That's not the end of this, though! I expect to see you at Dornton Manor within the hour!'

Ben bowed. 'I will be there.'

'No!' Lady Alyssa cried in furious protest. 'It's unthinkable that you should incur any blame in this! Return to London! I'll sort it out.'

Ben suppressed a sigh. Obviously, she hadn't yet realised there could be no 'sorting out'. Not for a man who really *was* a gentleman.

'You must know that's not possible now,' he said gently. 'I'll see you at Dornton later.' He managed to dredge up a smile—as if his life hadn't just been thrown off course right before his eyes with the speed of a runaway carriage. 'Make sure you are a convincing invalid. Ladies, you'd best get on the road.'

When Lady Alyssa opened her lips again, he held out a hand to forestall further argument. 'Indulge me on this, please. Go with your mother and Lady Fulton. We'll sort it out at Dornton.'

'But this is insufferable!' Her cheeks pink with anger and vexation, her eyes bright with distress, she stood motionless, staring at him. Finally, yielding to the plea on his face, she marched to the bedside chair, tossed her cloak about her shoulders and jammed the bonnet on her head.

'Very well, I'm ready,' she told her mother, who wrapped an arm around her shoulders to 'support' her. As she walked out, leaning against Lady Aldermont, she looked over her shoulder at him. 'This isn't finished yet!'

*Oh, yes, it is*, Ben thought as they exited the room. *Wiggle, squirm and protest all you like, there's only one way out for us now.*

Still wrapped in that curious sense of detachment, as if he were only an observer to the tragedy unfolding in his life, Ben descended to the taproom to pay the innkeeper. The hefty tip he added induced the man to send him off with hearty wishes that his ailing cousin soon recovered her health.

Would that their position were so easy to fix.

But after examining the situation from every angle as he followed them back to Dornton Manor, Ben could see only one honourable exit from this disaster.

Both Lady Alyssa's mother and her hostess had seen him embracing her in an upper chamber of a posting inn. Even if the story of her 'being taken ill on the road' managed to damp down any gossip in the village, those two ladies thought they were interrupting a seduction—a charge his kiss only reinforced.

They could try—Lady Alyssa would probably insist on it—to explain the tangled web of wagers, courtships and botched elopement that had led to their being discovered alone together. They might even be able to have the innkeeper testify it was the Earl who hired the carriage Lady Alyssa arrived in. But with Denbry and Rossiter nowhere to be seen when they'd been discovered, and with neither of them likely to confess their parts in the scheme, such accusations were not provable and would probably sound ridiculous.

Instead of trapping Lady Alyssa into the marriage Rossiter wanted, Denbry trapped Ben instead. And doubtless considered it a fine joke and a fitting revenge on the man who'd spoiled his wager.

Of course, Ben could insist on standing by the truth, flatly deny he'd attempted to run away with Lady Alyssa and leave. But she'd still be ruined. With the guests at Dornton Manor agog at the sudden departure of Rossiter and Denbry and a plethora of gossiping servants, Lady Fulton and Lady Aldermont's early-morning drive to the village to bring back Lady Alyssa was bound to come out.

She'd be laughed at, pitied. Ruined.

He thought about the small manor in which he'd grown up, his mother an outcast, known as a nobleman's former mistress who'd borne a bastard. She'd been ostracised for that sin every day of her life.

There might not be a bastard child involved, but ruination would isolate Lady Alyssa just as completely, in ways that she, for her whole life an accepted member of society, couldn't possibly imagine. Having grave doubts about her ability to use scandal to convince her father to let her live independently, he hadn't been able to square it with his conscience to leave while the scheme went forward, too worried that Denbry or Rossiter would somehow achieve her ruin. He certainly couldn't walk away now that *he* was thought responsible for it.

He couldn't, wouldn't let Lady Alyssa suffer as his mother had.

So it appeared, like it or not, he was going to be married.

Unless Lady Alyssa's family believed ruin was preferable to having an earl's daughter marry a viscount's bastard son.

That slender hope quickly died. Most likely, they would consider ruination worse.

Having reached that unhappy conclusion, Ben tried for the rest of the ride to Dornton Manor to find a cheerful face and drum up some enthusiasm for a match he knew initially Lady Alyssa would oppose. She had a sharp eye and no tolerance for empty flattery, so if he wanted to be convincing, he'd have to pull up something that came from the heart.

First, he likely face the gauntlet of Lady Aldermont and Lady Fulton.

Once he'd turned his horse over to a groom and announced himself to the butler, he was immediately ushered to a small study near the kitchen entrance—probably to forestall his discovery by the other members of the house party. Instead of the ladies, however, it was Lord Fulton who came in to meet him.

As soon as the door shut behind him, Lord Fulton exploded, 'Damnation, man, why resort to some crack-brained elopement? Granted, your pedigree might be a bit…marred, but your father acknowledges you and you've built up a good reputation in Parliament. No need for anything so havey-cavey! With his daughter so long on the shelf, Lord Aldermont would almost certainly have given his permission for you to marry. I suppose a girl nowadays think it romantic to imagine herself a star-crossed lover, forbidden by her father to marry the unacceptable man she loves, but the chit should have had more sense!'

'A star-crossed lover?' Ben repeated, completely mystified.

'I should have been more suspicious when Lady Alyssa cornered me in my library to ask about the Reform Bill! As if a female would have any interest or understanding of politics! But m'wife told me she had some proper suitors here, so until *this* happened, I didn't recall that she'd asked about all four of you "Hadley's Hellions"—and you in particular. I gave you a good character. Hah!' he said with a snort. 'It appears now I shouldn't have. She must have been leading on those other men, just to throw her mother off the scent.'

'She asked you about me?'

'Didn't I just say that?' Lord Fulton replied irritably. 'Now the deed's done, we need to wrap it up as much as possible in clean linen. Fortunately, you weren't daft enough to admit to the innkeeper that you were eloping, so we can squelch any gossip from the village. If you arrive today and we let it be known your father is a longtime friend of the Lambornnes, you can woo the girl and propose in the usual way. No one but her mother, my wife and I need know the truth. I'll even pressure Aldermont to accept your offer, if that becomes necessary. Hardly a good match for an earl's daughter, but under the circumstances, better than none. You do intend to offer for her?' he asked, turning a stern eye on Ben.

'Of course.' There was no other acceptable answer, he thought on a wave of desolation.

'Good. Didn't think you were the sort to seduce a girl and then abandon her, even if you do have a reputation as a rake. We shall come out of this all right and tight, then. M'lady wife is laid upon her bed at present, recovering from the shock of it, so I'll get the housekeeper to assign you to a room. You can join the rest of the party later today.'

A knock sounded at the door, followed by the entrance of the butler. 'I'm sorry, my lord, but upon being informed that Mr Tawny was with you, Lady Alyssa insisted on intruding.'

Despite his efforts to block the doorway, the lady herself pushed in. 'My lord, would you allow me to speak with Mr Tawny? Alone? I assure you, it is very important.'

'Haven't you had enough of closeting yourself alone with this gentleman, miss?' Fulton retorted. 'Your lover will be presented to the party later today. You'll have plenty of opportunity to speak then.'

'I shall speak to him now,' Lady Alyssa said evenly. 'Alone. Or, if you will not permit that, I shall pack my things and ride away with him.'

Lord Fulton uttered an oath, followed by comments critical of her good sense and breeding, which Lady Alyssa, signalling Ben with a wave of her hand not to intervene, endured in silence. When her agitated host at last paused for breath, she said, 'Will you leave so I may speak to him? Or should I call for a horse?'

For several long moments, they stared at each other, Fulton irritated and discomposed, Lady Alyssa unflinching.

At last, Fulton said, 'Oh, very well! Since the damage is already done and he's agreed to wed you, I'll allow it. But don't tell your mother or Lady Fulton.'

'I shall not. Thank you, Lord Fulton.' Nodding a dismissal as calmly as if this were her salon and he the intruder, Lady Alyssa waited for Lord Fulton to walk out.

Which he did, after pausing on the threshold to give them both a black look. 'Young people today! What happened to manners and breeding?' Shutting the door with a decided slam, they heard him stomp down the hall.

As soon as his footsteps faded, Lady Alyssa came to Ben. 'I won't let them do this to you.'

For an instant, his spirits leapt with the wild hope that he might escape matrimony after all. But then reality intervened, plunging him back to earth.

Summoning a smile, he said, 'It's beyond that, I'm afraid. I think we should rather be discussing how we're going to make the best of this.'

She stamped her foot, uttering an oath that shocked him. 'I never thought you, of all people, would give in so...spinelessly! It's beyond enduring that, after all the trouble you took to ensure my safety, *you* were the one trapped by the plot! As you well know, I am quite happy to be ruined. But I never meant to entangle you in it! If I could find Denbry now, I *would* shoot him!'

'I'd give you the pistol,' Ben said, attempting to lighten her mood. 'I admit, I'm...not very happy to be entangled. But it's foolish to imagine I can simply step aside now. It was one thing for Lord Denbry to ruin you and disappear, with no proof of his involvement. Or for Mr Rossiter to be found with you, when marrying you was what he wanted anyway. But now *my* name is the one your family will identify as your seducer and, if we don't marry, it is *my* name and reputation that will suffer almost as much as yours.'

'You would marry a woman you don't want, to salvage your reputation?'

'I would marry a woman of character, intelligence and charm, with whom I expect I could live with quite happily for the rest of our lives, to save her reputation and my own,' he replied, choosing his words carefully.

'One you could live with "quite happily",' she repeated. 'And what happens when you encounter a woman whom you desire with every fibre of your being, whose very presence fills you with joy and without whom you know your life would be blighted for ever?'

Before he could reply, she shook her head. 'No! I cannot let you do it. I *have* known a man who made me feel complete, whose presence and understanding and tenderness filled me with joy. You deserve to experience that, too. I won't let society's expectations, or your own sense of honour, rob you of it.'

'Not everyone experiences a love like that,' Ben countered. 'I'm nearly one-and-thirty; if I were going to encounter such a thing, I probably already would have. Perhaps I'm not capable of it.'

Nor did he truly want to experience a love that robbed one of reason and could plunge one into despair. A marriage of convenience would spare him that, he suddenly realised.

'A man as honourable, compassionate, and understanding as you?' she said. 'No, we shall not marry. In the eyes of my family, I shall be ruined, just as I want to be. Some whisper of the scandal will likely leak out, troublesome perhaps for a while, but it will fade. In the interim, you can return to the life you've planned, free to pursue your dreams, as I will be free to pursue mine.'

So she was still counting on the scandal to help her achieve her aims. Knowing the way autocratic men acted, Ben was much less sure disgrace would gain her what she sought. 'Are you so certain being ruined will induce your father to release your trust? He's sure to be outraged by your refusal to wed and could well conclude that obstinacy shows you possess so little sense that you haven't the wit to manage your own funds.'

She flinched at that assessment. 'He already thinks

I haven't any sense, else I would have accepted one of the respectable offers I received during my Seasons. I'm betting that his desire to rid himself of a daughter he's never liked, who has involved the family name in scandal, will outweigh his desire to control my funds and my life. But let's say it does not. Even if I don't gain the means to control my future, you, who are entirely blameless, should be free to pursue yours. *I* was the one obsessed with foiling Denbry's aims; it should not be *you* who pays for it.'

'Now who's being noble?' He gave her a wry smile. 'You insisted on following your plan, but I insisted on remaining in Dornton Village, against *your* advice. I was fully aware of the risks. And I'm fully prepared to face the consequences and do my duty.'

She flinched. 'What makes you think I want to marry a man who considers me a "duty"? When once I had a suitor who considered me his "beloved"?'

He was struck by the hurt she tried to mask. Had she felt all her life that her family regarded her as a burden, to be handed off to another man as soon as possible? 'Duty can also be pleasure, Lady Alyssa,' he said quietly. 'I find you lovely, intelligent, principled, courageous and very talented. Many couples have built strong marriages on far less. I shall do everything I can to make you happy. That, I promise you.'

She turned away from him, swiping at eyes now sheened with tears. 'My dear Mr Tawny,' she said, a tremble in her voice. 'Honourable to the very end. Don't worry, I shall take care of this for us both.'

She held out her hand. 'I'll say goodbye now, with my most sincere apologies. You wanted nothing but my good; I'm sorry to have repaid your noble intentions with a tawdry scandal. As I don't expect to see you again, I hope you soon get your Reform Bill passed and wish you a glorious future in Parliament.'

Ignoring her hand, Ben said, 'Not see me again? What do you mean?'

'I shall stay in my room, refusing to see you. I'll inform my mother I will not consider your suit and want to return home at once. I couldn't live with myself if I took advantage of your honour and compassion to ruin your life because of my own stubbornness.'

And then, instead of seizing his hand to shake, she reached up and pulled his mouth down to hers.

Her kiss was wild, fierce, angry, a testament to the passion he'd sensed in her. Swept beyond thought, he responded with an answering hunger, plundering her mouth as she opened to him, seeking out her tongue and tangling his with it, while she murmured low in her throat and urged him closer.

Ah, how he loved the softness of her bosom against his chest, the delightful roundness of her bottom. Need—sharp, deep, compelling—sang in his blood as he deepened the kiss, desire rippling across his skin, travelling to every part of his awakening body.

She kissed him with just as much fervour, her hands sliding down his back to caress his buttocks and pull his burgeoning erection closer. Not until his hands went of their own volition to tug at the tapes of her gown, did she push him away and break the kiss.

For a moment, they simply stood, their panting breaths loud in the silence of the salon. Her face was flushed, her breathing rapid, her eyes dilated with desire, while her kiss-reddened lips begged him to pull her back into his arms and begin again.

But before he could move, or retrieve his absent wits to point out what a good omen mutual desire was for happiness in marriage, Lady Alyssa stepped back.

'Goodbye, Mr Tawny,' she said breathlessly. Then whirled around and hurried out the door.

# *Chapter Six*

In the committee room three weeks later, Ben surfaced from his abstraction to find Christopher Lattimar waving a paper in front of his face. 'Penny for your thoughts? Or perhaps I ought to make it a crown, since you've been so distracted.' Putting down the document, Christopher said, 'Giles and Davie won't be back for another week. We have plenty of time to review these proposals. Since I can't get you to pay attention anyway, why don't we repair to the Quill and Gavel for a few rounds?'

Inwardly revolted at the idea of visiting the place, he said, 'You're right; I can't concentrate. But I'd rather we go back to the town house.'

Christopher shook his head. 'You haven't wanted to visit the tavern once, this whole week. What is going on?'

Maybe he should confide in his friend. As of yet, he'd heard nothing further from Lady Alyssa or her family. No rumours of her ruination at a country house party had filtered back to London, as far as he knew.

But he didn't mix much in society; Christopher, who

was much better socially connected, would be more likely to hear all the latest *on dits*.

Perhaps he should disclose what happened to Christopher. His friend could alert him at the first whisper of scandal, so he could take the appropriate action.

Because he was still not convinced that yielding to Lady Alyssa's refusal to marry had been the best course of action.

What was he to say to Lord Fulton, should he ever encounter that gentleman? Or to Lady Alyssa's sire, in the unlikely event they met?

Regardless of Lady Alyssa's refusal to marry him, in the eyes of several society members, he was still considered an amoral seducer. For a man who prided himself on his honourable dealings with ladies, for whom the imperative to protect women had been burned into his soul since childhood, it was a slur that continued to burn, like salt rubbed into a wound.

'Ben?' Christopher said, snapping his fingers in front of his nose. 'You're beginning to worry me.'

His friend's handsome brow was furrowed with concern. Making up his mind on the instant, Ben said, 'Very well, I'll tell you. But over ale at Queen Street. You'll soon understand why I no longer favour the Quill and Gavel.'

The two friends summoned a hackney to carry them into Mayfair, where Ben's father had insisted on loaning him the use of a town house.

Once ensconced in the library, glasses of port in hand, Ben said, 'This is long, complicated and almost unbelievable, so please hold any comments until I reach the end.'

He proceeded to fill his friend in on the convoluted train of events, from the ill-fated evening at the Quill and Gavel to his eventual return, alone, from Dornton Manor.

'Damnation!' Christopher exploded when at last Ben had finished. 'I *knew* I should have insisted you come with me to Wiltshire. You would never have been drawn into this business!'

'Despite how it all worked out, I can't truly be sorry I was drawn into it. If I'd not gone to warn Lady Alyssa, Denbry or Rossiter might have been able to make off with her. Not that, after discovering what an intelligent, discerning woman she is, I think either would have managed to seduce her. But if Rossiter were intent on forcing her into marriage to obtain her dowry, she wouldn't have been able to resist him. And once he'd...deflowered her, she might have reconsidered her refusal to marry him.'

'You're still uneasy about the rumours getting out, destroying her reputation and tarnishing yours.'

'Yes. Although I don't see what else I could have done to prevent that. Lady Alyssa kept her pledge not to see me again. I hung about Dornton Manor for several days, sending her notes pleading that she reconsider, to no avail. I'm sure her mother and Lady Fulton harangued her endlessly, but she was adamant. Finally, Lady Aldermont told me I might as well return to London, as it was clear her daughter would not relent.'

'So at this point only the Fultons and her mother know what happened?'

'And Denbry, Rossiter and Quinlen. Although I warned Denbry if any word of it got out, I'd know who to blame and he'd never use his hands again. In any event, embroiling me in this, after I'd tried to ruin his scheme, is probably revenge enough for him, whether I end up married or not.'

Christopher bent a penetrating gaze on him. 'Do you *want* to be married?'

Avoiding a direct answer, Ben said, 'I can't shake the uneasy feeling that, at some point, the scandal is going to rise up to damage me. Cutting a swathe through the *demi-monde* is one thing; it's almost expected. But compromising a woman of good birth, and then not marrying her, would earn me condemnation from more than just society, it would damn me in the eyes of the honest folk of my district. How could I claim to want justice and fairness for all, then ruin an innocent, without appearing to be, at best, a hypocrite? Even if only the Fultons and her parents ever learn of it, they still believe Lady Alyssa was compromised. By failing to marry her, I've proved myself less than a gentleman.' He paused. 'What would my mother say?'

Christopher clapped him on the back, no words necessary to convey his understanding. 'And the lady couldn't be convinced that marriage was a better option than having her family disdain her?'

'Sadly, she's used to their disdain—which is such a pity! If I weren't already conflicted enough, she insisted *her* sense of honour won't allow me to sacrifice myself, when my intention was only to save hers. How can one argue with a sense of honour?'

'She sounds very unusual. I can't think of another single female who would choose ruin over the regrettable necessity of marriage. Especially not to a handsome, charming fellow like you who knows so well how to delight the ladies. Maybe you should have tried to make love to her.'

Ben had no intention of confessing to Christopher just how close to that he'd come. Nor did he intend to admit that, deep down, he couldn't shake the insidious suspicion that though her family was willing to take him, Lady Alyssa couldn't bring herself to marry a bastard son.

Shaking off those thoughts, he continued, 'She has some bird-witted notion that being ruined will make it more likely she can persuade her father to release the money left her by her great-aunt, so she can set up her own household. If only I had more confidence that she *could* persuade him! I wouldn't mind so much having a slur against my character, if Lady Alyssa were to end up getting what she truly wanted.'

Christopher looked at him with surprise. 'She wants to live all alone? Whatever for? Is she…malformed?'

Picturing Lady Alyssa's lush, petite figure and mesmerising eyes, Ben laughed. 'Far from it! She's not the classic blue-eyed, golden-haired English beauty, but she has a lovely form, handsome, expressive eyes, a keen intelligence and a great deal of courage and fortitude.'

'Then why does she want to live like a hermit?'

In a few more words, Ben described the lady's exceptional talent and even more exceptional goals. 'I've seen her sketches and they are superior. I think it's quite likely a publisher would want to bring out her remarkable work.'

Christopher studied him. 'You're not entirely indifferent to the lady, are you?'

'I'm not,' Ben admitted. 'If…all this had not happened, I would have considered seeking her out later, to see what might develop.' *To see if she'd send the bastard packing for my effrontery in wanting more.*

'So, what do you intend to do now? Repair to her family home, woo her and persuade her marry you?'

Ben smiled wryly. 'I have been considering that very thing. But she's too intelligent for me to be able to bamboozle her with sudden vows of everlasting love. I am at a stand, not sure *what* I ought to do next. Not just to squash any rumours before they surface to tarnish my reputation, but to make sure the rest of her life doesn't become a misery, if her father refuses to let go of her funds. She didn't ask me to involve myself in her life; I chose to do that and feel…responsible, now, for her well-being. But on the other hand, if I travel to Aldermont Hall, she might refuse to see me.'

Christopher shrugged. 'At least then you'll know you've done everything you could to make the situation right.'

Ben took a deep swallow of ale. 'We should have a few more weeks before we'll need to start preparing in earnest for the next session. Enough time to travel to Lincolnshire and back.'

'Returning, perhaps, with a bride?'

'Would you wish me well?'

Christopher regarded him steadily. 'You said she described you as honourable, compassionate and understanding. All of which you are. You've described her as intelligent, honourable, independent, courageous and lovely. Seems to me that two individuals who begin with that much mutual admiration have as good a chance of making a successful marriage as those who go into it in the throes of ecstatic passion.' He chuckled. 'Perhaps more. Ecstasy isn't sustainable. So, would I give you my blessing for wedding a lady more or less forced on you by circumstance, when wedding her would uphold your honour and fulfil your responsibility? A lady you admire and would have sought out anyway? Of course! Though that means I'm probably going to lose my carousing partner, if she accepts you.'

'Openly carousing would certainly be bad form,' Ben agreed. 'As for something more discreet—I'll have time to consider that later. First, I need to finalise the situation with Lady Alyssa.'

The vague outlines of a plan he'd been harbouring ever since he rode away from Dornton Manor began crystallising. Glad now that he'd confided in his friend, he said, 'Thank you for letting me talk things through. I've a much clearer idea now of how to proceed.'

'Following the dictates of honour and conscience can never be wrong.'

'Even when it gets you into trouble?' Ben replied with a laugh.

Before Christopher could answer, a knock at the door was followed by the entrance of Russell. 'A letter for you, Captain,' he said, holding out the folded note. 'Came by express messenger.'

While Christopher looked on curiously, Ben broke the seal and swiftly read through the missive. A rueful grin on his face, he turned to his friend.

'It seems Lady Alyssa has been having second thoughts herself. Apparently she's changed her mind and begs me to visit her at Aldermont at my earliest convenience.' *Apparently she'd decided a bastard son was good enough after all.*

'That seals it,' Christopher said. 'To get back before the next session, you'll want to leave immediately.' Raising his mug, he said, 'To a successful marriage.'

After they drained the rest of their ale, Christopher said, 'Relieved, or regretful?'

'Some of both, I suppose,' Ben admitted. 'But there's also…anticipation. Lady Alyssa is so unique, life with her will always be full of surprises.'

And pleasure, he thought, recalling her scorching goodbye kiss. That they would prove well matched in the physical side of marriage he had no doubt whatsoever. His body was already stirring in anticipation of showing her all the ways to pleasure.

'Call on me—any of us—if you need anything,' Christopher said, standing to shake his hand. 'Know you carry my best wishes with you.'

'See you in a week,' Ben said as his friend walked out.

He'd return in a week, soon to become a married man. The notion seemed so foreign, Ben couldn't get his head around it. But honour required marriage, if Lady Alyssa could be persuaded to it. He might not be able to vow everlasting love, but he could pledge a good-faith effort to make her happy.

And he'd be able to look his mother in the eye without flinching.

For the first time since leaving Dornton Manor, he felt…at peace. And resigned to what he was about to do.

Now, on to Aldermont Hall, to woo Lady Alyssa… the unique and volatile lady he meant to make his bride.

Several days later, Ben urged his mount past the gatehouse and up the long carriage drive to Aldermont. During the hard ride out from London, as he thought about the future, he'd had plenty of time to realise how little he really knew about his prospective bride. He looked forward to filling in the vast gaps in his knowledge of her life and upbringing, looking for areas of common interest.

He was certain of the essentials, though: her sterling character, a sense of honour as fierce as his own, a keen intelligence and exceptional artistic talent—all contained in a body he was eager to explore.

He also knew that she'd loved a man who'd been taken from her, a man she might still mourn. A man who had considered her his 'beloved' rather than a women wed from a sense of duty.

He'd have to do his best to convince her of his sincere regard. He wouldn't try to trick her with false vows of love, but he knew at least one way in which he could demonstrate his appreciation with complete conviction. Desire fired in his blood at the thought of their imminent physical union.

Reluctantly pulling his thoughts from envisioning that delight, he forced himself to consider his even more imminent arrival. Lady Alyssa's note hadn't given him any idea about her parents' feelings on the matter of their marriage. He didn't know whether he would be welcomed as a future son, treated with icy civility for having involved the family in scandal, or harangued by an irate father who felt his daughter could have done much better than the natural son of a viscount.

With such uncertainty over his reception, he'd taken a room at an inn in the nearest village, which had also given him an opportunity to bathe, shave, and don a fresh set of clothing. If her father were going to read him a jobation, he at least wouldn't incur any criticism for his appearance.

Dismounting before an impressive, porticoed entrance, he turned over his horse to the groom who come trotting up. Brushing off his lapels, he straightened his shoulders, raised his chin and knocked on the front door.

An austere butler admitted him, betraying only by a flicker of an eyelid that he recognised Ben's name. He was led down a long gallery into another wing, deposited in an ornate salon filled with lacquered furniture and told that Lord Aldermont would be informed of his arrival.

Thus crushing the faint hope that he might see Lady Alyssa first and be forewarned what to expect before having to confront her father.

Girding himself for a possible lambasting of his character, honour and breeding, Ben paced the room, too agitated to sit on one of the uncomfortable-looking chairs.

A few minutes later, the butler announced Lord Aldermont. A grey-haired gentleman with a vague resemblance to Lady Alyssa strode into the room, a scowl on his face.

Ben bowed, a greeting his host acknowledged with a bare incline of his head while he looked Ben up and down. 'Tawny,' he said after a moment.

'Benedict Tawny, my lord,' Ben said evenly.

'Chilford's by-blow, aren't you? You have the look of him. Can't deny I'd hoped for better for her, but at least your father acknowledges you, so you have *some* prospects. About time you got here. I assume that means you are still cognizant of your duty to marry my daughter, in spite of her disgraceful behaviour?'

'I have been ready to do so ever since the…incident, but deferred to your daughter's wishes.'

'Don't know why my lack-witted wife didn't see the engagement finalised before the chit left Dornton,' Lord Aldermont said with irritation. 'In any event, get it done now and there's still a good chance we can avoid a scandal. Although I don't understand, if you claim to call yourself a gentleman, why you didn't insist on it three weeks ago.'

Masking his irritation, Ben said mildly, 'I could hardly force Lady Alyssa into accepting my suit.'

'Why not?' Aldermont waved an impatient hand. 'She's female! Which means she has no idea what she wants—or what's best for her. Oh, I imagine she spouted off at you—been nothing but trouble since she was old enough to open that impertinent mouth—but that's no excuse. A good cuff to the cheek usually silences her. All I require now is that the marriage be legal and immediate, so you can take her off my hands as soon as possible, ensuring there is the smallest chance of embarrassment to the family.'

*'Nothing but trouble...a good cuff to the cheek usually silences her...'* Appalled and affronted on Lady Alyssa's behalf, Ben could hardly rein in his anger enough to make a civil reply. 'I feel honoured to secure the hand of so lovely, intelligent and principled a lady,' he said at last. 'And one who is so very talented.'

'You mean her little scribbles?' Aldermont gave a bark of laughter. 'Indulge her in that if you like, but I'd burn that sketchbook. Get her in the bedchamber and get her breeding—that's all a wife's good for. Then take your bed sport elsewhere—I hear you're quite the man for it,' he added, giving Ben a look that held a glimmer of admiration.

*For his reputed prowess as a rake,* Ben thought disgustedly. Though that fit, given what else the Earl had revealed of his character. No wonder Lady Alyssa was so determined to escape her father's control.

Eager himself to quit the presence of a man who made him more inclined to plant him a facer than shake his hand as a future son-in-law, Ben gave the briefest of bows. 'If you would have me conveyed to Lady Alyssa, I'll pay my addresses at once.'

'I won't wrangle over the settlements; she'll have a fair portion, little as her behaviour warrants it. Chambers, my solicitor in London, will see to it.' After crossing to tug the bell-pull, Lord Aldermont said, 'Brewster will show you to her. Good day, Tawny.'

With that, he nodded to Ben and strode from the room.

Waiting for the servant to return and escort him to Lady Alyssa's parlour, Ben paced the carpet, trying to force down his anger, outrage, pity…and awe. In the face of such belittling disdain and discouragement, it was nothing short of amazing that Lady Alyssa had grown into the strong, determined, fiercely independent lady he'd met in the woods at Dornton.

All the more reason to get her away from her detestable father with all speed.

As the butler returned to usher him down yet another long hallway, he squelched once again his lingering regret that marriage had to be the price for accomplishing that.

So occupied was he in trying to calm his tumultuous thoughts, the better to play the ardent suitor to the lady he must woo, it didn't immediately sink in that, instead of guiding him to another salon, the butler had lead him up several flights of stairs. They then proceeded down a long hallway past what could only be…bedchambers?

Not slowing until he'd reached the room at the very end of the hall, to Ben's further surprise, the butler produced a key and unlocked the door. 'She's in there,' he said, gesturing for Ben to enter.

## *Chapter Seven*

Ben walked into a damp, chilly chamber so dim, he at first couldn't make out either furnishings or occupant. As the door clicked shut behind him, he halted, his appalled brain initially too shocked to function.

Once his vision adjusted, Ben was able to tell that locked shutters blocked any outside light from penetrating through the two windows. The shadowed outlines of what seemed to be a four-poster bed took up the far side of the room. Empty andirons in the bare hearth glinted dully in the light of the stub of a candle set on a table before the fireplace, that bit of tallow providing the only heat or illumination in the room. From within a wing chair facing it, a dull voice said, 'Tell him I haven't changed my mind.'

Lady Alyssa's voice.

His mind kicked back into motion on a wave of sensations—darkness, cold, the quiet desolation of her tone. *'My father locked me in my room until Will's ship sailed for the Indies...'* Was that why she'd written to summon him?

His chest tight with fury, concern and compassion,

he hurried to the chair. 'You're safe now, Lady Alyssa. I'm here. It's over.'

Blinking, she raised the wax-splattered candlestick to peer at his face. 'Mr Tawny?' she said at last.

'Yes, it's Ben Tawny,' he confirmed, kneeling before her in the brightest of the candle's feeble light.

She shook her head, as if she couldn't believe he was not an illusion. Tentatively, she reached out to touch his face. 'Ben Tawny,' she whispered wonderingly. 'It really is you. But...why have you come?'

His heart turning over with pity and distress, he took her hands—her small, icy hands—in his large, warm ones. 'I came as soon as I got your note. You wrote that you'd changed your mind, remember? You finally gave in to my pleas and agreed to become my wife.'

In the candle's glow, he could see she was wearing another outdated, high-waisted gown, the material thin with wear, with not even a shawl to ward off the chill. Her hair, though neatly pinned, was dull, as if she'd not washed it for some time. A quick glance revealed neither washbasin nor towels on the dresser.

Had her father denied her those comforts as well? he wondered, another wave of fury rippling through him.

She was shaking her head. 'But I haven't changed my mind. And I didn't write you.'

Ben sucked in a breath, the implications almost too much to comprehend. If Lady Alyssa hadn't written him—who had? Her father, hoping that seeing for himself the cruel conditions in which she was being held would spur him to greater eloquence in trying to convince her to marry—and take off Aldermont's hands the daughter he disdained?

Perhaps. But seeing her like this also spurred in Ben a desire to take Lord Aldermont apart limb from limb.

Reining in his rage, he said, 'It doesn't matter. I'm here now.' But when he tried to gently stroke her cheek, she gasped and recoiled.

His fingers froze in mid-caress. *'A good cuff on the cheek usually silences her...'*

Was she bruised and battered, as well as frozen?

It was too dark to tell.

Fury erupting, with a growl, Ben seized the poker off the cold hearth and strode over to the first barred window. Wishing it were her father he was assaulting instead of the shutters, he slid the poker under the frame and yanked savagely, jerking the iron rod back and forth until the wood shattered. Pounding the frame until the shutter lay in jagged pieces on the floor, he went to the other window and disposed of the shutter blocking the light there, then came back to the hearth.

Gently pulling Lady Alyssa from her chair, he led her to the window, where, as she blinked against the sudden brightness of the afternoon light, he could better inspect her. Although he'd already suspected what he would find, the outline of bruises on her cheeks and forehead—some the livid purple-red of new injury, some fading to green and yellow, sickened him.

Under the law, a woman was the property of her husband or father, who could beat her as he willed. Even kill her, without much danger of prosecution.

He wanted to howl in outrage and anguish.

'I'm so sorry. So very sorry! I should never have left you at Dornton.'

'It's not your fault. You couldn't have known what he would do.'

'I should have known,' Ben ground out. 'You told me plainly enough what he did before. He starved you, as well?'

'Bread and water.'

'And he…beat you?' He had to ask, though the answer was clearly written in the bruises on her face.

She nodded. 'I thought he might…kill me. Sometimes I hoped he would. Then it would be over.' Her dull eyes sparked in sudden fury. 'I asked for Aunt Augusta's money. He laughed at me, told me I'd never have it—but my husband would, if I gave in and agreed to marry. I told him I would never g-give in.'

Her voice broke, along with the last of Ben's control. Shaking with anguish, remorse and fury, he wrapped her in his arms, relieved beyond words when, after a second's hesitation, she buried her head against his chest and clung to him.

For a long time, he simply held her, heating her chilled body with his warmth while he wrestled to bring his rampaging emotions under control. Bad enough for her to be mocked, pitied and ruined. But to be physically assaulted on top of that, by the person who should have been charged with her well-being was…unendurable.

As a child, he could do nothing but look on helplessly when men made crude jokes about his mother. When women cut her, crossing to the other side of the street if they encountered her walking into town. When, under cover of darkness, boys from the village pelted their windows with rocks, the ugly taunt 'whore!' echoing among the shattering glass.

Rage and years of remembered torment burned away any remaining hesitation, regret, or longing for the life that might have been. As Lady Alyssa trembled in his arms, Ben hardened his resolve to proceed down the path honour dictated.

He hadn't been able to rescue or protect his mother. But he could rescue and protect this innocent. Whatever it took, he must convince her to let him.

A few moments later, with a deep sigh, she pushed away. With infinite tenderness, he let her go.

'I don't know who wrote to you, Mr Tawny, but I appreciate your coming. Though I still can't marry you. I refuse to yield to my father's bullying. Nor can I allow him to use his treatment of me to try to force you into it.'

Her resistance wasn't logical, but he understood it. He'd seen the same phenomena in the army near the end of a fierce and prolonged siege: exhausted, wounded and overwhelmed men, so battered by fatigue and paralysed by a desperate resistance they initially refused to yield their posts to a relief force.

Having already resolved to oppose her father to the death, she wouldn't be convinced to abandon that stand by appeals to her own well-being. He'd need a different argument to persuade her.

As he led her back to the chair, he said, 'I was going to come anyway, even before I got the letter. To try again to convince you to marry me. Because I think it would be best for both of us.'

'I already told you—'

'Please, hear me out,' he interrupted. 'It's not just the reputation you don't care about that our marriage would safeguard. As I told you at Dornton, I think we would be well matched. We're already friends, aren't we? I admire your lively intelligence, your compassion, your sense of honour. I find you attractive, and there's a passion between us that I can't wait to explore. I think we could build a mutually satisfying marriage. But more than that, I am now pleading with you to do me, not just the honour, but the *favour* of marrying me. A confidential consultation with my closest associates confirmed what I already suspected: should word of this scandal get out—and the longer we delay marrying, the more likely it is that some word *will* get out—the odds are that it would quite adversely impact my career.'

'Impact your career?' she repeated.

'Yes. It would be hard for electors in my district to believe I am sincere in my appeals for a government that values the worth of every citizen, should they find out I callously ruined the life of an innocent lady. Not only would electors have doubts, but leaders of the party would have to seriously question my morals, integrity and honesty. It could be the death knell for any chance I might have to occupy high office and gain the influence to move forward the reforms I see as vital for our nation.'

He watched her face as he spoke, hoping his appeal would engage her compassion on *his* behalf and sway her resolve.

'Isn't it just as likely the scandal would be a nine days' wonder, soon supplanted by the next and eventually forgotten?' she countered.

'Perhaps within the highest levels of "polite" society, where morality is sometimes...lax. But not among the more responsible gentry, to whom we have been espousing the highest of ideals in arguing for reform. How could others believe I am truly interested in promoting principle, rather than merely seeking political power, if my behaviour shows I *have* no principles?'

She nodded slowly. 'So...you believe the chances

of the scandal surfacing to harm your career are great enough to justify marrying a near-stranger?'

'If that near-stranger will do me the honour of accepting my hand,' he said with a smile. 'What's more, if we marry, you will finally have access to the money that belongs to you.'

'If we marry, it becomes *your* money,' she said bitterly.

'Not if the settlements are written to reserve it for your use.'

Another glimmer sparked in her dull eyes. 'You would agree to that?'

'I would. Marry me and you can claim what you say you desire most: the funds to pursue your art when, where and how you want. I admire your drawings and believe in your talent. I'd be delighted to do all I can to help promote your work.'

He could sense the hope stirring in her. 'It would be a…marriage of convenience, then? You would allow me the funds to travel all over Britain, whenever, wherever, and for however long I wished, so I might complete my sketches before the publisher's deadline? And not object to my publishing them?'

'I would support you in that aim,' he confirmed.

'In return, I'd pledge to allow you to go *your* own way, not interfering with your life or your…choice of companions,' she vowed, excitement beginning to colour her voice. 'You're certainly welcome to whatever dowry you can wangle from my father, to use for your campaigns and political work. It could be a…a bargain between friends.'

'Friends, yes, though I'm not interested in your money—keep that for your own work. There's also the passion we'd no longer need to restrain—a most attractive inducement to marriage.'

To his surprise, she looked away, avoiding the intensity of his gaze. 'I suppose you'd insist on…a husband's rights.'

'And a wife's. The pleasure goes both ways, you know,' he replied, puzzled by this unexpectedly missish reply from the woman who'd previously responded to him with abandon. Why this sudden reserve?

'Passion is for a man's enjoyment, not a woman's. All she gets is the risk of pain and death in childbed. Which would be worth it, I suppose, if she wanted a child.'

'Do you truly believe that?' he asked incredulously. *After the kisses we've shared?*

'All I want now is a chance to pursue my work.'

Ah, her *work*… Did she fear succumbing to passion would saddle her with responsibilities that might threaten her ability to continue it? he wondered, struggling to understand this unexpected change. Or did she suspect that permitting him to bring her pleasure might give him some kind of power over her, at the very moment that freedom from her father would finally allow her to control her own life?

To be fair, after what she'd endured at her father's hands, he could understand why she would resist anything she feared might drag her back into bondage to another man—despite the depth of attraction between them.

How long would it take him to convince her that passion would liberate, rather than limit her?

Could he be happy with a *marriage blanc* until he did? Persuading a body already starving for another taste of her to keep its distance would be both disappointing…and difficult. Despite her offer to let him seek 'other companions'.

'I…I wouldn't deny you, if you insisted on claiming my body,' she said, drawing him out of his thoughts.

'Insisted on it?' he echoed, torn between insult and amusement. He might not be happy at the prospect of an initially passionless marriage, but he would make sure this very minute that she understood he would never impose his desires on her. 'There'll be none of that, *ever*, I promise. You do believe me?'

She studied his face before slowly nodding. 'Yes, I believe you.'

'Good. I'll have you know I've never taken a lady who wasn't actively encouraging.'

She looked back at him with a shrug.

'*Enthusiastically* encouraging,' he amended.

She raised an eyebrow.

'Passionately demanding,' he countered.

She gave him a sceptical glance that practically shouted a challenge to his skill at seduction. If she were throwing down that gauntlet, he was more than prepared to snap it up.

'I repeat, there will never be any intimate contact between us, unless and until you desire it.'

*Rescue her first, work on that later*, he told himself. Having already tasted the passion of which she was capable, coaxing it to emerge would be a highly satisfying challenge.

As long as he didn't expire of frustration before the ultimate victory that, he had no doubt, would eventually be his. Or rather, *theirs*. But he couldn't expect her to long for a bliss she'd never experienced.

'I realise that forgoing your husbandly rights will

not pose any problem,' she said with a twisted smile. 'I'm not attractive enough to make avoiding my bed a hardship—not when there are so many *enthusiastically encouraging, passionately demanding* women in the world.'

*And I won't rest until you are first among them, fully convinced of your attractiveness*, he thought, suppressing a grin at her emphasis. 'On the contrary; having to forgo intimacy *will* be difficult for me, as you must certainly realise,' he replied. 'But in this matter, I shall always bow to your wishes. You do believe that, don't you?'

When she nodded again, he said, 'Good. Shall we move on to discuss the immediate future? I had intended to ask whether you'd prefer to be married at Aldermont Hall or in London. But after seeing how you've been treated, I don't want you to spend another night under your father's roof. I'll seek your mother at once and ask her to send you and Molly to the inn in the village until she can accompany you to London, under my escort. Once there, you can stay with my friends until the lawyers complete the settlement agreements, securing your money to you, and then we can be married. If that meets with your approval?'

'Leave here now, today, never to return?' Her eyes finally taking on the brightness he found so attractive, she smiled. 'I've never heard a more wonderful offer!'

'Then show me where I might find your mother and get your things ready. I'll send her to fetch you as soon as I finish speaking with her.'

She nodded. 'I'm ready now.'

As she started to rise, he gently pushed her back into her chair. 'I think you've forgotten something.'

While she looked at him enquiringly, he went down on one knee. 'Lady Alyssa Lambornne, will you do me the honour of becoming my wife? I promise to protect and cherish you, respect your talent and your work, and give you free rein to pursue it.'

Blushing a little, she said. 'Then, yes, Mr Tawny, I will marry you.'

When she would have hopped up, he once again stayed her. 'It's customary, I believe, to seal such a bargain with a kiss.'

Eagerness lit her face, sending his hopes soaring. Then she must have recalled her resolve to keep her distance and the enthusiasm faded. 'If you wish.'

'No,' he corrected. 'Only if *you* wish.'

He didn't move towards her—but he didn't retreat, either. He could sense her indecision as she wavered, as wary and poised for flight as one of the birds she sketched. Yet held in place, as he was, by the intensity of the sensual pull between them.

Sure as he was of its power, he was still relieved when, with a little sigh, she leaned down to offer her lips.

He reined in the desire to kiss her deep and hard. They were beginning again on entirely new terms and, if he hoped to lead her to eventual surrender, he would have to proceed with caution.

So he merely brushed his mouth against hers, keeping the pressure as slight as the breeze stirred by that bird taking wing. Suppressing the urge to lick and probe and invade, he kept his lips closed, warming hers with his breath, exploring her with glancing little touches, from the centre of her upper lip to the corners of her mouth, the contact so minimal he was almost not touching her at all.

With a whimper, she leaned closer, pressing harder against him, opening her lips. He allowed himself a single, brief brush of his tongue against hers—even that tiny contact sending a heady rush of arousal through him—before moving away, leaving cold air where there had been the warmth of flesh against flesh.

Her lashes fluttering open, she looked at him, surprise, confusion and an answering arousal in her eyes. He gritted his teeth against the compulsion to kiss her again, amazed such a simple caress could affect him so profoundly.

If there were any justice in the world, her lips were tingling as fiercely as his, her heartbeat stampeding just as wildly, her body warming, melting, awash like his with desire and anticipation.

Though he sensed, even this soon, he could have taken her further, he made himself resist the urge to proceed.

When at last she came to him, he intended for her to be the most *enthusiastically, passionately demanding* lover ever to seek him out.

Even if he ended up half-dead from frustrated desire first.

'Now,' he murmured, 'take me to see your mother.'

Leaving the remote bedchamber, Lady Alyssa descended the stairs and led him down another hallway before halting to rap softly at a door. 'Mama? It's Lyssa.'

A tall, thin woman opened the door—to be pushed aside by Lady Aldermont. 'Lyssa! Oh, my darling! You are free at last!' With a sob, she seized her daughter and drew her into the chamber.

Ben followed Lady Alyssa in. Though he remained at a discreet distance during their tender reunion, Lady Aldermont soon spotted him over her daughter's shoulder. 'Mr Tawny, you came! Oh, thank Heaven!'

'Yes, Mama, he came,' Alyssa said, detaching herself from her mother's embrace. 'Molly and I are going to the Fox and Hare; I shall never spend another night here. Then, as soon as you can get away, Mr Tawny will escort us all to London. Now, I must find Molly and make myself presentable.' She stepped towards the door, pausing on the threshold to look back. 'By the way, Mama, I've agreed to marry him.'

And then she was gone, shutting the door behind her.

He'd been led to a small sitting room that must adjoin her ladyship's bedchamber. After her daughter disappeared, Lady Aldermont motioned him to the sofa. 'Won't you have a seat? Linden, will you bring us tea?'

After he seated himself, Lady Aldermont came over to seize Ben's hand. 'Thank you for coming, from the depths of this mother's heart! Thank you even more for somehow convincing Alyssa to marry you.'

'*You* sent me the note,' Ben said, suddenly piecing it all together.

Lady Aldermont flushed. 'Yes. I was about to confess it. I am sorry to have misled you…but I was so worried!'

Indeed, her tired, red eyes and the dark shadows under them spoke of weeping and sleepless nights. With a sigh, she seated herself beside him.

'I know it was wrong of me to have written in Lyssa's name. If the situation had not been so…desperate, I would not have done so. She was locked in a battle of wills with her father, one in which she would not yield…one I feared she might not survive.' Tears sheening her eyes, she added, 'You must think me the worst of cowards for not protecting her.'

Petite, like her daughter, Lady Aldermont looked so light, Ben suspected he could lift her with one hand. Had she tried to shield Lady Alyssa from her husband's wrath, the Earl could have knocked her aside with one blow—leaving her as battered as her daughter.

'Not at all,' he replied, compassion filling him. 'You did exactly what you should have to protect her. You sent for me.'

Tears started in earnest then, but with a shuddering breath, she wiped them away. 'Thank you for that. And for responding so quickly. I shall be grateful for ever! After her father began his…campaign of *persuasion*, I begged her to reconsider her refusal to marry you. But she was adamant that she could not take advantage of one of the few men of compassion and integrity she'd ever met. Her eloquence in insisting that a man of your character and talent should not be saddled with an unwanted wife led me to hope that, if your heart were not already engaged, you would take pity on her circumstances. And follow the dictates of honour—even though you are innocent of any blame.'

'She told you what really happened?' At Lady Aldermont's nod, he said, 'Does her father know?'

'I don't believe so—not that it matters. He wouldn't care in the slightest *how* she was disgraced, or by whom, only that the shame be covered up by marriage. As long as Alyssa is wed and off his hands, the character of her husband is a matter of indifference to him.' Lady Aldermont's lip curled in disgust. 'Which makes me glad there is no way Lord Denbry could be compelled to marry her. After what she has suffered, I should hate for her to be chained for life to such a man. The fact that she admires and trusts you—most unexpected, given her experience with the men of her own family—makes me hope you will treat her kindly.'

An unspoken appeal in her gaze accompanied those words.

The appeal of one who had lived the bitter reality of being chained to a husband who did not treat a wife kindly? 'I give you my word, I will honour and respect your daughter.' Though another quick inspection of Lady Aldermont revealed no apparent bruises, Ben felt compelled to ask, 'Does Aldermont strike you, too?'

Flushing again, Lady Aldermont said, 'Oh, no! I'm much too timid. Within a week of our wedding, he had me completely cowed. But Alyssa... While Aldermont despises me for being weak, she goads him to fury with her defiance. In many ways, they are so alike, though she has only the best of him—strength of will, intelligence, determination—without the cruelty and selfishness. And so many wonderful qualities that he lacks—compassion, a sense of fairness and honour.'

'Inherited from her mother, no doubt.'

Lady Aldermont smiled sadly. 'I only hope I gave her something of value. I confess, I feel some of Alyssa's guilt at taking advantage of *your* honour. I can't even assuage that guilt by assuring you Alyssa will make you an ideal wife. Oh, you couldn't find a woman of finer character! But even her fond mama must admit she lacks most of the virtues men expect in a bride. Though she is perfectly capable of managing a household, she has little interest in doing so; she has no patience with drawing-room conversation, and much prefers solitude—tramping in the woods with her sketch pad or withdrawing to the library to read a book—to entertaining. I only hope you can...appreciate her unique talent and not be frustrated or annoyed by her lack of conventional accomplishments. And that you will not, one day, come to regret what honour...and I...have forced on you.'

At least on that score, he could reassure her. Having already made the decision to marry Alyssa, he would never shame the woman he'd claimed for his bride, or himself, by repining later. What was done, was done and would be carried through with integrity and determination.

'I promise you, I will never regret it! Let me assure you, I find your daughter admirable and possessed of an outstanding artistic talent. I understand her goal is to pursue that talent, perhaps even publish some of her drawings, and I fully support that aim. Not every politician's wife enjoys playing the hostess. I'm fortunate to have a close friend whose wife does; since Lyndlington and I work on the same projects, any necessary entertaining can be handled by Lady Lyndlington. I spend most of my days at political meetings and assemblies, which will leave Lady Alyssa ample time to pursue her artistic interests. I believe we share a mutual admiration and appreciation; I see no reason why we cannot build a satisfying future together.'

Nodding, Lady Aldermont pressed Ben's hand as Linden returned with the tea tray. Famished after his long journey, after helping himself to refreshments,

Ben said, 'How soon do you think you could be ready to accompany us to London?'

'Tomorrow. Linden doesn't have to pack much; I can purchase whatever I need after we arrive. Aldermont expects his wife to be always in the height of fashion, and gives me a generous allowance for clothing and household furnishings.'

The melancholy look on her face said that largesse didn't in any way make up for being shackled to a husband who neither loved nor appreciated her. Stirred once again to compassion, Ben said, 'There's no need to open Aldermont House. My father has given me unlimited use of a town house on Queen Street, where Lady Alyssa and I will reside after the wedding. Why don't you remain with her there once we arrive? I can stay with friends until after the wedding. And you are welcome to sojourn at Queen Street as long as you like.'

Once again, tears sheened Lady Aldermont's eyes. 'How kind! But a mother-in-law residing with newlyweds—that would never do! You must have time and space to become acquainted with each other…since the cruelty of circumstance has not allowed you to become very well acquainted before the wedding. Having Lyssa wed and safely out of her father's charge, with a kind man to care for her, is everything I hoped for! You have convinced me that she will have that and more. I couldn't be happier or more grateful.'

Since the cruelty of circumstance had not granted her the same joy? Ben thought, still incensed on behalf of both the Lambornne ladies.

He'd always thought his mother led the cruellest of existences. But for all her wealth and comfort, Lady Aldermont was lonelier. Though, to Ben's disgust and fury, his father had succumbed to the lure of wealth and title in abandoning his mother, he had at least truly loved her.

Lady Aldermont had never known that.

He might not offer love, but he could offer Alyssa what neither of their mothers had attained: respectability coupled with respect and affection.

As they finished their tea, with promises to join them at the inn early the next morning, Lady Aldermont sent Linden to fetch her daughter. Going off to begin her packing, she left him to await Lady Alyssa.

Now, inevitably, to be his bride.

Despite his firm decision to marry her, Ben couldn't completely squelch the quiver of panic in his gut.

## *Chapter Eight*

Sighing with delight, Alyssa leaned back as Molly combed the tangles from her wet tresses. Freshly bathed, garbed in clean clothes, she felt lighter, not just freed from grime, but from the huge weight of defying her father's coercion.

Very soon, she would walk out of this house for the last time and out of his control for ever. Euphoria sent her spirits soaring.

Remembering she'd secured that freedom by stealing Ben Tawny's brought those high spirits back to earth.

Had she really agreed to abandon principle and let Lord Denbry's plot force Tawny to marry her?

Had she really agreed to hand over control of her life to another man? For once married, under law, she would become as much his property as she'd been her father's.

But Ben Tawny wasn't simply a younger version of the Earl, she assured herself, fighting down a sudden wave of panic. Like Will, he was kind and principled. With his unselfish decision to warn her about the wager, he'd already demonstrated his superior character. He'd also promised to grant her the financial assets to make her truly independent—and she would hold him to it.

How many years had she longed for the freedom he'd just offered?

Nor was letting him marry her completely an abdication of principle. True, his ending up in a compromising situation was her fault, but there was nothing she could do now about that. She could at least not worsen his position by continuing to refuse him, thereby making him appear a heartless seducer and placing a stain on his character that would compromise his chances of attaining high office.

After all, for most men, success in their career was more important to them than their choice of a wife. At least she brought him a handsome dowry to fund his parliamentary activities.

Best of all, his absorption in his career would leave her free to focus on hers. Unlike her father, he was fair enough to cede to her the money that rightfully belonged to her, funds that would allow her to travel, complete her sketches on time and see her book through to publication.

In return, he would be free to go his own way—and associate with whomever he chose.

She smothered an uncomfortable flare of protest by reminding herself why it was such a wise arrangement. Allowing him to seek his pleasure elsewhere would leave him too satisfied to bother with beguiling her.

She'd not escaped her father's iron-fisted control over her life to be lured into voluntarily offering power over her to another man—even one as principled and attractive as Ben Tawny.

Especially one as principled and attractive as Ben

Tawny. She already liked and admired him; it would be all too easy to fall further under his spell. Not only could he distract her from the work she yearned to accomplish, but it would be foolish in the extreme to let herself become too attached to a man who'd freely admitted he 'had a certain reputation with the ladies'.

A sudden image flashed into her head: waiting at home, yearning for his touch—wondering if he was with another woman and when or if he'd return to her. She recoiled, a sick feeling in her gut.

No, best not to let herself become fascinated by a man whom every other female found equally fascinating.

Even if she were not faced with the daunting prospect of having to share her husband with other women, it would be better not to become too attached to him. The ache of loss she felt every time she remembered Will should be enough to convince her not to risk losing her heart to any man.

She *would* honour her agreement to marry Ben Tawny. But she would also make sure the settlement terms guaranteed her a lifelong independence, get the wedding accomplished speedily and from then on spend as little time as possible in the company of her intelligent, charming, and seductive new husband.

Sure now of how she meant to go forward, Alyssa took a deep breath and began to help Molly with the packing.

But the difficulty of keeping her vow to maintain her distance became apparent soon after they rejoined her mother in her sitting room to await Mr Tawny.

'Are you feeling better, my dear?' her mother enquired as they walked in.

'Yes, Mama, I am.'

'Partly due to Mr Tawny, your ladyship,' Molly said. 'Never would have expected a gentleman to know just what to send up to a body what had been near starved! Now, I admit I had my doubts when I learned how he'd hoodwinked all of us, turning up to question the maids and valets in the servants' hall at Dornton like some sly rogue out of Bow Street! But my, how he's worked since to safeguard Lady Alyssa!'

'He is a most impressive gentleman,' her mother said.

With a sigh, Alyssa silently agreed. That he was as admirable as he was attractive did not help her resolve not to fall under his spell.

He must have some flaws—which she'd doubtless discover. Or not, if she followed her wise counsel to limit the amount of time they spent together.

Despite that rallying thought, she couldn't steady the shaky breath she drew as Brewster opened the door to announce Mr Ben Tawny.

Starved, beaten, numb, she'd found only comfort when he'd held her close in the cold, dark prison of her bedchamber. But washed, refreshed and revived by the meal he'd had sent up, she was conscious of his visceral appeal the moment he walked into the room.

She was equally unable to still the flutter in her pulses as he halted to bow before her.

'Lady Alyssa, I was so relieved when Brewster came to fetch me, saying you had completed your packing! I hope that means you are feeling better?'

'Yes, thank you, Mr Tawny. All the more so after the meal you ordered for me. Hungry as I was, I would probably have devoured anything, but the bread, broth and cold chicken settled particularly well.'

He shrugged off the compliment. 'A lesson from my soldiering days. After being on short rations, it's best to start with something light.'

'Well, it restored me wonderfully. And I am ready to depart.'

Suddenly she realised she'd left her hand resting on his far longer than courtesy dictated. *Liar!* a little voice in her ear whispered as she hastily removed it. *You are not at all prepared to turn yourself over to him. Just look at you, babbling on about broth and chicken!*

Somehow, she'd lost the wonderful ease she'd felt around him when she'd met him in the wood. That she'd still felt, even alone in the upper chamber of an inn, when he'd given her the most sensual kiss she'd ever experienced.

It was one thing to flirt, or share delectable kisses, when she expected she would never see him again. But how was she to stave off the advances he'd hinted at, once they were wed? Another wave of anxiety rippled through her.

After all, marriage would require a modicum of togetherness, at the very least until the settlements were completed and the wedding itself performed.

Would he try to persuade her afterward into granting those husbandly rights? Could she resist him, if he did?

'When do you think you will be ready to depart, Lady Aldermont?' Tawny asked, his voice jolting her out of her thoughts.

'If you can delay just a bit longer, Linden told me she can have me ready to leave this afternoon. I've already notified Brewster to have the travelling coach prepared. If that is acceptable, Mr Tawny?'

'Whatever will make the journey more comfortable for you and Lady Alyssa is agreeable to me, Lady Aldermont.'

'Excellent. Molly, will you bring us more tea? I expect by the time we've had some refreshment, the baggage coach will be packed and we can set out. We should have enough daylight to reach Romley before nightfall—there's a very fine coaching inn there. Will you ride, Mr Tawny, or can I persuade you to join us in the coach?'

'I shouldn't wish to crowd you, but if Lady Alyssa will permit, I'd be delighted to join you in the coach.'

Two questioning sets of eyes turned to Alyssa, pinning her like a botanical specimen on a tray. She hesitated, swallowing the refusal that sprang automatically to her lips.

It was dismaying enough to discover her mother would be ready to leave at once, so she would not have the several days at the village inn she'd been expecting in which to recover from the ordeal with her father—and think through more carefully all the implications of marrying Benedict Tawny. It was more alarming still to envision him in the coach, instead of riding beside it, as she'd assumed he would. Sitting opposite her where, at any moment, some bump on the road or sharp corner taken too quickly could bounce her foot against his, or jolt her against him…

Her mouth dried, her pulses leapt and swallows swooped and soared in her stomach.

She refocused to find Tawny looking at her in concern, her mother in surprise at her apparent lack of gratitude to the man who'd given up so much to rescue her. 'Of course I'd prefer that you ride with us,' she said, flushing with annoyance.

Heavens, it was time she stopped acting like a nervous virgin left alone with a practised seducer. Mr Tawny had assured her there would be no intimate contact between them unless she desired it. *Enthusiastically, passionately demanded* it, she recalled his words.

She had the uneasy suspicion he might be able to entice her to do just that.

But, at least along the road to London, her mother's presence would prevent both enticement and surrender.

He was still gazing at her, she realised. She forced herself to give him a smile, which he returned with a reassuring wink.

'I thought travelling together would give us a chance to become better acquainted. I already know you possess a keen sense of honour, courage, determination and a wonderful artistic talent, Lady Alyssa, but I know very little about your life up until now. I should like to learn more.'

Resigning herself to the inevitable, she said, 'If we are to spend much time together, you should probably call me "Lyssa". The only person I know well who still calls me "Lady Alyssa" is my father.'

'I would not like to be ranked with him,' Tawny said with feeling. '"Lyssa" it shall be and you must call me "Ben". Lyssa—a diminutive, for a small lady?'

Alyssa had to laugh. 'Hardly that! As I imagine you suspect, I was never one for sewing samplers or sitting decorously at Mama's knee. Once I was old enough to escape the nursery maids, I trailed after my brother. It was he who began calling me "Lyssa"—claiming he couldn't imagine a female "less a" lady than me. We remained close companions on his visits home from school—until he grew old enough to take my father as his model.'

'Not that his discouragement turned your interest to more maidenly pursuits,' Lady Aldermont said with a sigh.

'No, I simply went exploring on my own,' Alyssa acknowledged. 'Harleton had begun teaching me to use a fowling piece. After he abandoned me, the gamekeeper discovered me trying to slip a weapon out of the gun room. Deciding it was safer to teach me to use it properly than to let me experiment, a menace to grazing cattle or farmers working in the fields, he finished my training. He and the grooms made sure I could handle any horse or firearm on the property.'

'Because they knew you would simply go after it on your own, if they refrained from teaching you?'

Alyssa nodded, unable to stifle a smile. 'I could climb up and down trees or buildings like a monkey and pick any lock they installed.'

'In between the sketching and shooting and riding and exploring, I truly did manage to instil some notion of household management in her,' her mother said. 'Though, as I already warned you, she was never much interested in "feminine" pursuits. If she wasn't haring off, riding the wildest of her father's hunters, or sitting by some muddy pond sketching water birds, she was whiling away her time in the library, studying every book she could get her hands on.'

As she watched Tawny listening intently to her mother, Alyssa suddenly realised he might just as easily have bid them goodbye an hour ago and returned to

London, instructing the ladies to follow at their leisure. Instead, he had chosen to join them on the journey.

So she might have someone with whom she was comfortable to act as a buffer between them as she—and he—worked through the inevitable awkwardness of going from virtual strangers to marriage partners? While at the same time, giving them a leisurely opportunity to become better acquainted, which should further alleviate that awkwardness.

*'We are already friends, are we not?'* he'd said the first time he'd asked her to marry him, back at Dornton Manor. It seemed he intended to make sure that before she committed herself to him, they were friends in truth. And had already begun the process in her mother's sitting room.

He truly was a most admirable gentleman.

Though her mother's presence wouldn't lessen the sensual tension she'd feel every time their fingers brushed, or her thigh rubbed against his in the jolting coach… All too aware of the potent physical connection simmering between them, she considered whether she'd been too hasty in giving him permission to see any lady he liked after their marriage.

But he didn't belong to her and never would. Not in the way Will had.

For an instant, she recalled the look on Will's face when he declared his love, devotion shining in his eyes, an ardency of his expression. As if she were the sun around which his earth moved, the most brilliant star in his heaven.

*'I won't let you ruin yourself by running away with me,'* he'd told her. *'This new position will allow me to*

*accumulate the wealth, power and status to make me worthy of your hand.'*

She bit down hard on her lip to stave off a wave of desolation. Ben Tawny would never look at her the way Will had, never think of her as more than a wife forced on him by honour and necessity.

She owed him her gratitude and support, but when tempted to cease resisting his dangerous appeal, she must always remember that fact.

After their arrival, they would formalise their bargain, exchange vows and she would be free to go her own way. She could endure a few days of Tawny's too-appealing company in a too-narrow space to accomplish that laudable goal.

She came back to herself to find him still studying her, his gaze concerned.

Summoning up another smile, she said, 'I've finished my tea. Once you have yours, I'll be ready to depart as soon as Mama's trunks are packed.'

And she would be ready—in every way, she told herself firmly.

A few days later, the coach turned into the narrow lane leading to Queen Street. Having discovered on the first day that the close confines of the coach kept her forever on edge, bedevilled by a nerve-shredding awareness of Tawny's presence, Alyssa had elected to ride for the rest of the journey. Although Tawny had accompanied her one day, being on horseback made it possible to limit conversation and keep her distance, which did much to stave off both panic—and temptation.

Unfortunately, it also allowed her many hours alone in which to think through all the implications of the bargain they'd struck. By now, she was having increasing doubts about whether that bargain would work.

A few minutes later, the coach drew to a halt before the town house. Tawny handed them down and ushered them into the front parlour, where he introduced his small staff, informing them he intended to continue on to sojourn with his friends, Lord and Lady Lyndlington. 'They are out of town at present, but due back soon.'

'Will Lady Lyndlington not think it an imposition to return and find a guest?' Alyssa asked, not wishing to create still more problems for Tawny. 'Don't let us force you out of your own house! We could be quite comfortable at a hotel, couldn't we, Mama?'

'I much prefer having you here, where my own staff can look out for you,' Ben said before her mother could reply. 'As for the Lyndlingtons, since our political discussions frequently last into the wee hours, I spend the night there almost as often as I do here.'

'With so few of our own people accompanying us, I would feel more comfortable staying here,' her mother admitted.

*He wanted them where his staff could look out for them.* Alyssa felt a lump in her throat. This latest expression of concern underlined that his consideration for a lady wasn't a passing whim, but a trait that ran deep in his character.

'You do agree to stay here, don't you, Lyssa?' her mother asked with a pleading look.

'Yes, Mama. It's very kind of you to offer, Ben. I didn't mean to seem unappreciative. I'm just not used to having a man show much interest in my well-being.'

As he recalled her ordeal with her father, Tawny's expression hardened. 'That's about to change. I intend to ensure your comfort and well-being from now on. But here I am, prosing away, when you must be longing to rest and wash off the dust of the road. Mrs Ingleton,' he said, turning to the housekeeper who had been awaiting his orders, 'show Lady Aldermont to her room, please.'

Before she could follow her mother, he held up a hand. 'Lyssa, would you remain for a few minutes? Mrs Ingleton has sent for a maid to assist you until the baggage wagon catches up. May I pour you a glass of wine while we wait for her?'

At the thought of being alone in the room with him, the warmth of gratitude and relief at ending the journey dissipated as alarm warred with anticipation. Looking with dismay at her mother's form disappearing down the hallway, Alyssa gave him the only possible answer. 'Of course, Ben. I'd be delighted.'

## *Chapter Nine*

*At least she'd agree to remain in his company.*

As the journey progressed, Ben's initial satisfaction at rescuing Lyssa and his certainty that wedding her was the best option for them both began to waver. The lady who'd once been so passionately approachable seemed to have become more anxious to avoid him with every passing mile.

Though the physical pull between them remained as strong as ever, she gave unmistakable signs that she didn't wish to get close enough to be tempted to act upon it. Which was fair enough, given her tortured history with her father; he would need time to earn her trust and convince her that he would never harm her. But if she couldn't bear being in his company, he would have little chance of doing that—which would leave them both trapped in a union that promised only misery.

Maybe he shouldn't have pushed for her to accept his suit at once, waiting instead until she'd had time to recover from her ordeal, he thought as he poured them each a glass of wine. But he hadn't been able to tolerate the idea of leaving her with her abusive father for even one more night.

Perhaps, relief at being rescued had led her to commit herself to something that, when she'd had more time to think about it, she no longer felt comfortable doing. But, having given her word, she felt compelled to see it through.

Before they moved a step closer to the altar, he needed to find out. And regardless of the damage it might do his career, he would release her from her promise, if it did not appear they could co-exist at least in friendship.

He ignored the protest of a body that was not at all pleased about the notion of settling for a union that promised friendship only.

He handed her the glass, noting how carefully she avoided letting their fingers touch. 'What is wrong?' he asked, studying her. 'And please don't tell me there is nothing. The closer we got to London, the quieter and more distant you became. Are you regretting the decision? Do you want to change your mind? I admit, I would be sorely disappointed, but I would never coerce you into marriage.'

Her eyes widened in surprise before she replied, 'No matter how much refusing you might damage your career?' Then, flushing, she said, 'Mortifying as it is to realise I was not concealing my unease as well as I thought, neither is there any point pretending I don't know what you mean. After thinking of little else the whole of the journey, I do have some…reservations.'

'Please, sit,' he said, waving her to a chair, more than a little dismayed to know she *had* reservations about taking him as a husband.

'I do hate being cooped up in a coach. It's what I so disliked about London during my Seasons—being trapped in a crowd of people, the din of voices, the heat, the overpowering scent of perfume and wine and humanity. Add to that, hearing nothing around me but boring conversation about fashion or jewels or the latest scandal and all I wanted to do was *escape.*'

She gave a strained chuckle. 'Not the best reaction, you must agree, for the wife of a politician who spends most of his evenings at political dinners. I know we said we would each pursue our own interests after marriage, but I expect I would need to be present for a few functions. I wouldn't want you to have a wife who looked either bored, or desperate to escape. Then there are your friends and their wives. Lady Lyndlington is a skilled political hostess and I'm sure the Duchess is equally knowledgeable. My education has been…uneven at best. I'm about as prepared to hold my own at table with ladies like that as Aldermont's gamekeeper.

'No, please, hear me out,' she said, raising a hand to silence the reassurance he'd been about to give. 'Papa saw no reason to waste money on a governess to instruct me in anything as useless as languages or music…since the chief duty of an aristocrat's wife is to run his house and give him sons. Oh, I've taught myself French and Latin and a smattering of history and literature. But what an embarrassment it was during my Seasons, when all the young ladies were called upon to play or sing, and I had to confess I couldn't even manage a scale! I'm afraid you will soon discover that my education has been extremely deficient. With the exception of a substantial dowry, I offer nothing of advantage to a man in your position. Which, I cannot help but think, makes me a very poor bargain of a wife. Are you sure that refraining from wedding me would be more detrimental to your career that taking so ill prepared a bride?'

Her words sparked one last, brief hope that they might avoid a forced marriage. Reality quickly extinguished it. Unless she was truly averse to marrying him, marry they must.

Though she'd presented her reservations about wedlock as concern for what the bargain meant for him, he knew that couldn't be the sole reason behind her reserve. 'I appreciate your concern for my well-being. But what about you? How would you gain access to your money and gain your independence, if we don't wed? Setting off precisely the scandal your papa thought to avoid is unlikely to persuade him to grant you the funds. Nor could I reconcile it with my conscience to see you forced back under the control of...the man he has shown himself to be.'

'I've no intention of returning to my father's house,' she assured him. 'I will receive the money in any event, upon his eventual demise. Perhaps in the interim, I could obtain an advance on the expectation, enough to maintain myself until that happy event? Or maybe I could hire myself out as a gamekeeper. A job for which I am much better suited than becoming a politician's wife.'

The doubt he'd been suppressing fought its way free, bringing with it an anguish he'd spent years trying to bury. 'Is the prospect of marrying the Chilford Bastard that distasteful?'

'No, of course not! How could you think such a thing?' she said at once, her protest so vehement, he could not doubt its sincerity. 'It is *I* who would not be an embarrassment to *you*!'

Mollified, he forced the suspicion back deep, where he trapped all memory of feeling outcast and inadequate. 'You would never be that. Do you suspect I'll not allow you unlimited use of your money, once we are wed?'

'No! I don't believe you would try to cheat me out of it.'

'Or that I would limit your freedom of movement, insist on your remaining in London when you wished to travel and sketch?'

'N-no, not really,' she admitted.

'Then what is the real reason for your hesitation? Do you not believe my promise to…refrain from touching you, unless you invite me?'

She hesitated, her lack of immediate denial bringing a frown to his face. Seeing his expression, she added hastily, 'Oh, yes, I believe you about that!'

'Then what?'

After another moment of silence, she gave a twisted smile. 'I'm not so sure I trust *myself* to resist, if you try to…beguile me.'

Irrationally, he felt enormously relieved to confirm his instincts were correct and it was her doubts over whether *she* could resist *him*, rather than a lack of attraction, that caused her distress. Though that affirmation made him want her even more, he didn't mean to trick or drag her, unwilling, into acquiescence.

No, he wanted her warm and willing and actively pursuing him.

'Would you believe me if I gave you another promise?'

She met his serious gaze. 'I…suppose I would.'

'Then believe this: I promise I will not try to "beguile" you. What I *would* like to do is re-establish the rapport we had at our meetings at Dornton. If we can recapture that ease, would it set your worries at rest?'

The sudden lightening of her expression told him he'd hit upon the right response. The brilliance of the smile that followed lit those magnificent eyes, sparking a jolt of desire even as it set off a curious little ache in his chest.

'I would very much like to recapture the camaraderie we had at Dornton! If we could and you truly aren't having second thoughts about what a poor choice of a wife I'd be, I think I can…move forward.'

Reassured by that response, he nodded. 'I still believe marriage is the best solution for us both. As I mentioned before, Lady Lyndlington can hostess any necessary political gatherings; you'd need not attend them, unless you chose to. Nor should you worry over your reception by my friends; they will have only admiration for a lady of your intelligence and talent. So if your reservations are mostly on my behalf, you can forget them. Wedding you is a good bargain I am happy to make.'

'You're sure?' she asked, studying his face.

'I am. We are agreed, then?' he asked, holding out his hand.

Tentatively, those mesmerising eyes on his face, she offered hers in return.

Though his body protested, urging beguilement, he made himself give her a quick, businesslike handshake. Though even that brief touch sent a zing of connection through him.

How he wished he could have held on and caressed

the softness of her fingers! Leaned down to kiss her, his thumb resting at her wrist. Would he feel her pulse beating as erratically as his?

Sometimes patience and abstinence were the best aphrodisiacs, he told himself. If he ever possessed her, it must be because she chose to give herself to him. And to make that choice, she would have to be convinced he desired only what she wanted and trust that yielding to him would bring only pleasure. It would not threaten her fragile new freedom or prevent her from doing what she most wanted to do.

Having a friend for a wife was better than a wild but resistant lover who came to him fearing that succumbing to their attraction would mean losing control over who she was.

Although the connection—immediate, automatic, powerful—that flared at every glancing touch argued that the passion between them could never be bottled up into something as tame as 'friendship'.

His fingers still tingling in the aftershock of that brief handshake, Ben forced himself to sit back, reach for his wine glass and take a sip. His body might not like it, but he *would* forbid himself to try to entice her. What they could—would—eventually share would be well worth the wait.

Since he couldn't eradicate the sensual connection, he'd better concentrate on trying to recapture the ease and build trust. The best way to do that was to ensure she had the means to be independent as soon as possible.

Tomorrow, he would take her to visit the solicitor.

'I'm glad that's settled. After riding so far, you must be as tired as your mother. Finish your wine; I'll send that maid to you on my way out.'

'Thank you, I'd appreciate that.'

After draining his glass, Ben said, 'If it can be arranged, I intend to visit your father's solicitor tomorrow. Would you like to accompany me?'

Looking surprised by the offer, she nodded. 'Yes, I would.'

'I want you to be familiar with every detail of how your money is to be handled. You should know the total and begin to plan how you intend to use, or invest it. I imagine the solicitor will have recommendations.'

He could almost see some of the tension within her easing. 'You're right, I need to plan. We're already approaching winter and there are a number of birds in outlying counties I haven't yet been able to sketch. Some of them are migratory; if I want to include all the sketches required to make the collection complete by the publisher's deadline, I'll need to find them and capture their images before they leave the winter feeding grounds.'

Ben nodded. 'I'll see you tomorrow, then.'

He rose and walked out, reassured—but still troubled. Happy as he was to know that Lyssa would work with him to restore the rapport between them, he was more uncertain now than he wanted to admit about the inevitability of her eventually yielding to him. He didn't need her money, wasn't concerned about her reluctance to play hostess and not worried at all about her being an embarrassment to him—he was certain she would fascinate his friends as much as she did him.

The only thing more miserable than being trapped in wedlock with a female who couldn't bear his company would be marriage to a seductive *friend* for whom he must lust for in vain for the rest of his life. Somehow—without *enticing*—he had to convince Alyssa to embrace the passion between them.

The next afternoon, Ben stood at his mirror, putting the finishing touches on his cravat. He'd had his batman visit the solicitor early that morning to obtain an appointment, then confirmed by an exchange of notes with Lady Alyssa that she would be available to accompany him. He'd leave for Queen Street shortly to collect her.

And take the first step in the campaign to win her trust.

With Giles and Maggie still away, he'd had all of last evening to ponder the best way of beguiling without beguiling and had hit upon a scheme he thought just might work.

If he could create the proper atmosphere, while resisting the urgent need to take advantage of it. But if letting her beguile *herself* were the surest path to eventual fulfilment, he'd make himself resist—somehow.

After taking a carriage for the short drive to Queen Street, Ben was pleased—though not surprised—to find Lady Alyssa ready and waiting for him. He escorted her to the carriage, handed her up—careful not to let his hands linger—and gave the driver instructions to their destination.

Seating himself on the forward bench opposite, rather than beside her, he said, 'Have you any idea how your funds were disposed—according to the terms of your aunt's will? Or as a bequest during her lifetime?' At Lady Alyssa's raised eyebrows, he said, 'During my years in India, I read law with one of the John Company barristers. An interesting way to pass the time, and with my future uncertain, I figured acquiring a contact who might recommend me to study at the Inns of Court could be useful, if I should some day need to pursue an occupation.'

'This, during the hours when you were not skulking about in disguise, ferreting out information for the army?'

'One can't spend all one's time skulking and ferreting,' he replied with a grin. 'Sadly, one must occasionally wear a regular uniform. Studying at the barrister's office was much more entertaining than participating in endless drills in the hot sun. As it turns out, arguing points of law with Jeffries was good preparation for the debates that make up much of a parliamentarian's life.'

She shook her head. 'Do you also tame lions? Summon snakes out of baskets?'

'No lions and I only flush out snakes of the two-legged variety,' he replied, sobering as he recalled the curs who had tried to ruin her.

'Like Lord Denbry,' she said, seeming to read his thoughts. 'Sorry, but I have no idea how the funds were left; certainly my father never thought it necessary to enlighten me.'

'Your father's solicitor should have all the details. Though it would have been useful to have some knowledge of them before meeting him.'

'Do you think he will create difficulties?'

'He will be expecting your future husband, or his solicitor, to enquire about the funds allocated to you. He probably will not, however, be anticipating what we want done with your great-aunt's bequest.'

'Signing it over to me?'

'Exactly. Don't be offended if he strongly advises

against that. I expect he's met very few women who wish to handle their own funds.'

'And even fewer husbands who would allow their wives to do so.' Gazing up at him, she said softly, 'Thank you, Ben Tawny. For being the exceptional man you are.'

Smiling faintly, he took her hand and gave it a reassuring squeeze. When, mindful of his resolve, he would have pulled away, she held on, still gazing into his eyes.

He was acutely aware of her gloved fingers on his, their pressure sparking a warmth that seemed to flow through him, heating his blood, settling in his loins. She took a little breath and angled her chin up, as if inviting his kiss.

It took all the will he could muster to gently pull his fingers free, when all he wanted was to wrap his arms around her and press her to him as he gave her the kiss for which she seemed to be asking.

But when—if—he kissed her, the invitation would have to be much more plain. Nor did he plan to grant such a request until after he'd turned her away often enough to make her as eager—and frustrated—as he was.

By now, the carriage was slowing. Trying to shake himself free of the sensual spell, Ben sprang out as soon as it stopped and handed her down with businesslike efficiency—which, her expression told him, both confused and frustrated her.

*You must figure out what you want...and be absolutely sure you want it*, he thought as he escorted her into the office.

A clerk ushered them into Mr Chambers's private domain. 'Mr Tawny!' the solicitor said, rising from behind his desk to offer a handshake. 'Lord Aldermont wrote that you would be consulting me. And… Lady Alyssa?' he asked, with a puzzled glance at the female who had just invaded his office.

'Yes, I'm Lady Alyssa. I don't believe we've met. A pleasure to make your acquaintance, sir.'

'The pleasure is mine, my lady,' he said, bowing. 'There was no need to inconvenience yourself, coming to my office! It has been my privilege to serve your noble father for many years and I hope to serve your future husband as well. You, sir, will be wanting to know about the settlements,' Chambers said, inclining his head towards Ben. 'Shall we set a meeting to discuss them with your solicitor?'

'No, I prefer to discuss them with you directly.'

'As you wish, Mr Tawny. Lady Alyssa, may I invite you to a seat in my study? Lawler will be happy to escort you there and bring you refreshment while your intended and I conduct our business.'

Before he could summon his subordinate, Ben said, 'We prefer that Lady Alyssa remain. We wish to have the bequest left to her by her Aunt Augusta transferred into a fund for her use, so it would be helpful for her to know how it was left and the new arrangements for accessing it.'

Obviously surprised, the solicitor stared at Ben. Belatedly realising his hesitation might be considered disrespectful by his soon-to-be very wealthy prospective client, he stammered, 'I-if that is what you wish, Mr Tawny. Please, won't you be seated?' He waved them to the pair of armchairs. 'Although I fear Lady Alyssa may find the legal discussion rather tedious.'

*He doesn't believe she'll understand it*, he thought.

Giving Ben an exasperated glance that said she'd interpreted the solicitor's comment in the same way, Lyssa said drily, 'I shall attempt to remain awake, sir.'

Oblivious to her ironic tone, Chambers continued, 'Shall we discuss the bequest first, Mr Tawny? You want the funds transferred into an account upon which your future wife will be allowed to draw. Unless you anticipate that your duties will require you to travel extensively outside the city while your wife remains in London, I can envision few instances when you would be unable to obtain funds for her. Unless there *are* unusual circumstances, I recommend that the account be drawn up in your name only.'

'Circumstances are unusual,' Ben replied. 'It is my bride who will often be travelling, while I discharge my duties here in Parliament. We wish the bequest left to her by her Aunt Augusta to be placed in an account in *Lady Alyssa's* name only.'

'In her name only?' the solicitor repeated. 'Surely her aunt did not intend the funds to be used in such a manner! Bequests left to female relations are normally included with the rest of the lady's assets, dispensed as set out in the settlements into dowries for daughters, stipends for minor sons and a widow's portion, all the funds administered after marriage by her husband.'

'I'm sure that is correct,' Ben said patiently. 'However, we do not wish to use the bequest in that fashion. We want the funds deposited into an account in Lady Alyssa's name, for her sole use.'

'But...if the account is thus construed, you would not be able to access it, even after you become her legal husband. Or to impose any control whatsoever over the way the money is used!'

'That was the general idea,' Ben said drily.

The solicitor looked back and forth between Ben and Alyssa, his distressed expression saying he wished he could discuss the matter with Ben privately. Finally, leaning towards Ben, he said in a lowered voice, 'I am sure that Lady Alyssa is a most competent young lady, not prone to…fits of fancy. However, I doubt she has any experience handling funds beyond the pin money allowed for fans and gloves and such. To give her sole discretion over what is quite a substantial sum… If she were to fritter it away, you would have no power to prevent her!'

'I expect it will be quite the opposite,' Ben said. 'She'll probably protect her funds as fiercely as a recluse with a sack of gold coins.'

'In any event, Mr Chambers, it is only the bequest from my aunt in question,' Lyssa interposed. 'Over my dowry, which I've been told is even more substantial, Mr Tawny will exercise all the *usual* control.'

Brightening considerably, the solicitor said, 'There is that, of course. As you were correctly informed, your dowry is quite vast. Upon signing the parish register after the wedding, Mr Tawny will become a very wealthy man.'

Ben frowned, not liking the image of himself as a fortune-hunter eager to get his hands on a windfall. 'Could the dowry funds not be tied up as well—into a trust for children, or a widow's portion?'

'But I should like to allot some of it for you to use in furthering your Parliamentary career,' Lyssa said. 'That *was* part of the bargain. As a point of honour, I must insist on it.'

Ben gave Lyssa a questioning look, wishing they'd

discussed the matter more thoroughly before confronting the solicitor. On the one occasion they'd touched on the question, she *had* offered to turn over her dowry, as long as she could keep her aunt's bequest, but he hadn't imagined she'd consider conveying the funds an essential part of their bargain. As a mostly self-made man, the notion of claiming a fortune merely for having married her rubbed him on the raw—no matter that it was the customary way of things.

But to his silent query, she returned a little negative shake of the head.

'You feel strongly about this,' he said at last.

'I do.'

'Very well, if you insist, I suppose a part of the funds could be set aside to meet Parliamentary expenses,' Ben agreed, not wanting to brangle in front of the lawyer. 'Approximately what is the total available, Mr Chambers?'

The figure he named made Ben gasp and Lyssa emit an amused chuckle. 'I didn't realise Papa was that desperate to be rid of me,' she murmured.

'No more than ten per cent should be reserved for my use,' Ben said. 'Her ladyship should have an account set aside to meet her personal needs during my lifetime, with the remainder returned to her as a jointure upon my demise.'

'Fifty per cent should be for you,' Lyssa said.

'No, that's far too much! Fifteen, at most.'

'Forty-five.'

'Eighteen.'

'I can't accept your receiving any less than forty.'

Ben sighed. 'Very well, forty. Nothing says I actually have to use it, after all.'

'Agreed.' She held out her hand, which Ben shook solemnly.

The electricity that cracked between their gloved fingers at that simple touch momentarily distracted him from replying. They gazed at each other, both once again startled by the strength of that connection.

Belatedly releasing her fingers, Ben shook his head to clear it and reassembled his scattered thoughts. 'So, Mr Chambers, please set up the funds from Lady Alyssa's bequest into an account for her use only and allocate from the dowry an apportionment for her use, some for mine, with the rest to be held for the future—in some sort of investment, probably. We would appreciate your advice on what sort. Shall we give you several days to set up the accounts and draft the documents, then check back with you to finalise the arrangements?'

The solicitor, whose incredulous gaze had been bouncing back and forth from Ben to Alyssa during their exchange, like a spectator following a tennis match, took several moments to find his tongue. 'I... well, yes, I suppose I can establish funds in that manner,' he said at last.

'Very good. Shall we call on you in, say, three days' time?'

'You are *certain* you wish to proceed in this manner?' he asked Ben. At his nod, the man shook his head. 'Very well, I shall see you again in three days.'

'Thank you for your kind assistance,' Ben said, rising. 'I'm sure Lady Alyssa's funds will be in good hands.'

'Yes, thank you, Mr Chambers,' Lyssa said, rising as well. 'We both appreciate your honouring our...unusual requests.'

'I shall do my best to serve you both.' Emerging from behind his desk, the solicitor walked them to the door, calling for his assistant to fetch them a hackney.

As soon as they were settled in the carriage, Alyssa broke into a peal of laughter so merry Ben had to join in. 'Poor Mr Chambers!' she said between whoops. 'The look on his face when you confirmed you wanted me to have funds over which you would have no control! I feared he might suffer a seizure of the heart!'

'I imagine he's never had an engaged couple in his office discussing the arrangement of their finances.'

'I imagine he's never had an engaged couple in his office at all. Such matters are usually settled by the respective fathers, or between the prospective groom and the solicitors.'

'He'll be marvelling about it for weeks,' Ben agreed.

'Probably dining out on the story, entertaining his solicitor friends. If he can dine at all. Thinking about some idiot female frittering away her wealth is likely to spoil his appetite.'

'The hefty fee he'll earn for making the arrangements will console him.'

She chuckled. 'I hope it makes him feel better.' Her mirth fading, she looked up at him. 'As your insisting he set it up as we discussed made *me* feel so much better. Thank you.'

'I made you a promise, Lyssa, which *I* consider a point of honour to keep. Very soon, you will have the funds your aunt promised you and the freedom to use them.'

Her beautiful eyes brightened. 'It's been nothing but a dream for so long, I can hardly believe it.'

'Believe it.'

Her expression turned regretful. 'I just wish my freedom hadn't come at the cost of yours. Even if I could induce you to spend all my dowry, it would still not be a fair exchange for what you give up—the ability to marry, or not, as you choose. I do promise to be as light a burden as possible and restrict your actions as little as I can. I shall be very proud, though, if any of the funds I provide help you to achieve more quickly the success your honour, commitment and ideals merit. Never have I met a man who deserves it more.'

Impulsively, she leaned up to kiss him.

That unexpected gesture turned from casual to carnal the instant her lips met his. As if startled by that instant connection, she gasped, pulled back…and then brought her lips to his again.

His hands went automatically to her shoulders—before he remembered he'd vowed not to *entice*. Forcing his hands back to his sides before his rapidly disintegrating intellect could lose its grip over his control, he held himself rigid, letting her kiss him, resisting with all his strength the imperative thrumming in his blood to take her further, faster.

With a little murmur, she drew away and back again, brushing her lips against his, as if she couldn't quite force herself to stop. Sweat broke out on his forehead and trickled down his back as he fought the desire to part her lips, taste her, stroke her tongue with his. Finally, knowing he must end the kiss or risk having his control shatter completely, he pushed her away.

Her breathing sounded as uneven as his own.

'Sorry,' she muttered unsteadily. 'I didn't mean to… take advantage.'

His chuckle was half-amusement, half-pain. 'Please,

take advantage whenever you like! You don't have to deny what's between us to claim your freedom, Lyssa. You are free to enjoy passion, too. I shall do my best not to "entice" you to anything you do not wish. But I am also delighted to offer—whatever you wish to take.' *Thereby contradicting his resolve not to respond to her,* he thought with an inward sigh.

'You are damnably hard to resist—but proceeding makes it even harder to stop,' she said. 'I shall have to be more circumspect about starting.'

Not the reply he'd hoped, but at least she'd not retreated into chilly reserve. 'I must confess to preferring you *un*-circumspect, but it shall be as you want. I keep all my promises, Lyssa. Even the ones I don't want to keep.'

'Thank you for that.'

Soon after, they reached the town house on Queen Street. 'Should you like to come in?' Lady Alyssa asked, turning back to him after the footman handed her down.

'I would *like* to,' Ben replied as he exited the carriage after her. 'Unfortunately, I have some documents I must study before the Lyndlingtons return tonight. Once I inform them of our plans, I'm sure they will invite you and your mother to dine, so they may get to know the lady I'm to wed.'

She paused before the entry stairs, her expression turning troubled. 'I only hope they will not be horrified when they realise how ill suited a wife I am for a man in public life.'

Ben couldn't help it—he had to cup her chin and lift her head up to face him. Silently damning the father and brother who had instilled in her such a deep sense of her ineptitude in playing a traditional woman's role, he said, 'They will admire and respect you. As I do. You'll see.'

She gave him a sad little smile, not looking at all convinced. 'Well, I shall be out of your hair soon enough after the wedding, so I won't be an impediment to you—or them—for very long.'

'You will be a delight to us for as long as we can persuade you to remain in London. But I'll leave you to your mother's care now and see you tomorrow.'

Sighing, she made a face. 'Mama is eager to take me shopping. You're abandoning me to a torturous round of choosing trimmings, velvets, laces and being poked and prodded into half-made gowns that can be quickly finished.'

'Make sure you select one ensemble that looks appropriately managerial, for when we return to finalise the details with Mr Chambers.'

That made her chuckle, as he'd hoped it would. 'Thinking about our interview this morning will keep my spirits up through the coming ordeal.'

'Bravely said! I'll see you tomorrow.'

'Tomorrow,' she agreed, nodding. As he turned to walk off towards Brook Street, she stayed him with a quick touch to his elbow. 'Thank you for being a man of principle who keeps his promises.'

Those intense eyes gazed up at him, both fierce and somehow vulnerable. Unable to look away, he lost himself in them, as something sharp and poignant twisted in his chest.

He wanted to promise he'd keep her safe from every danger and help her realise the dream so dear to her. How he'd gone so quickly from disinterested concern for an unknown female, to an intense desire to protect and defend this particular lady, he didn't know, but that imperative now beat as strongly within him as his physical desire for her.

He couldn't deny regretting the loss of his freedom, but marriage to this unusual woman would never be a burden. He expected to be surprised, beguiled, entertained—and if she ever let the passion within her win out, *satisfied*—for the rest of their lives.

He doubted any syrupy notion of romantic love could offer a stronger basis for a successful union than that.

## *Chapter Ten*

Two nights later, Ben handed the Lambornne ladies into a hackney as they set off for dinner at the Lyndlingtons'.

'I see the shopping expedition was a success,' he said as the ladies seated themselves. 'That celestial blue becomes you wonderfully, Lady Aldermont. You are lovely, too, Lyssa. That gold trim on that green brings out the fire in your eyes.'

While Lady Aldermont blushed and thanked him, Lyssa merely nodded. She also seemed as tense as she was lovely—as if already convinced the dinner would be a trial.

'Too bad this will only be a casual dinner, with no dancing. I'd be the envy of the gentlemen, squiring two such lovely ladies across the floor,' he said, hoping to set her more at ease. Without much success, for she only frowned.

After a concerned look at her daughter, Lady Aldermont said, 'Won't you tell us who will be present tonight, Mr Tawny?'

Hoping to set his intended more at ease, Ben said, 'It

will be a small group and you may well be acquainted with some of them, Lady Aldermont. Lady Lyndlington's father, Lord Witlow, and her aunt, the Dowager Countess of Sayleford, will be there, along with my colleagues, of course. Giles Hadley, Lord Lyndlington, David Tanner Smith and his wife, Faith, formerly Duchess of Ashedon, and Christopher Lattimar.'

'Your Hellions?' Lady Aldermont asked. 'I am acquainted with Lord Witlow—a fine, courteous gentleman. Lady Sayleford was quite the arbiter of fashion when I was coming out—all the girls on the Marriage Mart lived in terror of a blighting word from her! The younger set, I don't know. Could you tell me a bit about them?'

With a glance at Alyssa, who continued to sit in silence, looking grim as if girding herself for an ordeal, Ben continued, 'Giles's mother—as I'm sure you'll remember, for it was quite a scandal—was divorced by his father when Giles was quite young. Like me, he spent his early days with her in an isolated cottage. After his aunt's prodding, his father eventually was induced to send him to school and university. Whereas the Viscount sustained us in tolerable comfort—as much, I suppose, as can be expected for a woman who bears a child out of wedlock,' Ben said, trying to keep the bitterness out of his voice, 'he also provided for my schooling, which is where I met Giles and Christopher, at Eton, and later David, at Oxford. With all of us having an unusual family background to set us apart from our fellows, we became fast friends.'

He chuckled. 'The ladies are equally out of the common way. Lady Margaret, daughter of one of the Tory leaders in the House of Lords, wed Giles, the voice of the Reform opposition in the Commons, while the Duchess recently scandalised society by marrying David, a farmer's orphan. In her defence, he's both a long-standing friend of the family and an exceptional man. When still a lad, his courage and initiative won the respect and esteem of Sir Edward Greaves, who sponsored him at school and in Parliament.'

'You sound like a group of independent thinkers, who hold to principle rather than simply conforming to the norms of society,' Lady Aldermont observed.

'We are that. Which is why Lyssa will fit in beautifully.'

He'd hoped that remark might lighten his intended's sombre mood, but she barely glanced at him. Stymied, Ben cast about for some way of setting her at ease before they began an evening she was clearly dreading.

The carriage arrived at their destination before he could come up with anything.

He wasn't the only one concerned, for as her mother followed her from the carriage, he heard Lady Aldermont whisper, 'Why so uneasy, Lyssa? You've dined out among strangers many times!'

'I never before cared whether people approved of me or not. Now my inadequacies will reflect badly on him,' she murmured back.

*Drab...long on the shelf...no conversation and little wit*, Ben recalled the description Denbry had given of her. If she believed this was how society saw her, no wonder she was not looking forward to meeting his friends.

Such a deep-seated conviction wouldn't be dispelled by his offering a few facile words of encouragement. He'd have to trust his friends to see and appreciate, as he did, the uniqueness of this lady and let their reception demonstrate that her reservations were groundless.

Not to his surprise, although Lady Alyssa nodded and smiled politely, after introductions all around, she made no attempt to enter the conversation in the drawing room where the arriving guests assembled. While her mother was quickly drawn in, blushing and smiling at Lord Witlow's gallant remarks before being swept away by Lady Sayleford, even Christopher, renowned for his facility with the ladies, managed to draw only one brief smile and not a single word from Alyssa.

Though Lady Maggie had seated him beside her at dinner, with the Hellions reassembled for the first time since their dispersal and with the reconvening of the new Parliament imminent, Ben was soon caught up in answering questions from Lord Witlow and his fellow Hellions about his assessment of what might be accomplished in the upcoming session. With both Giles's lady and David's wife keenly interested in politics themselves, and with Lady Sayleford deep in conversation with Lady Aldermont, there was only one lull in the discussion into which Ben tried to introduce the topic of Llyssa's sketching. But to his exasperation, her monosyllabic answers and complete lack of enthusiasm in responding allowed the conversation to swing immediately back to politics.

He'd often wondered how the woman he'd found so magnetic could have been so undervalued by society's gentlemen and had concluded it must be because she was too out of the ordinary, too passionate and unconventional; most men preferred a more docile and biddable bride. But watching her tonight, he understood only too clearly why she'd been overlooked.

Small, silent, with her eyes staring lifelessly into the distance or fixed on her plate, she really did seem to have no conversation and little wit. It was as if the vibrant women he knew had disappeared somewhere deep within herself, leaving behind this wooden manikin with her size and features, but none of her personality or passion.

Told over and over by her contemptuous father and critical brother that she was hopelessly out of place in society, she made no attempt to participate. He needed to show her that not all in society were like the men and women who had been so dismissive of her, let her see that his friends would welcome and appreciate the woman she was—if she would only give them a chance.

With politics the overwhelming focus of talk during dinner, however, he couldn't manage to lead the discussion into anything else. But before the evening ended, Ben was determined to bring the real Alyssa into the light.

A short time later, Maggie rose to signal it was time for the ladies to withdraw. Seeing his chance, before she could lead them from the room, Ben hopped up and went over to place a hand on her arm.

'Maggie, I need your help,' he said *sotto voce.*

'Of course, Ben. What is it?'

'Lady Alyssa. I need you to focus on her once the ladies withdraw and work your magic to get her to talk.'

Maggie patted the hand clutching her wrist. 'She has been rather subdued. If she's not used to political discussions, the conversation at dinner had to be rather daunting! My fault—I should have turned the topic to something else.'

'That would have been difficult, with Giles, Davie and Christopher fired up to discuss strategy.'

'I'll make it up to you both and see if I can't draw out your shy wallflower.'

'Alyssa?' Ben laughed, shaking his head. 'I've never met a woman less like a shy wallflower in my life.'

'Truly? She certainly appears…quiet. How do *you* find her?'

'After suffering through too many overheated and under-stimulating parties during her Season, she's decided she doesn't fit into society. But when the topic interests her, she's…completely different. I first encountered her while she was in the woods, sketching, and so absorbed in her work that she didn't notice me at all. When I did catch her attention, she was entirely self-possessed and, unlike most single females, not a bit interested in impressing me. Get her to talk about her work. A London publisher wants to issue a book of her sketches.'

'Publish them! How wonderful. I will certainly ask about that.'

'She has a major talent and a most unconventional outlook. Quite unique.'

For no reason he could fathom, Maggie gave him a speculative look.

'What?'

She shook her head, an odd little smile on her lips. 'Nothing. I'll do my best.'

'Thank you, Maggie. I think you'll find her as fascinating as I do.'

'I'm sure I shall.' With that, she turned and said, 'Ladies, shall we? After the gentlemen settle the fate of the nation, they will join us for tea.'

With smiles and murmurs to their dinner partners, the other women rose and followed Maggie from the room. Except for Alyssa, who continued to stare down at the carpet and left without giving Ben so much as a glance.

Dinner had been even worse than she'd feared, Alyssa thought glumly as she trailed the others out of the dining room. While Lady Sayleford kept her mother occupied with commentary about society figures of their mutual acquaintance, the rest of the company had avidly discussed the upcoming Parliamentary session. Thanks to Mr Tawny's brief description and what she'd gleaned from reading Lord Fulton's newspaper, she at least knew who Lord Grey was and a few of the issues being addressed.

While the other ladies—led by the brilliant Lady Lyndlington, who seemed to have an intimate knowledge of every politician and every issue—were able to contribute an intelligent comment from time to time, she'd been completely lost.

If that were not intimidating enough, the Duchess was not only well spoken, she was the most beautiful woman Alyssa had ever seen. She'd always thought her mama would be the perfect model for any artist wishing to do the portrait of an angel, but she had to admit, the Duchess would make an even better one.

While these glittering butterflies danced and swirled with the conversation, she sat still and silent like a giant slug. They must think her as ignorant as a South Sea savage and wonder why on earth Ben Tawny intended to marry so uninformed and ill spoken a bride.

Only by shutting out the commentary flowing around

her and reviewing in her head the various birds she still needed to sketch, mentally composing the most efficient itinerary to get to all of them before winter ended, was she able to keep her face from flaming with humiliation.

If tonight hadn't convinced Tawny to call it off, she must quit London immediately after the wedding, before she embarrassed herself—and him—any further.

As they filed into the drawing room, Lady Sayleford directed her mother to a chair by the hearth with a plea that they continue the discussion begun at dinner. Wondering how long it would be before the gentlemen joined them, drank their tea, and she might finally seek refuge in her room in Queen Street, Alyssa walked over to the window.

Gazing into the darkness outside, caught up in her glum reflections, it was several minutes before she realised her hostess was addressing her.

'Sorry, I'm afraid I wasn't attending,' she said, turning to Lady Lyndlington, feeling her face redden in truth. 'Could you repeat that, please?'

Lady Lyndlington smiled. 'I wanted to apologise for allowing politics to completely dominate the discussion at dinner. I failed in my duties as hostess in not insisting we talk about something else, but with the new session about to begin, and so much at stake, I'm afraid I was quite as hopeless as the men. They are just now coming back together after having been apart for several weeks and are eager to plan for the session ahead. Having cut my teeth on politics, I became as carried away as they were. I am sorry!'

Surprised that her hostess would apologise, Alyssa stammered, 'H-how kind of you, but it's not at all necessary. It's my own fault that I know too little to contribute to the conversation.'

'Of course it isn't,' the angel-as-Duchess said, coming over to join them. 'I knew almost nothing myself before Davie came back into my life—my first husband was not at all political. The Hellions are so passionate about their work, you will soon learn. I hope you'll become enthusiastic about it, too, since it's so important to Ben. But even if you don't develop an interest, I know you'll be proud of the vital task they are doing for the nation.'

At least with that, she could agree. 'Yes. Even as ignorant as I am, I realise what a great vision it is they wish to accomplish. I *am* proud to be associated with men who are willing to work selflessly for the betterment of the nation.'

'We were so preoccupied with politics, we never got to what Ben wanted to discuss—your work, Lady Alyssa,' Lady Lyndlington said. 'He tells me that your sketching is of such high quality, a publisher wishes to put out a book featuring it.'

'Y-yes.'

'A published work!' the Duchess echoed. 'How impressive! I've never known anyone clever enough to have a book published. Please, won't you tell us more about it?'

'Very well—if you truly wish to know.'

'Certainly we do!' Lady Lyndlington said.

Perhaps Tawny's friends really would appreciate her, Alyssa thought, their encouragement warming her. Though she wouldn't get her hopes up just yet. It was only natural that they would politely try to include the woman who was to marry one of their husbands' best friends.

'If I can complete all the sketches by the end of January—and if the publisher still wants them—they may become a book.'

'How exciting! You shall become famous!' the Duchess said.

'Hardly,' Alyssa replied with a chuckle. 'Waterman doesn't know the sketches were done by a woman, of course. To get them published at all, I shall have to remain "A. Lawrence"—one of my mother's family names, as " Lambornne" is too recognisable.'

'Naturally,' Lady Lyndlington said drily. 'No man would be enlightened enough to publish drawings by a female, regardless of how exceptional they are.'

'How did the publisher learn about them?' the Duchess asked.

'A...a friend who believed in their worth initially brought the drawings to his attention. Once I have the sketches completed, I shall have to find another agent to contact the publisher to arrange the transaction, Duchess.'

'Aggravating, but necessary, I suppose,' the Duchess agreed. 'And you must call me "Faith", as the others do. Only my former mother-in-law and the solicitors still call me "Duchess".'

'And you must call me "Maggie",' her hostess added. 'With our men such close friends, we cannot stand on formality.'

'Very well, I should be "Lyssa", then,' Alyssa said, tempted to abandon caution and respond to their warm friendliness and what appeared to be genuine interest. Maybe...maybe they truly could become friends.

Which would be…delightful. Other than her mother, she'd never had a female friend.

'You haven't told us what you sketch,' Maggie recalled her.

'Birds.'

Maggie's eyes widened. 'Like Mr Audubon? One of Father's friends subscribes to his portfolios. They are magnificent!'

'They are indeed,' Alyssa said, enthusiasm for the topic dissipating the last of her reserve. 'During my second Season, I endured the company of the most boring fellow ever, because he promised to take me to the library of his cousin, the Duke of Northumberland, who was a subscriber. I was enthralled! Not that I am by any means Audubon's equal, but I had already begun a series of watercolour sketches of the birds in Mr Bewick's book. A wonderful resource, but the illustrations are all in black and white.'

'Bewick's *A History of British Birds*?' Faith asked. 'My brother and I loved that book, and always carried it when we were tromping about in the woods at Wellingford.' She sighed. 'Where I spent some of my happiest days.'

Alyssa shook her head. 'I can't picture *you* tromping about in the woods.'

'Can you not? If you had a Season in London, surely you heard me criticised—the "little dab of a duchess" with the "countrified ways".'

Alyssa stared, wondering if the Duchess were teasing her. She couldn't imagine anyone criticising so beautiful and charming a lady. 'You're not serious, surely.'

'You truly hadn't heard? You must be the only one ever to attend a society function who hasn't, then.'

'Well, to be fair, I didn't really listen much to what was said around me,' Alyssa admitted. 'Gossip, and talk of fashion and jewellery and houses and servants... it was all so boring. And the rooms so hot and over-crowded, all I wanted was for the event to end so I could get away.'

'I understand completely!' Faith said. 'I can't tell you how many times I wished I could escape, slip back to the town house and into some of my brother's old clothes, and go for a punishing gallop!' She sighed. 'But with everyone watching everything I did, all the time, I seldom had the opportunity. Maggie and I often ride in the mornings here. While you are in London, you must join us.'

'I should like that,' Alyssa said.

'So, it is your watercolour sketches of birds the publisher wishes to turn into a book?' Maggie asked.

'Yes. While I was viewing the Duke's folio, I mentioned my sketches to his librarian, who asked to see them. He was impressed enough by the watercolours that, unbeknownst to me, he contacted a publisher. With the tremendous success of Audubon's folios, he felt there might be interest in a colourised edition of British birds and the publisher agreed.'

'How exciting! But does it not take hours to complete such sketches? You must spend a great deal of time in the woods. How lucky you are!' Faith said.

'It does take time. Using Bewick as a guide, I make several preliminary pencil sketches of birds I expect to see, then observe them in the wild and use pastels to add in the colouration. Once I'm sure I have the right hues, I do a final sketch of the bird in its habitat, in flight or on a nest, and return to the studio to paint.' She gave them an apologetic look. 'I'm afraid I'm far more at home tromping through the woods than sitting through a dinner party. As was evident tonight.'

'Might I ride out with you, if you intend to sketch hereabouts?' the Duchess asked. 'I promise not to interrupt your work.'

'I'm afraid you would be terribly bored,' Alyssa said. 'My mother requires me to bring a maid if I'm anywhere but on Aldermont land and the poor girl just hates it.'

'Out in the woods, where I might ride and explore at leisure?' Faith exclaimed. 'I would love it! Take me when you go next and leave the maid at home.'

'Imagine, Faith, we shall be able to claim as a friend an artist who commands public attention for her work!' Maggie said. Turning to Alyssa, she added, 'No wonder Ben is fascinated by you.'

That comment extinguished Alyssa's enthusiasm as quickly as cold water poured on barely caught kindling. 'Did Ben not tell you how we came to be engaged?'

'I've hardly seen him since we got back,' Maggie said. 'If he informed Giles, my husband hasn't yet passed the story along to me.'

'Of course not, silly,' Faith said. 'Men never enquire about what one really wishes to know. Though he's one of the kindest, most principled men I know, Ben has quite a reputation with the ladies. He's never indicated any desire to trade admiring the many for devotion to just one, so you must have bedazzled him.'

It was tempting to say nothing and let that rosy illusion stand, since Tawny apparently hadn't informed his friends of the truth. Doubtless, an omission meant to protect her honour and reputation.

But it seemed dishonest, somehow, in light of the

ladies' open acceptance, to reinforce such a lie—if they were truly to be friends.

Though they probably wouldn't want to be, once they knew the circumstances. Buoyed by the heady feeling of being liked and accepted, Alyssa had to struggle with herself to confess what she knew they deserved to hear.

'I wish that were the case, but it isn't,' she said bluntly. 'Caring for Mr Tawny as deeply as you both do, it's only right that you know the truth. Which will also explain how he came to offer for a woman so clearly unsuited for being the wife of a politician.'

The two ladies exchanged a look. 'We do care about Ben,' Maggie said. 'But we would not press for details that are private between you and your intended.'

'Taking me to wife, he's going to need your help in meeting his social obligations. You should understand why he took so puzzling a step.' Girding herself for rejection, she took a deep breath. 'It's not a very edifying tale.'

While the two ladies listened without interruption, Alyssa quickly related the history of the wager, Ben's intervention, her insistence on challenging the perpetrators—and the calamitous conclusion, when members of the house party discovered her at the inn, tarnishing not the names of the rogues who'd tried to ruin her, but of the honourable man who'd tried to save her.

'I did initially refuse his proposal,' Alyssa explained. 'But when he tracked me down at my father's house, he insisted that if we did not wed, and the story got out that he'd seduced a lady of quality and refused to marry her, the charge would seriously damage his reputation and quite possibly compromise his political career.'

Maggie nodded thoughtfully. 'Yes, it could very well do that.'

'So you see, though I like to think we share a mutual respect and fondness…' *no need to mention the barely controlled passion that flared between them* '…this is hardly a love match. The only way I could salve my conscience about robbing Mr Tawny of his freedom was to insist he use my substantial dowry to further his political career.'

'Fondness and respect are a good beginning,' Faith said. 'That's what I felt for Davie, long before I realised I loved him.'

Alyssa didn't even want to consider going down that path. But neither did she feel comfortable admitting she'd given Ben Tawny permission to live his private life as before, seeing such ladies as he chose. A circumstance which would make it foolish in the extreme for her to allow herself any feelings warmer than friendship for him. 'I think we will rub along tolerably well. Especially since, with a bequest left by my aunt, I intend to travel a great deal to pursue my sketching, while Mr Tawny will of course remain in London, continuing his work with Parliament.'

'You'll both go your own ways?' Faith asked.

'Yes. That's the bargain we struck.'

Maggie nodded. 'A sensible way to start.'

*Start, continue and end,* Alyssa thought. Better to stay far from London, where it was too easy to be drawn in by his accommodating friends. Where she might conceive the dangerous notion that she fit in with them. With him.

'You mentioned that, initially, your mother and Lady Fulton intended to put it about that you and Ben had been secret sweethearts?' Maggie asked. 'If you truly want to protect him and his career, I suggest that you let us spread that notion around. Just in case any hint of the scandal should surface in London.'

'Yes, what better way to get your revenge upon the wretches who wanted to ruin you, than have it be thought you'd both ended up in a love-match?' Faith said. 'Ben can be the impetuous suitor, pressing you for a promise you weren't quite ready to make at Dornton. But after he followed you to Aldermont Hall and once again begged for your hand, you could no longer resist.'

Alyssa sighed. 'Romantic, if entirely untrue.'

'It fits the facts of your interactions and that will protect both your reputations, should any gossip surface,' Maggie said. 'And it will give Ben the chance to play the ardent lover.' She laughed. 'He should love that.'

*As long as he didn't try to play the part with her,* Alyssa thought. But then, he'd given her his promise not to 'beguile'.

He'd be able to save that talent for use on other women. Somehow, the thought didn't cheer her.

At that moment, the gentleman walked in, each coming over to claim his respective lady. 'You are right—she is fascinating,' Maggie told Ben after giving her husband a kiss.

Tawny claimed Alyssa's hand, brushing his lips across her knuckles in a gesture that sent a shiver down her body. Flashing him a frown of warning, to which he responded with an unrepentant wink, she pulled her hand free—with more reluctance than she should have.

'Didn't I tell you?' he said to Maggie. 'She's unique.'

'She is indeed! Alyssa has been relating to us the circumstances behind your engagement,' Maggie informed

Ben. 'Faith and I agree that we should put it about that Lady Alyssa has known you for some time, but, after your persistent wooing, found her feelings transformed from friendship to love.'

'The persistent lover?' Ben said with a grin. 'I like that role.'

Maggie turned a penetrating gaze on them—as if she could feel the sensual connection between them Alyssa was trying so hard to ignore. 'I don't think you'll have the least difficulty playing it.'

Alyssa feared he'd be all too good at that as well.

'Father, did Ben tell you about his intended's amazing talent?' Maggie said as Lord Witlow walked over to usher them towards the ladies by the hearth. 'She does watercolours of British birds, which are to be published in a volume similar to Mr Audubon's *Birds of America*.'

'Indeed? No, he didn't tell me. Congratulations, Lady Alyssa. You must have a superior talent! I hope you'll do us the honour of showing us your work.'

'She is wonderfully adept,' Lady Aldermont said, looking fondly at her daughter.

'So, when is the wedding to be, young man?' Lady Sayleford asked Ben. 'All that political discussion is well enough, but we ladies prefer to concentrate on domestic issues.'

'As soon as the solicitor has the legal documents prepared,' Ben replied. 'I've already obtained a special licence.'

'You must allow me to give the wedding breakfast,' Lady Sayleford said. 'No, Anne, I insist!' the Countess added as Alyssa's mother protested. 'You didn't open Aldermont Place and it's not fitting that the fête be held at the groom's house, since I expect the happy couple will repair there after the ceremony. They should have some privacy! I shall very much enjoy launching them. Of course, I can then vouch for their devotion, should any…rumours surface.'

'Rumours?' Lady Aldermont said faintly.

'I've already acquainted Lady Lyndlington and the Duchess with the circumstances, Mama,' Alyssa said. 'Though I wasn't aware Lady Sayleford knew of them.'

'If anything happens to anyone in society, Aunt Lilly will find out,' Maggie said. 'She has more sources of information than every newspaper in London combined.'

'Nothing I'd like better than giving a check to young men whose behaviour isn't as it should be,' Lady Sayleford said. 'You'll let me know the date for the wedding, so I can make my plans?'

'That would be most generous,' Lady Aldermont said.

'It would be, Lady Sayleford,' Alyssa said, feeling a sense of panic as the once-distant event suddenly loomed closer. 'But please, only something simple.'

'It will be just our small group of friends and family,' Lady Sayleford said. 'I would invite your father, too,' she added, turning to Tawny, 'but he's presently out of London.'

If she weren't so preoccupied by her own worries, Alyssa might have asked Ben how he felt about including the man who'd played so little part in his life. She knew her own father wouldn't bother to attend, even if he were in London, and was glad to know he was permanently out of *her* life.

'What of your mother, Ben?' Alyssa asked. 'Don't you wish her to be present?'

After an awkward silence, Ben said stiffly, 'She isn't received, Alyssa.'

Before she could retrieve herself from that faux pas, Ben continued, 'In any event, she never leaves the country.'

'It's a momentous achievement, getting this lad to the altar,' Lady Sayleford said, smoothly changing the subject. 'An event well worth celebrating—no matter how it came about.'

Forcing a smile, Alyssa tried to calm the flutters in her stomach. Yes, she was getting the dynamic Ben Tawny to the altar. How was she going to handle what came after?

*The happy couple will repair to the groom's house... they should have some privacy.*

All her attention focused on obtaining her bequest and the freedom it would allow her, Alyssa hadn't thought much about the wedding, except as a detail she must accomplish before leaving London to begin her work.

She'd like to do so as soon after the event as possible, but it would look odd in the extreme were she to depart immediately after the ceremony.

But spending the night...alone together. Just her and Ben Tawny?

He'd promised not to beguile her. But simply standing silently beside her, doing nothing more than gazing at her with those intense green eyes, his whole body radiated a masculinity potent as a siren's song, luring her towards shipwreck on the dangerous rocks of her own desire.

Could she keep herself from succumbing to the temptation he posed?

## *Chapter Eleven*

Three days later, Ben Tawny stood beside Christopher Lattimar in the front parlour of Lady Sayleford's town house, waiting for the guests to arrive for the wedding. After much consultation between Lady Aldermont and the Dowager Countess, it had been decided that the ceremony would be officiated over by the rector of Lady Sayleford's parish church, with both the wedding and the reception held at her home.

After which, the newlyweds would depart for Ben's town house on Queen Street. And he would have to work in earnest on the promise not to beguile her.

It wasn't going to be easy.

He had seen little of Alyssa the last several days, even having to visit the solicitor on his own after Lady Aldermont begged him to excuse her daughter so that they might finish the shopping necessary to complete her trousseau. He smiled, recalling the eye-roll Alyssa had given him behind her mother's back, but she was obviously too fond of her mama to deny her the delight of fulfilling what that lady saw as her obligation to see her daughter properly outfitted.

They'd dined in company each evening, once at Lady Sayleford's, so that the ladies could review the Countess's plans for the wedding, and then again at Maggie's. With her mother accompanying them in the carriage, and the guests coming over to speak with them before and after dinner, he'd hardly had a private word with his intended. He had, however, been gratified to see how much more at ease she'd seemed with his friends, who had been as supportive and encouraging as he'd expected.

After days of company and chatter and activity, tonight it would be just the two of them. The very thought brought a rush of arousal to a body that hungered for her, the need sharpening the longer he had to deny it. He couldn't seem to push his mind past that longing into planning some way to pass the time that would not end up with him leading her to his bed.

He'd better think of one, though, and quickly. He had a strong suspicion that if he couldn't keep his desires under control, she would reject him and quit the house immediately, angry and feeling betrayed by his failure to keep his promise.

Having her succumb to his overtures and letting him make love to her would probably be worse. She'd end up furious with him for breaking his word and with herself for allowing passion to lure her into doing what she'd vowed she would not.

Either way, he might lose her before he ever had a chance to win her. If he wanted to make a success of the marriage to which they were now committed, turn it into the union of friendship—and eventually passion—he knew it could be it, he must deny his own desires until Alyssa convinced herself it was safe to indulge her own.

'That's a profound sigh,' Christopher observed, pulling him from his reflections. 'Not having second thoughts, are you? Hardly useful at this late date.'

'No second thoughts about marrying,' Ben replied, surprised to realise it was true. He might have some doubts about how to conduct himself during the early days of the union, but he had no reservations at all about wedding her. 'Actually, it feels…right. The longer I'm around her, the surer I am that she will make me an admirable wife. Independent enough to go her own way, with work of her own to occupy her, not needing constant attention to keep her happy. Intelligent and thoughtful enough to provide a unique and different point of view.'

'I admit, I had my doubts at that first dinner, when she was initially so withdrawn and silent. But since then, she's shown herself to be intelligent, articulate, amusing, and enormously talented. That sketch she showed Maggie last night! I defy Aububon himself to produce a better one.'

'They are all just as excellent. The only reservation I do have,' Ben said, finally admitting the one doubt that still troubled him, 'is thinking it may not be quite fair, using the unfortunate circumstances to push her into marrying a man like me.'

'A man like you?' Christopher repeated, frowning. 'Educated, intelligent, personable, dedicated to serving the nation—what is wrong with a "man like you"?'

'An earl's daughter normally can do much better than a bastard. All of you may have had…difficulties in your upbringing. But the stain of illegitimacy can never be washed away.'

'I'd make light of it, except it obviously troubles you. I know, growing up, it must have been difficult. But you have your father's recognition and support now, in addition to the reputation you've earned on your own. You can't change the past, but your *present* has made the facts of your birth insignificant, to most.'

'It doesn't seem to matter to Alyssa—now. If I can help her achieve her dreams, maybe it never will. Having the resources and the time to pursue her drawing is all she wants.'

'I should think she'd worry more about whether you're ready to settle down. Hard to ignore the lure of the ladies.'

'Depends upon who is waiting at home. Neither Giles nor Davie have any problem with that.'

'True, but neither were as…active as you've been. Still, Lady Alyssa is arresting. When she speaks of her art, there's a passion about her that's almost palpable. What a honeymoon you'll have, you lucky dog!' Christopher said, giving him a jab in the ribs.

Ben resisted the temptation to confess that it would likely be more frustrating than fulfilling and that he had her permission to look elsewhere if he chose. The promises about intimacy given between them were for him and Alyssa alone; he'd not discuss the details even with his closest friend.

Another measure of how different this relationship was from every previous one, he realised with another little shock. He'd had no qualms before about discussing his amorous adventures with Christopher.

And with Alyssa to come home to, he had no interest

in looking elsewhere, for now. No matter how frustrating these first few weeks or months might be.

A murmur of voices in the hallway announced the arrival of the rest of the party. Lady Sayleford came first, escorting the vicar, followed by the Lyndlingtons and the Smiths. At the last walked Lady Aldermont and Lady Alyssa.

His bride.

She looked lovely, he thought, her unruly brown hair corralled into an intricate coil of braids beneath a fetching bonnet, her gown a subtly patterned deep green that whispered of forest glades and made him think of the day he'd first met her, sketching in the dappled shadows. The wide sleeves and full skirts emphasised the smallness of her waist, cinched by a brown-velvet belt.

The untamed beauty of a wildflower confined in a vase. His lips curved of their own accord into a smile as something tender, deep and aching swelled in his chest.

He must make sure he kept his promises, helped her achieve her dreams—and proved himself worthy of her.

She looked over to see him watching and their gazes met and held. But his smile faded as he noted that, though her expression was composed, in those expressive eyes, he read wariness and uncertainty.

'Ladies and gentlemen, shall we take our places?' the vicar said.

She drew in a sharp breath, panic flickering in her eyes, disappearing so soon he couldn't be quite sure he'd seen it. Ben had a sudden fear that she was about to call it all off when, with another deep breath, she squared her shoulders, lifted her chin and walked over to him.

While the small congregation took seats set up for

them before the hearth, Ben leaned down to kiss her hand. 'You look beautiful,' he murmured.

'Thank you. I convinced Mama to narrow the sleeves and leave off the lace, so at least I don't look as if a dress shop had exploded around me.'

He retained her fingers, so that she had to look up at his face. 'Are you sure you want to do this?'

'Are you?'

'Absolutely.'

She gave him a brave smile that was only partly reassuring. 'Then, yes, I'm ready.'

At that, she turned towards the vicar and nodded, and the service began.

The rest of the afternoon was a blur, the solemn ceremony followed by signing the parish register, after which Lady Sayleford ushered them into the dining room where a sumptuous repast had been set out. The party broke up into a constantly changing arrangement of small groups, conversations touching on politics, travel, fashion and current happenings among the notables of society threaded in and out.

Watching his bride closely, Ben observed that although she nodded and smiled and took part in the discussions, there was still about her a subtle tension that, having seen her relaxed and confident at their meetings in the woods at Dornton, he couldn't help noticing, even if no one else appeared to see it.

It was more than the sensual awareness that always hummed between them. There was a defensive edginess to it, an unease similar to what he'd first noted in her on the drive from Aldermont into London.

He didn't want that feeling to set the tone for their

marriage—or have her remember their wedding day as a trial of endurance. Somehow, he would find a way to put her at ease.

It wasn't until several hours later, after their friends sent them off in a flurry of well wishes, that Ben finally had his bride to himself. Having accepted an invitation from Lady Sayleford to stay with her for a few more weeks before returning to the country, Lady Alyssa's mother had moved her belongings to the Countess's town house that morning.

Not wishing to begin what might be a serious conversation on the short coach ride back to Queen Street, Ben occupied the drive with observations on the wedding. To which his bride returned monosyllabic answers, or none at all. Holding herself rigid, she perched at the edge of the seat, as far away from him as she could get in that small space.

Retreating from him, exactly as she had during their return from Aldermont.

Biding his time despite his impatience to discover what had made her so unsettled, Ben waited until they were seated in the parlour, glasses of wine poured and all the servants dismissed. 'What is it, Lyssa? What is bothering you?'

She took a sip before setting her own glass down with trembling hands. 'How do you come to be so observant? I thought I managed to look quite serene. No one else noticed anything—not even Mama.'

'She was too caught up in seeing all the plans carried out. And I suppose I watch you more closely than the others.'

'My father and brother have watched me closely on

occasion, without having any idea what I felt. You are unusually sensitive to a woman's feelings, for a man.'

'Neither of them is exactly a model of masculine sensitivity.'

'True. But I met many gentlemen during my Seasons, and after. None of them seemed able to discern what women were thinking, even those who claimed to care. You *are* more attuned.'

'Perhaps,' he allowed. 'I spent my early years with my mother as almost my sole companion. Though I was as self-absorbed as any child initially, by the time I was six, I couldn't help noticing how other people treated her—us—the few times we walked into the village. At first, she told me that people kept away from her because they thought she'd done something bad, although she hadn't. Later, when boys threw rocks at the cottage and called her "whore", she explained that meant a woman who lay with a man for money, but she'd never done that. She'd only been with my father because she loved him and that acts done out of love couldn't be bad. She would soothe me when I got angry or frightened after the other boys mocked or tried to bully me. As I got older, I realised she must feel the same hurt and anger and outrage herself, but she gave little outward sign of it. I learned to watch for subtle changes of expression in her eyes and the set of her body. So I was better able to help and cheer her when I could.'

'She must be so brave.'

'She is. The bravest, most unselfish person I know. Despite our circumstances, she tried to give me a normal childhood, never letting me doubt I was worthy of love and loved completely. From the first, she's wanted what was best for me, no matter the cost to herself. It would have been much easier for her to go to some distant place, where she could have started a new life claiming to be a widow, her husband killed by war or accident. But I was a viscount's son. To claim the future my heritage offered, I needed to be educated and make friends among the class of my birth. So she settled in a nearby village, accepted my father's help and, when I was old enough, let me go away to school. And lived her life ostracised from polite society as a fallen woman.'

'I wish I had her courage. It's silly, I know, but I can't seem to stop these…mindless fears. I trust you, truly I do, but then I remember that, as my husband, you have complete control not only over my wealth, but my person, too. Beat me, starve me, lock me up—no one would stand against you and the law would do nothing to help.' She shivered. 'It's as if there are little demons trapped deep in my bones, screaming out a warning, and there's nothing I can do to silence them.'

Scoured with anger and pity for what she'd endured, he held out his arms and, to his relief, she came into them. 'You hear ghosts of the demon who beat you and starved you and locked you in the dark?' Ben asked, fury intensifying as he spoke the words. 'I've seen something similar in the army, men who'd survived horrific battles having recurring visions of the nightmares they'd seen. For some of them, the memories disappeared over time. I will do all I can to help you banish them. And I hope, after you know me longer, the thought of being with me won't revive them.'

She snuggled closer. 'I hope so, too. Please remember that in my head, I know you are the one who *protected* me.'

The idea that being wed to him could frighten her revolted him—a timely brake on burgeoning desire. Even so, it wasn't wise to keep holding her. For the moment, the need to offer comfort kept his physical longing in check, but the attraction between them was too strong to be subdued for long.

Gently, he released her and handed her back her glass. 'We've had almost no time to talk the last few days. I should give you the particulars about accessing your account and you can tell me the plans you're making for setting out on your sketching expeditions.'

'The thatched plover, one of the most popular birds on the downs, leaves by mid-November for winter feeding grounds in France, according to Mr Bewick. There are several other migratory species in the area, some that fly in only for a brief time.'

'Who will accompany you?'

'Molly, of course.'

'How will you travel?'

'Hire a post-chaise, I suppose.'

'Have you any idea how to do that?'

'Well…no. But it can't be that difficult. Harleton does it all the time.'

'Do you know which inns you can stay at? How to bespeak a room, order food and provisions? You don't, do you?'

'Just because I've never done those things doesn't mean I can't,' she argued.

'It's not a matter of competence,' he said patiently. 'Even if you knew how, you must take into account the view of the innkeepers and ostlers. No lady of good birth travels without male escort unless she's in her own private carriage, attended by a host of servants and retainers who ride ahead to order rooms, meals and provisions. Men in the trade would suspect a lone woman of Quality travelling with a single maid to be a runaway wife or daughter, or a girl cast out by her family. In other words, potentially a source of trouble from an outraged noble family, who could make the merchant's life quite difficult. The respectable inns probably wouldn't take you and places that might would also harbour all sorts of unsavoury individuals. It simply isn't safe for you to travel like that.'

'So I'll need to purchase a coach and hire a staff of grooms, outriders and maids?' she asked with exasperation. 'Before you point that out, no, I've never hired staff before, either. That could take weeks! I'll just have to risk it. I simply can't loll about London that long, if I am to reach all the places I need to go to complete my work.'

Ben shook his head. 'I can't, in good conscience, allow you to set off into certain danger. Please, Lyssa, be sensible! If you absolutely *must* leave soon, let me come with you. The new session won't start until December, so I can be out of London for another few weeks. Let me hire the carriage and grooms for this first journey and accompany you to the locales you must visit immediately. You can watch me during the journey to see how it's done. In the meantime, here in London, Russell can find you a suitable coach, grooms and horses, and Mrs Ingleton can hire the additional staff.'

'You, go with me?' she asked, her eyes widening with alarm.

Ben sighed. 'Trust, again, Lyssa. Do you not believe I will honour my vows on the road, just as I have tonight?'

She bit her lip. 'I—I guess I believe it. But…it will

be much easier for us both to resist temptation, if you remain in London.'

Relieved she at least admitted to being tempted herself, he said, 'I will treat you as chastely as a brother. I'm eager for you to make progress towards finishing your sketches. But surely you can understand how imprudent it would be to set off without proper organisation and protection.'

After a moment, she nodded reluctantly. 'Your argument is persuasive, much as I hate to admit it. I have travelled very little and never on my own. Arrangements have always been made by others; I wouldn't know where to begin. And we've always journeyed in our own vehicle, with a substantial party of servants and baggage.'

'There may be an additional advantage to having me on this first trip.'

As she cocked an enquiring eyebrow, he said, 'I don't see how you can exorcise the demons warning you against me, unless we spend more time together. Enough time for the absolute certainty that I will never harm you to penetrate so deep into those bones, it displaces the fear. I'd like that to happen sooner rather than later, Lyssa. It's…wounding to imagine you fear me, even though you know those fears are groundless.'

'I'm sorry—'

'No, you don't have to apologise. It's irrational, something you can't control.'

He reached out for her hand and, after a moment, she gave it to him. 'Words are easy; I want to prove by my actions that I keep my promises. To give you the funds that belong to you. To never touch, or attempt to entice you, unless you invite it. Today, I added vows to love, cherish and protect you, for the rest of our lives.'

Her lips trembled and one tear slid down her cheek. He longed to kiss it away, but made himself remain motionless.

With a gusty sigh, she released his hand. 'How lucky I am, Ben Tawny, that you happened to be in the Quill and Gavel that night. Thank you for your patience and your caring, and your trust. What can I do, but try to be worthy of them? Yes, I will be grateful to have your help on my first expedition.'

Ben hoped she might seal the bargain with a kiss, as she had impulsively kissed him after their interview with the solicitor. But after a tantalising moment, she drew back.

*Since proceeding makes it even harder to stop, I shall have to be more circumspect about starting.* Sadly, it looked like she was going to be.

Accepting her retreat, he said, 'Why don't you spend the rest of the evening finalising the itinerary? I'll head out first thing tomorrow to obtain the carriage and provisions. You'll also need to assess whether you need any additional art supplies, as we may not be able to find them in the countryside.'

She nodded. 'Very well. I'll do both—and thank you again. For your…understand and forbearance. You could have…insisted on claiming what is now yours.'

'What is now mine is the right to protect and defend you. Everything else—*everything*, Lyssa—still belongs to you. It always will.'

Brushing away another tear, she nodded briskly. 'I'd better get started.'

He was relieved to see her already looking more like

her normal, confident self. 'I thought you would prefer to retain the bedchamber in which you've been staying. I'll return to my own, at the back of the house. Do you want to work here in the parlour, or shall I ring for Molly to meet you in your chamber?'

'I'll ring for Molly, thank you.'

'Then I'll bid you good night. Sleep well, Lyssa—and dream only of the wonderful drawings you're going to create.'

Much as he craved a kiss, Ben made himself nod and walk out of the room.

Good thing he would need to busy himself being a pathfinder and intelligence-gatherer, he thought as he mounted the stairs, painfully conscious of his still-aroused body. He needed something compelling to distract himself from the temptation of being near her day after day...denied the intimacy his body craved.

Now that he understood her fears, he was even more determined to keep his word. And even more convinced that, some day—in the not-too-distant future—she would overcome them. And come to him.

# *Chapter Twelve*

Sunlight danced on the waves in the cove below, the sound of crashing breakers, muted by distance, provided a soothing background hush, while sea birds swooped and soared in the windy sky above her. From her hidden spot in the tangle of low bushes, Alyssa worked rapidly to fill in with colour her sketch of the plover perched on a nearby branch. She'd just finished the markings of his head and chest when the bird flew off.

She gazed at the drawing with satisfaction. The sketch was nearly complete, the still-empty sections tagged with a slash of colour that would allow her to finish at the inn tonight, even if she didn't find another specimen to observe.

A 'halloo' made her look up, to see Ben Tawny waving from a spot on the cliffs overlooking the sea where a blanket had been spread. He mimed pouring wine into a glass and made a questioning gesture. Smiling, she nodded and waved back, signalling her readiness for the picnic he'd prepared.

Closing her sketchbook and latching the box of pastels, Alyssa rose and walked towards him. Her heart as light as the wispy grass blowing in the wind, she felt more fulfilled and carefree than she ever dreamed possible in the dark days of her confinement and despair.

Ben walked over to meet her. 'Did you finish the sketches you needed? I didn't want to rush you, but I am famished.'

'Near enough that I can complete it tonight, if I have to.' She hoped he'd take her arm, but he didn't. Keeping to the letter of his promise, he hadn't touched her at all this entire trip—not even with such commonplace gestures as offering an arm while walking or a hand to assist her into a carriage.

Not that she felt any less the subtle physical attraction that hummed between them whenever he was near. But he'd made absolutely no move to act upon it, a fact she'd initially found helpful and reassuring. But which, after nearly three weeks on the road, as wariness decreased and trust built, she was finding increasingly… frustrating.

'What an excellent forager you are!' she said, inspecting the picnic lunch he'd assembled for them. 'Or commissariat officer, the army would call it?'

'Forager is more apt,' he said, taking her sketchbook and pastels box—careful not to let their fingers touch. 'The commissariat generally kept the permanent compounds provisioned, but they often trailed behind when we were in the field. Of course, when out gathering intelligence, one was on one's own to scrounge up victuals.'

'The army may have honed the skill, but you must have been born with it. You've managed so efficiently this entire trip! Rooms bespoke before we arrive, hot water at the ready for bathing, supper waiting by the time we've washed off the dust of the road, extra candles in the rooms for additional light to complete drawings in the evenings… Picnics in the coach, if we're travelling, or in the most picturesque spots near where I'm sketching.'

He made her a bow. 'With no marauding tigers or snakes to watch out for and no hostile troops looking to use me for target practice, it's like reliving the best of my free-ranging days with the army, with none of the drawbacks. I hope it's allowed you the maximum amount of time and daylight to work.'

'It has. I admit, I couldn't have completed nearly as many sketches without you taking care of the arrangements.'

He smiled at her, affection and that *something more* lurking in his gaze. 'You positively glow when you're sketching, you know. I'm glad I've been able to give you the chance to work, free of constraint.'

'How can I thank you enough? I can't remember ever being this happy. Not even when I was tromping the fields with Harleton, before we…fell out.' *Though she could imagine one more thing that might make her happier...*

Pushing that temptation out of mind, she chuckled. 'Molly adores you, too. With you riding out with me, locating the best birding sites and remaining to stand guard, she's been able to stay at the inn, having meals at leisure, and finishing her duties with plenty of time left over for gossiping with the maids and flirting with the grooms.'

'I'm happy to exchange places. I'd much rather be in the saddle, exploring—and keeping watch—than trapped back at the inn, twiddling my thumbs.'

'Or winning the cost of this lunch at cards from some unsuspecting traveller?'

Gesturing her to a seat, he gave a lazy shrug. 'One must maintain one's skills. Never know when it might be necessary to fund that next meal.'

'Skill developed at Eton and Oxford?' she guessed. 'You told Mama you never developed a taste for town entertainment, as you tried to spend as little as possible of your mother's blunt.'

'Yes, I did begin gaming there. Though some of my opponents I'd rather have punched in the mouth, doing that could get one expelled. Relieving them of some of their generous allowance was almost as satisfying.'

'I hope you won some off Harleton. I'm sure Papa provided for him handsomely.'

'Though he was temptingly plump in the pocket, as I once told you, I avoided your brother. He was too prone to remarks that would have strained my resolve not to plant him a facer.'

Taking a seat just a tempting arm's length away, he poured them wine from a jug and handed over a glass. This time, she wrapped her fingers over his as he handed to her—and left them there.

His gaze shot to hers, the molten depths of his green eyes sending a blaze of heat through her. For a long moment, they stared at each other, conversation silenced by the connection flowing between them, hot as the sun on her shoulders, powerful as the breakers crashing against the rocks below.

Helplessly drawn to him, she leaned forward and angled her face up, thirstier for his kiss than for the wine he offered. His scorching gaze roved over her face, making her lips tingle, then dropped to her chest, setting a jolt of awareness to her breasts. Filled with a strange urgency, heart thudding in her chest, she could scarcely breathe.

Then, just as her eyes fluttered shut, he turned that lighthouse beam gaze away, seizing a loaf of bread from his haversack and pulling off pieces. She thought his hands were shaking. She hoped so; hers certainly were.

Should she take the bread from him, climb on to his lap, claim the kiss she yearned for? *You are free to enjoy passion, too.*

She could be, couldn't she? So far Ben had kept every promise. He'd induced Mr Chambers to set aside Aunt Augusta's bequest in an account for her, giving her the thrill of walking into the bank and withdrawing funds—every clerk in the place staring in horrified fascination. He'd supported and assisted her desire to travel, masterfully arranging this trip to give her the maximum amount of time to sketch. He'd scrupulously—too scrupulously—honoured his pledge not to touch her or beguile her into intimacy.

Every day, the dark demons of fear receded further.

Why not indulge in the passion between them and give herself to him completely? Losing herself in passion didn't mean she had to lose who she was, nor would it give him some sort of control over her.

Or would it?

Though she might belong to him in that way…so might others. She doubted he'd avail himself of her permission to seek pleasure elsewhere now, when they were still in the first days together. But after she gave in, gave herself, and they'd had weeks—or months—to slake that hunger?

Would he then be ready to taste passion elsewhere?

Perhaps that was the final doubt she'd not been able to resolve, the one stricture holding her back from claiming what she hungered for. Which made no sense. She'd been almost ready to give herself to him at Dornton, before there was a hint of anything permanent between them. When he'd certainly go on to other lovers after her.

So why hesitate now?

If they had trysted just that once, and he moved on, she wouldn't have to wonder when he came back to her after each time apart whether there had been someone else. Whether there still was someone else.

She could reopen the discussion, tell him she wanted to withdraw her approval of his seeking companionship elsewhere. But, having thrust him in a situation which left him virtually no choice but to marry her, curtailing the only freedom left to him didn't seem fair.

Especially when she'd already promised it to him. And he had kept all his promises to her.

While she dithered, Ben cut up ham, cheese and apple, piled it on a napkin, and passed it to her. He whistled cheerfully as he did it, seeming nowhere near as frustrated and conflicted as she was, she thought, disgruntled.

'Have you thought how you are going to approach the publisher, once your sketches are complete? Mr McCalister acted as your agent before, didn't he?'

'Yes,' she answered, the mention of Will's name bringing with it an echo of sorrow, less sharp now than it had once been. 'I shall have to find someone else. However enthusiastic Waterman may have been when he saw the drawings, his ardour would swiftly fade, if he knew they had been done by a female.'

'Fair or not, he knows the work wouldn't be as

well received,' Ben agreed. 'Would you like me to ask around to find a suitable agent?'

'I would very much appreciate that,' she replied, pleased and gratified that he'd offered—for she hadn't intended to ask the favour. 'I wouldn't know where to begin. I need someone who believes strongly in the work, strongly enough not to be put off by the fact that it was done by a female. I expect most men would have as many reservations as the publisher.'

'I don't see how anyone who sees your drawings could fail to appreciate them. But I'd be happy to find someone who is suitably enthusiastic.'

'As long as you're sure doing so won't further impede your own work. Trekking to the wilds of Devon and Cornwall, rather than remaining in London with your friends, determining strategy for the next session of Parliament, has to have already set you back.'

'I can manage. Travelling with you, riding the countryside, watching you work, has been a pleasure.'

His obvious sincerity, and the genuine affection in his gaze, created a curious tightness in her chest. 'You've made it a pleasure for me, too. After your performance with the merchants in Dornton Village, I knew you would be good at arranging food and lodging. But I hadn't anticipated you would be able to nose out locals who know the best places to find the birds I needed to observe. Being guided to just the right locale has saved me hours and allowed me to finish more sketches than I'd thought possible on this one trip.' She sighed. 'It won't be the same in future, travelling without you.'

'I wish I could accompany you on every trip! But another week at most and I must return to London. By then, Russell should have a coach ready for your inspection, a coachman and grooms to ride escort, and Mrs Ingleton will have selection of maids for you to choose from to assist Molly. You can be off again as soon as all is ready.'

Travelling about England, observing nature, producing not just the sketches wanted by the current publisher, but other works painted in the field...it was the fulfilment of the dream she'd cherished for years. She was thrilled to be able to finally be living it.

But somehow, after the time they'd shared together, setting off again without Ben by her side wasn't nearly as appealing as it had been a month ago.

She was going to miss him far too much. Which was the best reason to set out again immediately, before she became too attached to a man who had her permission to go his own way. 'Yes, if I'm to finish everything, I shouldn't tarry long in London.'

Refilling her wine cup, he handed it to her and, this time, let his fingers cover hers. 'Unless you want to linger,' he said, his voice rough and low. His eyes never leaving her face, he put the cup to her lips, tipped it up to let her swallow, then caught a drip on his finger before it could dribble down her chin. Moving the cup away, he held his finger out, offering her the drop.

Mesmerised by his eyes on hers, she licked his finger—and then sucked it into her mouth, thrilling at the taste of wine and salty flesh.

Heat spiralled in her belly, sending a wash of arousal throughout her body. Ben groaned, or maybe it was her own moan she heard. His breathing uneven, he pulled his finger free.

This time, his hands were definitely shaking.

Before she could say a word, he jumped to his feet. 'I'll take another ride around the cliffs, see if I can find a better clump of brush for you to sketch from. Tiddle at the inn said there are several places where the plovers roost.'

And then he was gone, catching up the reins of his horse and swinging into the saddle.

Her own fingers trembling, Alyssa finished the wine. After putting the remnants of bread, ham and cheese in the basket, she gathered her supplies and headed back to the copse, her senses still swirling.

For the first time she could remember, she went back to sketching wishing she might be doing something else.

The next day brought a return of the bright sun and mild weather for which the West Country was famed. One could hardly believe winter loomed ever closer, Alyssa thought, lifting her face to the warmth.

The birds knew the secret of the Devon coast, too, and flocked here, drawn by the warm temperatures, steady sunshine, bountiful supply of fish, seeds and insects. Today, she was in search of the sea birds Tiddle had told Ben nested in some of the caves. Ben had ridden out with the man earlier this morning, to be shown which caves she could safely linger and sketch in, without threat of being caught by the rising tide.

Leaving their horses to graze on the hillside above, they picked their way down the steep path to the beach, Ben bringing the blanket, picnic and supplies. 'I'll walk along the sand and explore the other outcroppings while you work, but stay within hailing distance,' he said as they approached the wide opening of the cave. 'Tiddle and I checked this out thoroughly, so you shouldn't encounter anything menacing, but it's a wild area. One should always remain on alert.'

Like a wide mouth opening in the hillside, the cave curved back from the sea, the water side offering first beach, then a jumble of rocks like a pile of blocks a child had sent tumbling—the spot where the sea birds liked to nest, they'd been told, the overhang of the cave protecting the nests from the worst of the wind, but open to the sky, with a supply of food from the sea just before them. Behind the rocks, still open to the sky, were smaller outcroppings, before the earthen roof closed over the back of the cave and its floor of rocks and dry sand.

Ben deposited the blanket and basket for their picnic lunch under the shade of the overhang. 'Did you see the nests, on the outcropping there? I'll help you climb to a place where you'll have a good view of the birds as they come and go.'

Pleased that he offered a hand, she took it, sighing a bit at the instant spark of connection. Only the need to pay close attention to her footing, lest she slip on the irregular surfaces, distracted her from the sweet pleasure of indulging in his touch.

How she wanted more of it!

Thankfully for her concentration, if not for her needy senses, Ben left her as soon as he'd seen her safely settled among the rocks. Just after he'd climbed away, one of the magnificent sea birds swooped in to its nest, gliding on the wind like a feral kite. Captivated, she at first remained perfectly still, not wanting to scare it from its perch, while she catalogued in her mind the exact hues of its head, beak, eyes, wings, so she might mark the colour on her sketch in case the bird flew off before she could get her supplies out.

Perhaps her presence was masked by the wind that blew her scent landward, or the roar and hiss of the surf, or perhaps, knowing it could soar away as quickly as it came, the bird considered her no threat. To her delight, as she slowly opened her sketchbook and brought out her pastels, the creature didn't stir.

For several hours, she lost herself in drawing the magnificent wildness perched so close to her. At length, the bird stood, spread out its magnificent wings as if stretching and flew off. She smiled as she watch it go, awed, humbled, and satisfied to have her sketch almost complete; she'd not need to work by candlelight in her room tonight.

Closing the sketchbook, she looked around to find Ben seated among some rocks nearby. Smiling, he clambered over to her.

'Finished?'

'Nearly.'

'Satisfied with it?'

'Oh, yes. What a wonderful spot, Ben! The breakers, the wind, the sand—it's perfection. I almost wish I could be a sea bird and stay here for ever. Thank you so much for finding it for me.'

He leaned over to catch a strand of dark hair the wind had teased loose from her coiffure. 'You might be a sea sprite, washed up among the rocks,' he said, pulling the strand through his fingers. 'A naughty siren, come ashore to torture poor mortals with nearly unbearable temptation.'

Her breath caught as she gazed into the green depths of his eyes. Did he mean that she'd been tempting *him* to the breaking point? That he hadn't been as cool and indifferent as he'd seemed for most of this journey?

The suggestion that he might have found it difficult to keep his hands off her—that he'd hungered for her as much as she'd been wanting him these last few days—sparked her always simmering desire. A heated urgency warmed her from her stomach down to her core, while her toes and fingers tingled.

Before she could get her stunned brain to summon any words, he said, 'Let me tempt you with some wine and ham. I have everything ready.'

Her tongue still too clumsy for speech, she gathered up book and pastels, eagerly taking the arm he offered, relishing the jolt of sensation as her fingers touched his sleeve. She would have pulled closer, into his arms, had the slick rocks and uneven surfaces not demanded she watch her steps. By the time they'd reached the beach, her heart was pounding and not just from the difficulty of the descent.

To her delight, Ben offered his arm again as he walked her into cave where, under the outcropping of rock, he'd spread out a blanket on the dry sand. She gave herself up to enjoying the thrill of his arm under her fingers, a thrill that intensified when they reached the blanket and he urged her to sit, massaging her shoulders before taking a seat beside her.

'You must be stiff after sitting still so long, sketching.'

She nodded, though 'stiff' was not at all what she felt. Everything within her was flowing, swirling in rhythm with the throb of her pulse, as heated sensations sparked in her breasts, at her lips, in her centre.

Her attention glued on Ben, she was barely conscious of the ham, cheese and bread he set out before her, watching him as he seemed to imbue every gesture with sensual overtones.

Her mouth dried and her brain stuttered as his fingers traced over the surface of the apple like a caress before he cupped it in one hand, drew his knife slowly through it and broke it into halves. He bit into his half, giving her glimpses of tongue and teeth as he ate slowly, licking the sweet juice from his lips.

Alternately tearing ham, cheese and bread into strips, he trailed each morsel over his lips, as if feeling as well as tasting it. He closed his eyes and inhaled deeply of the aroma, before popping it in his mouth to consume.

Scarcely conscious of what she was doing, she managed to eat some of what lay before her. But when he once again offered her the wine cup, then brushed his thumb over her mouth after she'd swallowed, she reached the limit of her endurance.

Pushing the wine away, she reached up, seized his head and pulled him down for the kiss she craved.

To her surprise and chagrin, he caught her hands and pushed her away.

'Do you not…want to kiss me?' she asked in a small voice.

He made a sound that was half-laugh, half-groan. 'I've wanted that, and much more, since the first moment I saw you in the woods at Dornton.'

'Then why refuse me? Punishment for resisting you so long?'

'No! Not at all. I just want to make sure you really know what you're doing. That you have no regrets. It would kill me to taste you and have you withdraw again.'

'But you would, if I asked you.'

He sighed. 'I would, if you needed me to. But it would be deucedly difficult.'

That reassurance seemed to cinder the last of her caution. 'Then I'm sure. No doubts and no regrets. I want you now! Please, Ben.'

'You are certain.'

'Yes, yes!' she cried impatiently. 'Absolutely certain.'

'Well, you do appear…actively encouraging.'

She smiled, recalling the indignant words spoken so long ago. '*Enthusiastically* encouraging,' she said, reaching for him.

His eyes blazed with a sudden heat that sent fingers of flame sparking all over her body. Slowly, he ran one finger down her cheek. 'Passionately demanding?'

With a little huff of frustration, Alyssa pulled his face down to hers for a kiss that was as fierce as it was needy. Clambering on to his lap, she pressed herself to him, opened to him as his tongue probed her lips.

She ran her hands down his back, over the firmness of his buttocks, and felt his hardness jerk against her belly. Heart pounding, as she rubbed herself against it, he groaned and cupped her bottom to bring her closer, his tongue laving hers hard and fast.

He brought one hand to her breasts, his thumb rubbing against her taut nipples, sparking another surge of sensation even though the layers of fabric. She craved to feel his hand on her bare skin, but that was hopeless, she'd never be able to peel herself out of the layers of shift and corset and bodice without a maid and she couldn't wait until they returned to the inn.

Ben, fortunately, was encased in fewer layers. One hard jerk and she dislodge the knot of his cravat, tearing at the folds until she could claw open his shirt. Sighing into his mouth as she found naked skin, she rubbed her fingers against the bareness of his chest, down to the hard nipples, wanting more, closer.

Thrusting her hand lower still, she eased away from him and popped open the buttons of his straining trouser flap, freeing his erection. She took him in her hand, marvelling as she stroked the hard shaft down to the velvet tip.

'Take me now. Please,' she whispered against his mouth.

'I don't want…to hurt you,' he gasped out between panting breaths. Staying her exploring fingers, he said, 'A bed…would be better. Cushion you. Make it easier.'

She squeezed him gently, eliciting another groan. 'Though I'm still, technically, a maid, I do have…some knowledge.'

'Did he…claim you?'

'Not with this,' she replied, freeing her hand to stroke him again. 'But he did explore me with these.' Taking Ben's hand, she thrust it under her skirts, up to where her thighs spread wide as she straddled him, through the opening of her drawers, to the sweet spot at her centre that was moist and plump and waiting.

'Like this?' he asked as he stroked there.

'Yes,' she gasped, driven to move her hips against his hand.

'And this?' He slipped a finger between the folds, into her passage, while his thumb massaged the little nub above.

'Yes. But…I want more. You…within me. Now.'

Pushing him back against a boulder, she lifted herself, dragged up her skirts and straddled him. Bracing herself against his chest, she urged his hands around to cup her bare bottom as she guided him to the entrance of her passage and rubbed herself against the tip of his shaft, which leapt as it touched her. She gasped at the exquisite feel of him, pressing against her.

For long tortuous moments, she kept him there, caressing her moist folds as the sensations built to greater and greater intensity. Moved by some inner compulsion, she lowered herself on him, taking him inside inch by cautious inch.

She had some dim expectation that pain might force her to stop, but apparently nimble fingers had done their work, for she felt none, nothing more than a tightening and stretching as he reached her depths. With a long slow sigh, she settled herself over him.

But remaining immobile didn't seem possible. Following some nameless imperative, she rocked against him, small movements that brought a surge of sensation.

'Are you…all right?' he asked.

'Wonderful,' she gasped, kissing him hard. 'What… now?'

'This,' he whispered and began to thrust upward.

Driven by instinct, she caught the rhythm immediately. Hands gripping her, arms rigid, Ben moved with her, faster and faster, until she seemed to surmount some precipice and with an explosion of sensation more intense than anything she'd ever experienced, shattered into a rippling, pulsing waves of pleasure.

Crying out, Ben wrapped his arms around her and bound her against his chest.

For long, slow, minutes, the incredible sensations shimmered and danced until slowly fading away, like the glimmer of fireflies as they disappear into the night.

Filled with a languid sense of well-being, Alyssa reclined against his chest, her head tucked under her chin.

'I guess we gave the birds and bees a lesson,' he murmured at last.

Filled with an exuberant joy, Alyssa felt no sense of awkwardness or embarrassment. Instead, she raised up to give him another kiss. 'I'm an idiot. Why did you let me wait so long?'

'I promised that passion would be your choice. Though I admit, I might have helped you along a bit today.'

A daunting thought pierced her euphoria. 'How could *you* wait so long?' she asked with a frown. 'Or maybe you didn't find the experience as…wonderful as—'

Laughing, he cut off her sentence with a kiss. 'I found it astounding. Unforgettable. An embrace of passion as unique as you are.'

Reassured, she subsided back against him with a sigh. 'I don't think my brain or arms are capable of doing any more sketching today. But if we return to the inn…could we do more of this? How long do we have to wait for—' she bounced on him '—you know? Oh!'

He grinned, knowing she'd felt his member stirring within her. 'I think I'll be ready again by the time we get back to the inn.'

She gave him a long, slow, lazy kiss, laving his tongue—and felt him stir again, more forcefully.

'I want to do that to every part of your body,' she murmured.

'And I to yours. That's another promise.'

'And you always keep your promises.'

'Always.'

'Excellent.' Slowly she eased herself off him. 'Then why are we not already packing up?'

# *Chapter Thirteen*

Late the next afternoon, Alyssa sat in her hiding spot among the copse of high bushes and low trees, the wind-swept headland before her, the cliffs and the sea to her back. The winter migrant she'd been sketching had flown off half an hour ago and had not returned. She'd wait another thirty minutes and, if no likely specimens arrived, hunt out Ben, if he didn't stop by for her before that.

Arriving back at the inn early offered definite benefits, she thought, a ripple of remembered pleasure warming her as she recalled the delightful activities they'd indulged in when they returned from the cliffs the previous afternoon. Though Ben had been outwardly calm and unhurried, Alyssa was in a fever of eagerness she couldn't have hidden if she tried. Evicting Molly, who'd been taking a nap on the trundle at the foot of the chamber they shared, she'd stuffed her art supplies on the low bench, pulled Ben in after her and attacked his neckcloth.

He'd laughed and caught her hands and given her a long, slow kiss, exploring her mouth and tongue at leisure, leaving her on fire with urgency. But he refused to be hurried, tormenting her by insisting that they undress each other slowly, garment by garment, he inspecting her after each unveiling as if she the sitter for a portrait he needed to view from just the right angle.

Though he teased her, letting his fingers trail down bare skin, placing little biting kisses on her shoulders, her elbows, the back of her knees as he unveiled them, he made no move to touch where her body cried out most for caressing—her breasts, heavy, turgid, the nipples puckered and aching, the tingling insides of her thighs and her already throbbing centre.

But, ah, after he'd bared her completely and held her at arm's length, caressing her with his gaze until she whimpered with need, he'd led her to the bed and proceeded to fulfil his promise from the beach, kissing, licking, sucking and caressing her from the soles of her feet, her toes, up her legs. Then moving to her ear lobes, the hollow at her throat, her collarbones, and a long, lovely interval exploring her breasts and nipples with his mouth while, with a few caressing probes of his fingers inside her passage, he brought her to completion.

After holding her gasping, boneless, in his arms until her breathing calmed, he began again, moving his mouth downward from her breasts, his tongue burnishing the skin of her ribs, her belly, and ever lower, between her legs, where he outlined each ridge and fold with the tip of his tongue before pressing harder, nibbling, laving and suckling her to another shuddering climax.

Magnificently naked, he fetched wine from the sideboard and poured her a fortifying glass, cradling her in his arms until her limbs revived. After which, she kept *her* promise, exploring his body with the same thoroughness he'd explored hers, until with mouth and hands she brought him to satisfaction.

After another languid rest, he positioned her against the pillows and entered her, driving deep with a single thrust. Kissing her, he moved at first long and slow, then faster and faster, pressing her down into the softness until all she could feel was him, above her, around her, within her, possessing her completely, driving her to the edge of exquisite madness and over.

They slept then, Alyssa awaking to near-darkness and a sense of awe. He was right; pleasuring in a bed allowed for a closer, more complete union.

Even so, she wouldn't have traded for anything that magical first time, discovering the full meaning of pleasure while the sea wind played over her body and the sound of crashing surf echoed in her ears, the wildness without mirroring the explosive release of the passion she'd kept trapped within.

How could she separate from him, after so complete a union?

But she wasn't going to complicate this pure pleasure with doubt or worry. She would take this time together as a gift—and figure out what it meant for the future later.

The raucous 'caw' of gull flying overhead jolted her back to the present.

It was fortunate she'd made such good progress on her sketches earlier on this trip, she thought wryly, since she'd spent half today's sketching excursion staring sightlessly into the distance, dreamily reliving the events of yesterday. Half-a-dozen plovers could have roosted beside her and she wouldn't have noticed.

But since her quarry had not returned, she'd declare the day's work finished, look for Ben—and claim another round of pleasure as soon as possible.

Heated anticipation coiling within her, she closed the sketchbook and shut the box of pastels. She was making her way out of the tangle of bushes when she heard the sound of approaching hoofbeats—and smiled.

It appeared she wouldn't have to seek out Ben. Perhaps he'd been thinking that returning from their expedition early was a good idea, too.

But the mounted figure that crested the headlands and trotted down the trail towards her wasn't Ben—it was Lord Denbry.

Belatedly spotting her, he pulled up hard. 'Well, well, Lady Alyssa! What are you doing here, in the back of beyond?'

She glanced down at her sketchbook and pastel box. 'Drawing, obviously. What are you doing here? As far as I know, there's no society around for miles.'

'There most certainly is not.' His handsome face hardening, he dismounted and blocked her path. 'My presence in this benighted locale is all your fault.'

'My fault?' she echoed sceptically.

'I'd been counting on the blunt from the wager to see me through to Quarter Day. There was enough of a bad odour afterward that m'father refused to pony up early. Had to travel to this devil's backwater to charm my old maiden aunt, who can always be counted on for a bit of the ready for the inconvenience of making the trip. Not as inconvenient this time, since remaining out of London for the moment seemed wise. Yet another sin to lay at your door.'

'Why?' she asked scornfully. 'Did you lose face

among your sycophants when your sordid little plan failed?'

'Rossiter insisted I remove the wager from the betting book.' Anger contorted his face. 'Retract it! Me! The humiliation of it! I've never been bested at a wager in my life!'

'Except by my brother, apparently. Though I'd feel better about the future of England if you'd been shamed by *proposing* the wager, not by withdrawing it.'

'I imagine you're proud of yourself!' He rounded on her. 'Leading me on with that shy, backward act. Even managed to turn the disgrace at the inn respectable, though it did harness you to a bastard. For an earl's daughter, that couldn't be accounted a triumph.'

Wishing she had a palette knife to run him through with—his removal should be considered a boon to decent society—Alyssa said, 'I've heard quite enough. Step aside so I can continue on my way and find someone else to vent your ill humour on. Goodbye, Lord Denbry. I truly hope to never encounter you again.'

'Not so fast,' he snarled, seizing her arm. 'Showed your true colours that day at the inn. A wild little piece, aren't you? Maybe I'll take a little restitution for my losses, here and now. No servants or reckless bastards to intervene this time.'

She could twist her arm free, but she'd never outrun him in skirts. Fury boiling in her, Alyssa was calculating how and when she might manoeuvre to land a kick to his groin when she heard Ben's voice, emanating from behind the copse of bushes.

'Unhand my wife, Denbry. Now,' Ben said as he paced out from behind the outcropping.

Though Denbry took a step backwards, he held on

to Alyssa's arm. 'I did ensure that you had to make her your wife, didn't I? Although there was that sumptuous dowry. Rossiter hasn't forgiven me for losing him that. Unfortunate to have to temporarily curtail your freedom, though I don't expect you'll keep your London mistress pining for long. I wonder who the little doxy will service then, while you're off with your tarts.'

Face expressionless, Ben approached at an unhurried pace—though the look in his cold green eyes made Alyssa shiver. In the next instant, he reached Denbry and, before Alyssa could blink, delivered a blow that ripped Denbry's hand off Alyssa's sleeve and sent the man spiralling backwards.

To Denbry's credit, he did not run for his horse—which Alyssa thought would have been the prudent reaction. Instead, struggling to his feet, one hand on his jaw, he said, 'Once again, the bastard's response. Pretend what you like, put on airs and graces in Parliament, but you'll never be more than a nobleman's illegitimate get.'

'If you are the example of a "gentleman", I'm glad to be a base-born. Army-trained, too, you might remember. I warned you before, if you ever maligned my wife or her reputation again, I'd give you an exhibition of that training. Apparently your memory is faulty. A pity. I'm afraid you're going to need a much longer repairing lease with that maiden aunt than you thought.'

With that, he advanced on Denbry and this time discretion won out. Looking around wildly to locate his horse, he made a run for it.

But Ben was faster. Catching up, he grabbed Denbry's shoulder, jerked him around and, as Denbry brought up his fists to repel a blow, kicked his feet out from under him. More frightened than hurt, the Earl cried out as he hit the ground and skidded, trying to right himself. Ben followed, kicking him to his hands and knees each time he tried to get up, driving him backwards, until Denbry was crouched with his back against a rock outcropping, one arm down to try to protect his legs, another up over his face.

Ben towered over him, his hair dishevelled, a murderous look on his face. Afraid he might do the man a serious injury, Alyssa ran up and grabbed his arm. Hard muscle tensed beneath her fingers.

'Let him go, Ben! He's not worth the trouble.'

For a moment, she was afraid she might have to tackle her husband to keep him from attacking again. But then, the ferocity seemed to leave him and he stepped back.

'Pummelling your miserable hide is the second-greatest temptation I've ever had to resist. Since I don't think I could manage it again, better make sure I don't set eyes on you after today. Or you *will* be sorry. Because there won't be any tender-hearted ladies around to save you.'

Struggling to his feet, Denbry looked from his torn cravat to the ripped knees of his breeches to his ruined boots, scratched from scrabbling across the rough ground. 'No, it's *you* who's going to be sorry,' he spat out and limped to his horse.

Alyssa kept a restraining hand on Ben's arm until the Earl had ridden out of sight. 'That's the last of him, I hope. Would you fetch our horses?'

With a terse nod, he headed off. Alyssa couldn't help admiring his tall frame and powerful shoulders as he disappeared into the copse. How could a lady not feel gratified at being defended by a man with such brutal efficiency?

Though she reminded herself Ben would have come to the defence of any lady who was being threatened, his response today did seem several degrees more ferocious than when he'd punched Denbry at the Dornton Village inn. Could their deepening friendship and their new intimacy have made him more attached to—and protective of—the woman to whom circumstance had bound him?

What would it be like to live with his tender care, engaging companionship and fiery passion every day, for the rest of their lives?

Except that when they returned to London, he would remain to carry out his duties in Parliament, while she set out again alone. Remain in the metropolis where, Denbry said, his mistress was pining for him.

Not that she could put much credence in anything the Earl uttered. But...was there a woman waiting in London for Ben?

She didn't think so—but she didn't know much about such relationships. Quite a few gentlemen—her father among them—had no difficulty going from their wives in the country to their *chère-amies* in the capital.

Before she skipped down the fanciful road of imaging their intimacy had bound them together too closely for anyone to come between them, she needed to remember that the lovemaking she found so unique and powerful had not been a new or perhaps even a memorable event for Ben. This self-admitted 'man of great address with the ladies' had pleasured many women before her...and quite likely would go on to pleasure many more.

That daunting thought was enough to dissipate the last remnants of the romantic dream that he'd been the gallant knight galloping up to rescue his one true love.

'You're very quiet, Lyssa,' Ben said he led their horses back up. 'Are you all right? He didn't hurt you, did he? By Heaven, if he did, I'll track him down—'

'No, Ben, I'm quite all right. Though I admire your science—you must show me some time how you take someone's feet out from under them like that—I could have handled him,' she said.

'Could you, now?' he said with a grin. 'How were you intending to do that, my warrior princess?'

Steeling herself against the warmth that endearment evoked, she said, 'Since I didn't have brushes or palette knife to stab him with, I intended to kick him where he'd remember the blow for a long time. These walking boots have thick heels.'

Ben chuckled. 'I'd liked to have seen that. Might have made up for being denied the pleasure of beating the stuffing out of him.'

'He is a miserable weasel. I only hope we're done with him.'

'If he does bother you again, I'll get him some place with no witnesses and this time you won't stop me.' Ben sighed. 'That's why we need to reform Parliament—so self-important wastrels like that can never take a seat based solely on their birth. But enough of that unpleasantness. Come, my sweet.'

Much as she was trying to listen to the voice of prudence that whispered she mustn't read too much into what was probably no more to him than a pleasant interlude, as he looked tenderly down into her eyes before giving her hand a kiss, she couldn't help being pulled back into that intoxicating sense of intimacy.

Prudence be damned, she thought defiantly. Maybe this sense of belonging together *was* an illusion. Still, she intended to enjoy every moment of the euphoria. They would be back to London—and reality—soon enough.

'What was the first temptation you had so much trouble resisting, by the way?' she couldn't help asking.

He stopped to give her a hard kiss. 'What do you think?'

Grabbing his shoulders, she pulled him down for another fierce kiss, revelling in his strength and masculinity. 'Time to return to the inn, then,' she said, releasing him. 'And resist no more.'

## *Chapter Fourteen*

Two days later, Ben sat at a table in Alyssa's chamber at the inn as she packed up her art supplies, while Molly folded the rest of her belongings and deposited them into her trunks. After three glorious weeks of exploring the countryside with his ardent bride, it was time to return to London.

For the first time ever, Ben regretted having to sit in Parliament.

He'd undertaken this journey so Alyssa could begin immediately, in safety, to complete the drawings that would make her dream of publication become reality. True, he'd also hoped that riding, dining, talking and spending the best part of every day together would erode her fears and teach her heart to believe what her head already knew: that he would never take more from her than she freely offered. He trusted, once her heart *was* convinced, she would release the hold over the passion he'd sensed in her that first morning in the woods at Dornton and come to him.

He'd succeeded spectacularly on all counts, he thought, a smile curving his lips as he watched her—

the hands and fingers that could fashion the image of a bird so cleverly it seemed ready to fly off the page could also tease and arouse and stimulate, drawing from his body a response more intense than anything he'd ever experienced.

Such a contradiction she was—all practical housewife now as she secured pencils, pastels and charcoal for the journey, and then out at the seashore that first astonishing afternoon, and in the bedchamber of the inn ever day after that, the most fearless, inventive and insatiable lover a man could wish for. Truly, the woman of a man's fondest sensual daydreams.

And it wasn't just the matchless lovemaking that drew him, though he enjoyed that immensely. He'd told Christopher he believed she would intrigue, surprise and delight him, and he'd been correct on that count, too. Her far-ranging interests, her keen eye for detail, her unconventional approach—every day brought new and surprising revelations, leading him to see everything from everyday objects to conventional behaviour in a new light.

He didn't think the fascination was likely to fade any time soon. Nor was his insatiable hunger for her likely to be slaked—since she would be leaving London again almost as soon as they arrived.

A good thing he would be caught up in strategy and planning for Parliament. He'd expected to like his wife and been certain he would revel in their lovemaking, once she allowed him to possess her.

But he hadn't anticipated he would regret not being able to spend every day with her, or how keenly he would miss her when they were apart.

'That's all of my things,' Alyssa said, pulling him

back to the present. 'Molly's taking it down to the coach. Have you anything to add?'

'No, I gave my trunk to the grooms earlier this morning.'

After the maid walked out, Alyssa came over to stand behind him, wrapping her arms around his neck and leaning down to kiss the top of his head. 'You're very quiet this morning,' she observed. 'Thinking about the upcoming session? Or a little fatigued...after our long night?'

With a growl, he pulled her around and on to his lap. 'Never tired from that,' he promised, cupping her bottom and giving her for a long, slow kiss. She leaned into him, meeting his tongue with hers to lave and play, caressing his neck with her fingertips and slipping one under his neckcloth, to the base of his throat where the pulse beat strongly.

'I don't suppose there's time...' she said regretfully when he broke the kiss.

'Not if we want to leave this morning,' he replied with a sigh.

To his delight, instead of hopping up briskly, she tucked her head against his chest. And giggled.

'What?' he asked, smiling down at her.

'I was just thinking what delicious gossip we must have provided for the servants—our own and the inn's. First, engaging separate rooms, then sending poor Molly up to the attics with the other servants. Disappearing for hours in the afternoon, not emerging until late in the mornings...'

'Does that concern you?' he asked, worried about the sensibilities of a gently born maiden only just introduced to intimacy and probably uncomfortable that all the world knew what they were doing in their chamber.

'Not a bit,' she said cheerfully, confounding—as she so often did—his expectations of what a girl of her sheltered upbringing would think or feel. 'We are wed, after all, and they will always gossip about something. Probably the maids are envious that I have a husband of such impressive vigour.' Rubbing herself against his burgeoning erection, she gave him a naughty smile.

'While the grooms are envying me a wife with such a gluttonous appetite. Who, I'm afraid, my wicked angel, will have to wait until this evening.' Giving her a pat on the bottom that was both affection and promise, he helped her to her feet.

'How many days do you expect it will take us to return to London?'

'We can make it comfortably in three, although I might want to spare one more. Which leads me to a question.'

'What's that?' she asked as she tossed a bonnet over her carelessly braided curls.

'We'll be passing through Hampshire. I'd thought to visit longer another time, but it seems a shame not to take an afternoon, since we'll be so close. Would you be amenable to stopping in Andover, while I go visit my mother in Whitchurch?'

'Of course. You will to take me to meet her, I hope.'

'I…wasn't sure how you'd feel about it.' Their travelling route had been well known from the start, but Ben had put off talking to Alyssa about this particular possibility until the last moment. He knew many of her views differed from those typical of her sex and class. But she'd been more or less compelled to wed him and, though she'd protested that it was his reputation she wanted to protect, he hadn't quite managed to banish the niggling fear that secretly she regretted having stooped to marry a bastard.

Conventional views about the treatment deserved by 'fallen women' were even harsher, and inculcated from childhood. Though he would like his mother to meet Alyssa, he'd been ferociously protective of her his whole life and didn't want to risk even the possibility that she might feel snubbed or disdained by his wife.

'She's the classic example all young females are warned against. And as you may remember, she's not received by anyone in society. Of course, I would love her to meet you, but…'

'But you want to know she'd be treated properly, with respect and courtesy, not condescension or thinly veiled distaste,' Alyssa said.

'Well—yes,' he admitted.

'Did you fear I might look down on her because I'm an earl's daughter and she a disgraced governess? Oh, Ben, I would be insulted at your lack of faith in me, if your concern didn't also reinforce how fiercely you protect your mother—and how could I resent that? I told you once I admired her courage. I expect she's far more virtuous than many "respectable" society matrons, who take lovers on a whim. How could I not wish to meet a woman who gave up so much to raise so honourable, principled and courageous a son?'

After enduring a lifetime of taunts—some from Alyssa's own brother and most recently from Denbry—her affirmation was like soothing rain soaking into the parched ground of the boy who'd been mocked, teased and rejected. An outsider all his life, until he found a place first with the army, then with the Hellions at Oxford.

Gratitude, relief and some deep emotion he couldn't put a name to welled up, closing his throat so he couldn't speak.

Reading the feelings that must be playing across his face, Alyssa cupped his chin in her hands, her gaze tender. 'How could you not think yourself a thousand times more worthy than men like Denbry and Harleton, men blessed with titles and wealth, but empty of any virtue? After my experiences with my father and brother, I have even more reason than you to know that it isn't birth that matters, but character. That's the truth you want to incorporate into the governing of England. Surely you believe it yourself! Or is that another something one knows with the head, but which must gradually be learned by the heart?'

He smiled wryly. 'When some of the lads found out I was base-born, my old sergeant major told them the army preferred bastards. They fight harder, he said, because they always have something to prove. I suppose he was right.'

'You proved your character to me the day you travelled all the way to Dornton to protect the sister of a man you despise—a woman you'd never even met. Your friends, your fellow Parliamentarians and your constituents all recognise that character. I'd be honoured to meet the woman who helped shape it.'

His heart still full, Ben rose and gave her a hug. Releasing her at last, he said, 'I'll be honoured to introduce the special lady I was lucky enough to marry. Let's get on the road.'

* * *

Three days later, the maid-of-all-work answered the door of his mother's small cottage. Poignant memories had begun to well up the moment their carriage turned into the long drive, but now, as the girl ushered them to the parlour, they submerged him.

How many times had he sat with Mama in that parlour while she read to him? When she'd held the little boy in her arms as he sobbed at another child's cruelty, or patched up his cuts and scrapes? Calmed the adolescent who stormed in, furious and longing to pay back the village boys for their taunts?

Welcomed back from India the defiant young man who'd rejected his father's offer of support and run off to take the King's shilling, counselling him to accept the Viscount's help now, so he might finish his education and establish the career she'd sacrificed so much to give him.

Always surrounding him with her unfailing love, nurturing, protecting, and guiding him towards the better life she'd wanted for him.

He'd written to his mother explaining his hasty marriage, so his arrival with wife in hand wouldn't be a shock. She hadn't been expecting this visit, though, as he'd not decided to make it until so late, a note would have arrived about the same time they did.

And then she was at the parlour door. 'My darling son!' she cried, embracing him, love and pride and welcome in her face, as there was every time he came home. No matter how long it had been since he'd last visited.

'Mama, how good it is to see you!'

'And you, too, my son. But you mustn't stand there!

Alice,' she called to the goggle-eyed maid, 'would you bring tea? Now, Ben, you must introduce this lovely young woman.'

Alyssa, who'd been standing back as they embraced, predictably didn't wait upon protocol. Dropping a curtsy, she said, 'I'm Lyssa, Mrs Tawny. And I'm so pleased to meet you. What a wonderful son you raised!'

One arm still around his mother, Ben turned towards her with a grin. 'Yes, this is Lady Alyssa Lambornne, now Mrs Ben Tawny.'

'You could say nothing that would delight a mother more,' his mother told her. 'Welcome, my dear! Please come in.'

They took seats in the neat front parlour, the maid returning soon after with the tea. As they drank it, his mother asked about their wedding trip, his work in Parliament, Alyssa's drawings, all the while, he could tell, watching and assessing his wife.

As Alyssa had informed him, he needn't have worried. The meeting between the two women closest to his heart went splendidly, Alyssa answering questions about her work, but then going on to admire his mother's needlework, asking about her garden and remarking on the book she'd left lying on the table beside her chair, which led to a discussion of what sort of literature they preferred.

After several hours, having acquiesced to his mother's urging that they remain for an early dinner before returning to their rooms at the coaching inn in Andover, the maid bore Alyssa off to wash and rest.

Giving Ben and his mother time for the tête-à-tête he knew she wanted.

Once his wife had left the room, his mother turned to Ben. 'I like your Alyssa very much.'

Ben smiled. 'So do I, Mama.'

'Which is fortunate, given that circumstances virtually forced you to marry her.'

'Well, I did have some notion of her character. If she weren't the confident and independent woman she is, she probably would have fainted dead away when I revealed the threat to her and, upon reviving, rushed home in hysterics, so there never would have been that unfortunate confrontation at the inn. But in any event, I couldn't have abandoned her to face ruin and scandal.' *Like my father did to you*, he left unspoken, anger over that fact still smouldering.

As if she knew what he was thinking, his mother said quietly, 'Now you know first-hand what it is to marry out of honour rather than free choice. It has always grieved me that you are so bitter towards your father.'

'What, did his father lock him in his room? Beat him? Starve him into accepting the fortune and title?' Ben spat out.

'There are other sorts of coercion beyond beating and imprisonment.'

'I know you've always loved him, even after what he did to you. And I admire you for forgiving him. I… I just can't.'

'As a child, you wouldn't have understood and as a young man, you were too angry to listen. Even after you returned from India, you refused to let me speak of it. Perhaps now, after your own experience, you will let me tell you what really happened between us.'

'I know he gave in to his family's pressure and repudiated you, left you pregnant and disgraced. What else is there to know?'

She sighed. 'A very great deal. Family is so very important, Ben. I should know, after having to live without it for so many years. I would like to heal the breach between you, while there is still time for the two of you to become closer.'

Ben had expected his mother to beg him to tell her everything about Alyssa—not rehash the old scandal. But from the imploring expression on her face, revealing what she wished to relate meant a great deal to her—and he wasn't any longer that angry, impatient young man who'd refused to listen.

Well, not impatient, anyway. He didn't expect that anything she disclosed would alter his opinion, but if it would bring her peace to tell him, he wouldn't deny her the chance.

'Very well, Mama. Say what you wish.'

'You like to claim Robert abandoned us for wealth and a title, but that's not true. His parents never approved of their younger son's love for a governess, not because of my birth, for my family was gentry—only because I had no money. But we had determined we would run away to marry, if necessary, and I think eventually they would have accepted me. All that changed when Robert's older brother was killed. There was no wealth to inherit, you see. The estate had been virtually bankrupt for years, his father borrowing against the expectation of his eldest son marrying an heiress. And Julien was supposed to—Cecily Daubennet was one of the wealthiest young women of her debut year. She was only a baronet's daughter, their fortune derived from a grandfather in trade, so her family prized above all her chance to become a viscountess. After Julien died, when Robert's father discovered that her family would be amenable to her wedding the new heir, enormous pressure was put on Robert to acquiesce.'

Touching his impassive face with a finger, she shook her head. 'It wasn't just his immediate family that would have suffered if he'd refused. The Deane's Hill estate encompasses hundreds of acres, a neighbouring village, dozens of tenant farmers, a huge household of servants, grooms, cooks, maids and retainers. If he did not marry Miss Daubennet, loans would be due that would require dismissing the staff, closing the house, selling off most of the land and throwing a whole community into economic distress.' She paused. 'How could we be selfish enough to claim our happiness at the expense of so many people? Could you have done so?'

Ben wasn't sure what to answer. He'd been willing to risk his life to defend his country's interests in India. Would he give up his love to prevent the distress of so many innocents?

'Maybe not *that*,' he allowed. 'But I would never have abandoned the woman who carried my child.'

'But he didn't. I knew I had to let him go—as a curate's daughter, I knew what it was to be poor, how if the estate failed, so many unfortunates would have had no recourse but the workhouse. But...but I was selfish, too. I wanted one night with the man I loved, before I had to give him up for ever. And I wanted to belong to him completely.'

She smiled sadly. 'He didn't put up much resistance. And despite what happened later, I have never regretted stealing that night. Robert married Cecily two months later—just as I discovered I was with child. I didn't tell him. So you see, all you have suffered, all you have missed out on by not having your father live with you, is my fault. Not his. I've carried that guilt since the day you were born.'

Astounded, Ben shook his head. 'You never told him? Then how…why?'

'I intended to go away quietly, live somewhere far away where I wouldn't be tempted to see him. But the pregnancy was…difficult. While going to bid my family farewell, I became too sick to travel. I don't know what might have become of me had not my old governess taken me in, for my family disowned me. But after he threw me out, my father sent an angry letter to Robert, castigating him for having ruined his daughter. Had he not, you might now be a congressman of the United States, for I intended to take passage after you were born.'

'But my father asked you to stay in England?'

'Yes. Knowing what it meant for me, he was horrified when he learned I was with child. But he begged me not to go away, for although you could not be born in wedlock, you were his son, child of the woman he loved, and in England he could provide for you. Perhaps I could have begun a new life somewhere else and spared you growing up with the stigma of being a bastard. But then your father would never have known you, or been able to help you, or have taken any part in your life. It was selfish of me, but I wanted the man I loved to know his son.'

Too shocked to take it all in, Ben said, 'What did Miss Daubennet think of this?'

'There was never any illusion of love between them. Robert honoured her wishes that you not be brought to live at Deane's Hill, for which I was grateful. If she had been amenable to it, I would have had to send you and losing you, too, would have broken what was left of my heart. In exchange, Cecily promised to make no objection about Robert supporting us, seeing to your schooling and establishing a relationship with you. It was easier for her to bear, you see, because what was between us happened before she even met Robert. Although I imagine she believed that once *she* gave him a son, he would lose interest in the one that could never inherit his title or estate.'

'Except she didn't,' Ben said. His father's marriage had produced three daughters, half-sisters he had never met, but no sons.

'No. Although I don't believe having a legitimate son would have ended his interest in you, there never was another. The money Cecily brought rescued the estate, but it was Robert's hard work that has restored it to the prosperity it enjoys today. As his means increased, Robert tried to provide more for us, as much as I would allow him. Once, when you were older, you asked why I never seemed to mind the disgrace. Do you remember what I replied?'

The moment was graven on his memory. 'You said there was so much love for me in you, there was no room to feel disgrace.'

'Yes. What I did not tell you is that, having chosen to remain here, knowing the disgrace it would bring, I had no right to mind it. I do regret that my choice caused you so much pain, much more than I ever anticipated. Knowing what I do now, I'm not so sure I would make that choice again. It's far too late to undo the past, of course. But the blame for the taunts and abuse and loneliness you suffered, blame you have always laid upon your father, should more fairly be directed at me.'

Ben stared at her, his mind reeling. To him, his mother had always been the wounded innocent, left by his callous father to face the consequences of a passion that should never have been indulged. It would take some time to get his mind around the fact that she had chosen to risk conceiving him, knowing that she and his father could never marry. That she had chosen to remain in England, with all the stigma that would mean for her—and him—rather than starting over again elsewhere.

'I...don't know what to say.'

She patted his hand. 'It's a great deal to take in. You'll need to think about it. After you have, I hope you'll be able to forgive me...and give your father another chance. Fortunately, you've been luckier than we were. Doing the honourable thing allowed you to rescue, rather than ruin, the woman you love.'

'The woman I love?' Ben echoed.

'You do love her, don't you?'

'I...well, I'm very fond of her, but...'

His mother laughed. 'Oh, my dear, love isn't always the *coup de foudre*—the lightning strike. Sometimes it happens quietly, so quietly you may not even notice. Something else for you to think about, yes?'

Before he could reply, she turned towards the door. 'Ah, Alyssa, my dear. I hope you've had time to rest? Alice will have dinner ready soon. If you'll excuse me, I'll go check on that.'

Giving Ben a kiss on the cheek before she walked out, she left Ben with his mind in turmoil.

His father had known only that he was giving up the

woman he loved. He'd not abandoned Ben. He'd begged Ben's mother to let him have a place in his life.

'Did you and your mother have a comfortable coze?' Alyssa asked, her question cutting through his turbulent thoughts. As she studied his face her smile faded. 'Oh, dear! She doesn't approve of me, does she?'

That was so far off what really troubled him, Ben couldn't help laughing. 'Of course she does. But after expressing her delight with you, she explained some circumstances from my childhood that were…rather disconcerting. Shocking, almost.'

'Shocking—good or shocking—bad?'

He shook his head. 'I'm not sure. When you discover that something you've believed your whole life is in error, it takes some…readjustment to put it all in perspective.'

'I don't have much experience with anything, but if you want to talk about it, I'm happy to listen.'

'Thank you. Later, perhaps, after I've had time to… digest it all.'

The maid came in then to escort them to dine. It wasn't until he was leading his wife to the table that Ben recalled the other thing his mother had mentioned—that he must be in love with Alyssa.

Could he be? The implications of loving her were so far reaching, he didn't want to deal with that now. It was all he could handle at the moment to sort out how he felt about his mother's revelations.

## *Chapter Fifteen*

After a long day's travel, they reached London the next evening. They'd both been rather silent on the journey, Ben looking over his notes about the upcoming session—when he could keep his thoughts from wandering back to the shock of what his mother had confided—Alyssa studying her drawings and compiling lists of which birds she still needed to sketch.

Usually, as the coach approached the last toll gate and the outlines of the city appeared in the hazy distance, Ben felt a rising excitement. This time, even the imminent reconvening of Parliament and his determination to finish their vital work did not pull him from his melancholy. Whether because the sunshine and stimulation Alyssa brought to his days would soon be lost, or because he was so unsettled and uncertain about what he should do regarding his father, he wasn't sure.

The first of the notes waiting on his desk when they arrived back at Queen Street brought him face to face with the second of those problems. Writing that he was sorry he had been out of town and unable to attend the wedding at Lady Sayleford's, Viscount Chilford asked that his son call upon him as soon as convenient.

There was also a note from Giles, informing him the Hellions planned to meet the next day to discuss their plans for the opening of Parliament. And Russell and Mrs Ingleton both informed him they had arranged a carriage and servants for him and Alyssa to review.

Had he been the Viscount's legitimate son, he would have made a courtesy call on his father to inform him of his intention to marry and arrange to introduce his intended, before the wedding took place. Since under law, he was the 'child of no man', that had not been necessary—he didn't need to consult his father about anything he did.

Still, he probably ought to introduce his wife to the Viscount. But although he couldn't imagine his father would have any objections to his marrying an earl's daughter with a fat dowry, it might be better to find out why he'd been summoned before he took Alyssa to meet the Viscount.

Not that his father had ever enacted any scenes. In fact, to be fair, it had always been Ben who was stiff and formal and frigidly polite on the few occasions when they met. The Viscount, he now realised, had been forbearing—invariably displaying a calm, quiet concern for his prickly eldest child, which was as warm an emotion as Ben would accept from him.

He'd always believed his father tolerated his near-contempt because of the guilt he felt over his treatment of Ben and his mother. Had he maligned his father all those years?

The next few days would be very busy, as he met with his friends and helped Alyssa ready herself for her next journey. The mantel clock having just chimed eight in the evening, he decided on the instant to visit to his father this very night.

Of course, proceeding at once without first sending a note meant it was quite possible the Viscount might be out. But if he were at home, Ben could settle the business at once, before embroiling himself in the many tasks he needed to accomplish over the next week. And he had to admit, ever since his mother had related the full story of their relationship, he'd been unsettled, driven to talk his father even though he wasn't sure exactly what he meant to say.

Leaving the library, he tracked Alyssa down in her chamber. Smiling as she saw him walk in, she said, 'Mrs Ingleton has a cold collation ready for us, whenever we choose to eat it. I'd prefer to finish the rest of the boxes first, unless you are famished…for food.'

Her hint of intimacy momentarily distracted him from his other concerns. Pulling her into a hug, he murmured, 'I'll claim what I'm most famished for later.' Releasing her, he continued, 'I've had a note from Giles informing me that we'll be meeting tomorrow afternoon, so perhaps we can look at the coach Russell procured and interview the maids and grooms in the morning.'

'That would be fine.' She chuckled. 'There was a positive mountain of invitation cards for us. Lady Sayleford must have done her work well, spreading the story of our "fairytale romance". I'm sure everyone who knew me during my two Seasons is astonished I found someone who liked me enough to propose and can't wait to observe the happy couple. Fortunately, I'll have left London before most of these events take place, but I thought we should attend the rout Lady Sayleford is giving in our honour two nights hence.'

'Yes, I suppose that's obligatory, though you can use my need to prepare for Parliament as an excuse to avoid any others you don't wish to attend. I've had another card, too—a summons from my father. I thought to go now, see what he needs and arrange a time for you to meet him before you leave. Go ahead and eat if you choose; I'll get something when I return.'

'Is anything amiss?' she asked, studying his face.

Since he hadn't yet decided how he felt about the situation of his mother and father, he hadn't said anything about it to Alyssa. 'No, nothing amiss. I'll give you a report when I return.'

Dropping a kiss on her head, he turned away, feeling her speculative gaze on him as he walked out.

The stroll from Queen Street to the imposing Chilford House on Berkeley Square took him just a few moments. His father's butler answered his knock and, though he had only called there a handful of times, in the way of butlers, Travers not only recognised him, he seemed to be expecting him.

'Good evening, Mr Tawny. Won't you follow me? I'll let the Viscount know you are here. Some wine while you wait?'

Accepting the wine, but too agitated to sit and drink it, after the butler bowed himself out, Ben paced the parlour. He knew he'd have to ask his father about the events his mother had described. He wasn't sure he was ready to hear the answers.

After holding himself aloof, anger smouldering within him his whole life at the man who'd condemned him to be born a bastard, it was hard to imagine seeing his father in a different light. But if it were true—and he had no reason to doubt his mother's word, especially as her account transferred to her own head the majority of the blame he'd always assigned to his father, another circumstance he wasn't sure yet how to deal with—in fairness, he *would* have to re-evaluate his attitude towards the Viscount.

A few minutes later, the door opened and Ben's father walked in.

No one who viewed the two men together could doubt that Ben was the Viscount's son. They were of a height, with the same dark hair and green eyes, the same lean face and prominent cheekbones. There were silver highlights now in the hair of the man of whom Ben was the mirror image, lines at the edges of the eyes and on the forehead. But his calm, measured pace and steady gaze had changed not since the first time Ben had met him, when he arrived at Eton as a boy.

Hating him then for taking him away from his mother and being the cause of the teasing and scorn the other boys directed at him, Ben had initially refused to speak to him.

His father walked over and offered a hand. 'Good evening, Ben,' the Viscount said as he shook it. 'Thank you for stopping by so quickly. I understand you only returned to London this evening.'

'How did you know? Are you having the house watched?' Ben asked before he could stop himself. He grimaced, finding it hard to stifle the adversarial response ingrained in him over so many years.

As usual, his father didn't seem to take offence. 'Actually, yes. I won't be in London long and didn't want to miss seeing you. Won't you have a seat?'

After they both took an armchair and had a sip of wine, his father continued, 'First, let me congratulate you on your marriage. As I said in my note, I'm sorry I wasn't in London to attend Lady Sayleford's reception. I…assume she had your permission to invite me. In any event, I'm not acquainted with your bride, but the Countess tells me she is quite a little beauty and extremely talented. I hope you will be very happy.'

'Thank you, sir. I hope to be. If you would like, I will bring her to call.'

'I should very much like to meet her, perhaps at another time. I only came to London to see you and must return to Deane's Hill as soon as possible.' He paused. 'Lady Chilford is quite ill.'

'I'm sorry to hear that.' Although in his younger days, Ben had hated the woman who prevented his parents from marrying, as he grew older, his attitude towards his father's wife had softened. A young lady, he'd learned, would have little choice but to wed the man her family chose for her.

'I had intended to offer your bride some jewellery as a wedding present, but after talking with Lady Sayleford, I thought she might appreciate this more.' Setting down his glass, the Viscount walked over to the secretary, opened the top drawer and brought out a large, flat tin box.

'One of the Audubon folios!' Ben said, recognising it instantly from the large size.

'I've also obtained a copy of the commentary Audubon and his Scottish ornithologist, Mr MacGillivray, recently published to accompany the engravings. I've located two more of the already issued folios and have arranged to subscribe to the series. I hope your wife will enjoy them.'

'That's extremely generous, sir,' Ben said, taken aback at the cost—and the care the Viscount had taken in choosing something Alyssa would love. 'But won't you allow me to buy them from you? I had hoped to find a set myself to give her, but hadn't had time—'

'Please, let me do this,' his father interrupted gently. 'It would mean a great deal to me to give your wife something I know she will treasure.'

'Then what can I do, but thank you?'

'I'll have them sent over to Queen Street tomorrow.'

As the Viscount walked back to his seat, Ben said, 'On our way back to London, we stopped to see Mama.'

The Viscount's eyes softened. 'She is well, I trust?'

'Very well. While we were there, she...insisted that I hear the full explanation behind your marriage and my birth. Something I'd refused to listen to before. It... paints quite a different picture from what I'd always believed.'

The Viscount nodded. 'She explained that I felt compelled to do my duty to save the estate?'

'Yes. And that you didn't know, when you married, that she was with child.' Ben shook his head. 'You know I blamed you for years for deserting us! Why did you never tell me that you had no idea she'd conceived?'

'You were right to blame me. Knowing I couldn't marry her, I should never have taken her innocence. You cannot imagine the agony I experienced when I received her father's letter and learned she was with child. Knowing I could do nothing—nothing—to prevent you from being born a bastard and the woman I loved from being branded a harlot.'

The Viscount sighed. 'I probably should have let her go, let her build a life for you both somewhere else, where she was not known. But we were both too selfish. The only bit of our lives we could share was you and neither of us could let that go. Angelica suffered cruelly for it, but you suffered most of all. If you grew up hating me, it was only what I deserved.'

For the first time, Ben considered what it must have been like for his father—trapped by duty in marriage to a woman he didn't love, knowing the woman he did love and the child of that love would be scorned for life—and unable to do a thing to prevent it. How would he feel if the woman involved were Alyssa, and he knew because of him, she would be shamed and ostracised for the rest of her life?

'It must have been terribly difficult,' he acknowledged, adding with a grimace, 'and my ill-humoured, grudging acceptance of everything you tried to give us couldn't have made it any easier.'

His father smiled. 'You were a tempestuous lad from the first. I can't tell you how proud I am of what you've overcome and how hard you've worked to get where you are.'

'With some timely assistance from you.'

His father waved a hand. 'I did little enough. It was you, making the most of your opportunities, who did most of it.'

Out of the still-churning emotions, Ben heard the echo of his mother's statement. 'Mama said she wanted to tell me, not just because I was finally willing to listen, but because she hoped we might…put aside our differences. Put aside my anger and resentment, really. And become more like father and son.'

The Viscount's eyes lit. 'Nothing would please me more. Are you willing to forgive the sins of the past and let us move past them?'

His father as…friend. It was an odd thought, after all these years thinking of him as a villain, but…an appealing one, he decided. 'I think I am.'

The Viscount stared at him, gratitude, tenderness and the love Ben had never allowed him to offer shining in his eyes. 'Thank you…my dearest son.'

After a moment, clearing his throat, he said, 'There was one other detail I wanted to mention. Lord Aldermont caught up with me at Brooks's. He wants to propose you for membership and needed to verify he would have my support. As he is a very influential senior member, his nominee should have no trouble being voted in. Would you be agreeable to that?'

'Me, a member of Brooks's?' Ben shook his head. 'I've been an outsider so long, I'm not sure how I would act as a "member of the club". Nor, frankly, do I want Lord Aldermont doing me any favours. His treatment of his daughter was…less than desirable.'

'Perhaps. But we must take people as they are, not as we would wish them to be. Whatever he's done before, her father is looking out for her welfare now, by placing her husband where he can rub shoulders with some of the most influential men in the nation. Besides, being voted in doesn't mean you have to frequent the place. The connections you could forge there would, however, be of definite benefit to your Parliamentary career.'

That was indisputable. The rest of the Hellions had often ragged Giles, a courtesy viscount and member there himself, for being the only one of their group of outsiders who could hobnob at the seat of power.

Now, apparently, there would be a seat for him, too.

'As long as you don't object, I'll tell Aldermont to go forward. In the meantime, think about it. As I said, you don't have to frequent the club if you don't want to. But you would have the *right* to visit if you chose.'

Ben shook his head and laughed. 'I'm not sure I'd dare. There'd be this part of me expecting the members to come running to the entrance if I stepped a foot inside, holding up crosses to ward off the vampire.'

His father didn't join in his mirth. 'My fault that you grew up feeling that way.'

'Well, as Mama said, we can't change the past—we can only alter the future. I would like to do that...Father. Perhaps when you are next in London? Now, I should return to Queen Street. Thank you again for the magnificent wedding gift! Please present my best wishes to Lady Chilford for a swift recovery.'

'I would, but...she's dying, you see.'

About to take his leave, Ben halted, shocked. 'It is that serious?'

'I'm afraid so. I...never loved her, but we rubbed along together tolerably well. It's only right that I be with her at the end. However, our conversation tonight prompts me to bring up a matter I hadn't planned to address until after...her passing. Nothing can change the fact that when I'm gone, the title, Deane's Hill and most of the land will go to a distant cousin. But there are several unentailed properties that came from my mother's family, in particular my grandmother's estate, Oakgrove. Before my brother's death made me the heir, I expected to marry your mother and establish our family there. It would please me very much to have you establish *your* family there. If you would accept them, I would like to deed Oakgrove and the other properties to you.'

Ben blew out a breath. 'So I'm to contemplate becoming a respectable member of Brooks *and* an estate owner, all in one evening?'

'Your carefree days with nothing to consider but the wishes of your constituents could soon be over,' his father said gravely, a twinkle in his eye. 'You will have to steel yourself to dealing with lazy tenants, failing crops, ageing roofs that leak and the hosts of other problems that bedevil a landowner. Think about it, if you would. We can discuss it more thoroughly when I return to London.'

The Viscount held out his hand. 'Goodnight…my son.'

Ben shook it. 'Goodnight…Father.'

Feeling like the world his mother had set spinning two days ago was now revolving even faster, Ben walked out.

He couldn't wait to tell Alyssa all about it. This was far more than just his father recognising and supporting a base-born son. By implementing the actions he'd just discussed, the Viscount would be announcing to the world that, although he couldn't pass on his title to Ben, he considered him his heir in everything but what the law forbade. Giving Ben property and membership at Brooks's would mean elevating him to the position of landed gentry, making him socially and financially the equal of the boys who'd scorned him and looked down on him at Eton and Oxford.

Though he'd still not be equal in rank to an earl's

daughter, he'd be a good deal closer. With that realisation came a sense of lightness, making him for the first time feel easier about the fact that Alyssa had been virtually forced into marrying him. Although he knew their unequal status hadn't mattered to her, the euphoria that filled him now told him it mattered to him a good deal more than he'd realised. Now she wouldn't have to wait until he earned his way to a high position in government to have a husband worthy of an earl's daughter.

*Listen to you,* his indignant intellect answered back. *Haven't you spent the last ten years working to ensure things like titles and estates are no longer the measure of a man?*

Very well, it might not be logical. But apparently, caring about the distinctions of birth and class that had made his growing up such a misery was not dispensed with so easily.

Alyssa would probably tell him his father's gift of a landed estate would make him no more or less worthy than he was right now. But she would also understand how much having it meant to him.

He had a sudden image of the outrage on Harleton's face the first time he saw Ben walk into Brooks's and burst out laughing.

Alyssa would appreciate that joke, too.

## Chapter Sixteen

Two nights later, Alyssa sat in her bedchamber dressed for the rout at Lady Sayleford's, leafing with reverent gloved hands through the Audubon folio Ben's father had delivered to them the previous day. It seemed unbelievable that she actually had her own copy of such a magnificent work.

Ben had told her he'd been looking for a set when his father located these. She still felt awed and humbled that they were willing to go to so much trouble to find something they knew she would love. Few people in her life had ever cared what she liked, much less bestirred themselves to provide it. And only Will had understood how valuable these splendid drawings would be to her, to study and admire and emulate as she went about creating her own work.

She was tempted to take them with her when she left on her expedition, but it would be safer to leave them in London. Although she didn't need any further excuses to linger. With the coach readied and the new staff hired, she should have already chosen a day to set out, since she knew perfectly well where she needed to go—and had a very narrow window of time to locate the birds she most needed to sketch before they left their winter migration grounds.

Every day she remained with Ben made it harder to leave. If the publisher's deadline weren't so imminent, she probably wouldn't be able to make herself go at all, so charming and funny and stimulating he was, seeming to enjoy her company, most definitely enjoying their uninhibited lovemaking. After each tender interlude, hope would sprout like a persistent weed that maybe, just maybe he might be on the way to falling in love with the bride who'd been forced on him.

More serious was the danger to her own heart. She was being foolishly blind if she thought she could linger here, enjoying his company, revelling in their lovemaking, without being drawn closer and closer to turning over to him the last bit of her heart he hadn't already claimed. If she wanted to maintain enough emotional distance to survive, if...*when* his current fascination with her ended and he moved on to someone else as—a pox on her for being an idiot—she had promised him he could, she needed to go as soon as possible.

Just as serious was the danger to her own sense of self. Her art defined her—yet here she was, contemplating dawdling in London like some starry-eyed miss waiting around for the object of her affection to notice her, instead of setting out to do the work she loved, the work she'd been born to do.

Who would she be, if she lost herself? And how would she manage, if she gave up her heart to a man who would satisfy but never love her?

Before she could further mull over those unanswerable questions, Ben walked in, looking splendid in his formal evening attire. 'Still looking at the prints?' he teased. 'Although I suppose I should encourage you. You spend so much time gazing at them, you'll never be ready to leave on your expedition and I'll get to keep you longer in London.'

He came over to help her place the print carefully back in the tin. Once the lid was in place, she reached up to give him a hug. 'What a wonderful present! I shall never tire of looking at them. Though I do need to depart shortly. The last few sketches I need are of rare migrant species who only visit English shores for a short time each winter. When he accepted my proposal for the collection, the publisher specifically noted that he would not publish the volume unless he could include those images.'

Ben nodded. 'Then, regretfully, we must get you on your way as soon as possible. Russell says the coach is ready.'

'Yes. The provisions have arrived, I've mapped out the route and, using your guidebook, chosen inns along the way. It only remains to get to it.'

'I know what I want to get to,' he murmured, nibbling the tip of her ear.

She should pull away—but soon enough, she'd be on a long, lonely journey without him. So she leaned into him, rubbing her torso against his, feeling the burn of the fabric against her sensitised nipples. Feeling his hardness surge against her. 'I suppose there's no way we could cry off tonight's party?'

After holding her pressed against him for a few more beguiling minutes, he sighed and pushed her back. 'Miss the rout Lady Sayleford is giving specifically in our honour? Our lives wouldn't be worth a farthing. I'd have to resign from Parliament and flee with you to the Outer Hebrides.'

'I suppose we'd better leave, then. Will we have to stand in the reception line?'

'I'm afraid so. Brace yourself, my sweet. There will be music, I'm told, so at least I'll be able to dance with you.'

'At the rout—and later. I had some riding in mind, too.'

Heat flamed in his green eyes. 'I'll hold you to that. Now, minx, we must be off.'

Several hours later, Alyssa sat in the ladies' retiring room, having Lady Sayleford's maid stitch up a bit of lace that had pulled loose from her hem when an inept gentleman trod on it. They were to play a waltz soon, Lady Sayleford had told her, and she wanted to dance it with Ben.

For someone who tried to avoid society parties, she had to concede this rout had been rather enjoyable. Of course, Lady Sayleford's wine and refreshments were excellent and her guests chosen judiciously to include men from government and finance, landowners of skill and enterprise, and ladies who complemented them. The conversation had been about the changes being proposed in Parliament, or the most advanced methods of improving land, or spirited discussions of the current offerings at the theatre. Not even the ladies resorted to prosing on about fashion, jewellery, or the latest *on dit*.

'I think that's done it, ma'am,' the maid said.

'Thank you, Mary.' After handing the girl a coin, Alyssa walked back down the hallway, intent on reaching the ballroom so she could find Ben before the orchestra struck up the waltz.

In her hurry, she was two steps into the salon adjoining the ballroom when she recognised Ben's tall figure and broad shoulders on the opposite side of the room. In the next instant, she realised there was a woman standing beside him...a very beautiful woman. Who had her hand on Ben's arm.

Fortunately, as he was facing away from her, Ben hadn't noticed her arrival—and the lady facing towards Alyssa was apparently too absorbed in their conversation to have noticed, either. Heart hammering in her throat, feeling like she'd been punched in the stomach, as Alyssa silently retreated, the music from the ballroom ceased. Not wanting to walk back down the hallway in the sudden quiet for fear her footsteps might draw their attention, she slipped behind one of the twin Corinthian columns that set off the entrance to the salon.

Out of sight but not, unfortunately, out of hearing.

'You might have warned me you were getting married,' the lady said. 'I was shocked when Darlington told me. And what's this folderol Lady Sayleford's been putting out about a secret love-match?'

'You'd better ask Lady Sayleford.'

The lady wrinkled her delicate nose. 'Discreet as ever, I see. But really, Ben, Lady Alyssa Lambornne? Two Seasons and both disasters! No wit, no style! I am disappointed in you.'

'Now, Cressida, you know I won't discuss my wife with you.'

'So, does this mean there will be no more carousing with the Honourable Christopher Lattimar? Oh, how the ladies are going to weep!'

He shrugged. 'I've had my time to carouse. One grows out of it, I suppose.'

'Perhaps. But not out of the need for…satisfaction. One only becomes more discreet.'

'You would know, my dear.'

'Yes, I would, wouldn't I? So I hope you won't abandon your…particular friends.'

'I don't think I'll have time for that, with Parliament beginning.'

'Parliament won't be in session for ever. Just don't keep me waiting too long.'

Tapping his arm with her fan, the lady started to walk away. 'Don't bother waiting for me, Cressida,' Ben said after her. 'Not when there are so many other conquests to be made.'

'But few so splendid.' With that, the dark-haired lady blew him a kiss and returned to the ballroom.

What did they say about eavesdroppers never liking what they hear? Not that she'd intended to eavesdrop. Still feeling sick, Alyssa felt unable to move a muscle—until a hand placed on her shoulder made her jump.

'Don't worry about Lady Darlington,' Lady Sayleford said in her ear. 'She's ancient history, my dear.'

'She looked rather like current events to me,' Alyssa replied.

'That's just Tawny being gallant. He's always gentle with the ladies—though you will note, he gave her no encouragement.'

Before she could reply, possibly hearing Lady Sayleford's carrying voice, Ben turned and looked in their direction. She could easily imagine what he read in her face.

She didn't want to talk to him—not now. Clamping

her hand on Lady Sayleford's arm, she said brightly, 'Everyone has been raving about your crab canapés, but I've not had one yet. Would you show me where they are?'

'Of course, my dear.' As they proceeded into the salon, Lady Sayleford said, 'I'm taking your wife into the refreshment room, Tawny. Why don't you fetch her a glass of wine and join us there?'

'Of course, Lady Sayleford,' Ben replied, his voice sounding perfectly normal—she couldn't tell about his expression, since she was avoiding looking at him. 'Would you like a glass as well?'

'Yes, please. And do make sure no one *waylays* you before you bring them.'

'I will take care, ma'am.'

With the din of music and conversation, the press of guests and the other Hellions present to chat with, Alyssa had time to compose herself for the talk with Ben she knew would be coming. It wasn't until they'd thanked Lady Sayleford, bid everyone goodbye and climbed into the coach that they were finally alone.

The drive to Queen Street being short, Alyssa thought Ben might wait until they arrived home to broach the subject. Instead, he turned to her the moment the groom shut the door behind them.

'I know how it might have looked, but let me assure you, Lyssa, I'm not involved with Lady Darlington.'

'But you were at one time.'

Sighing, he nodded. 'Yes, I was at one time.'

'And she would like to renew the acquaintance.'

'Perhaps. Cressida Darlington lives to entice men—the result of wedding a much older and rather uninterested husband. But the important fact is that *I* don't wish to renew the acquaintance.' He reached over to tip up her chin, so she had to look in his eyes. 'There is only one woman I want in my life and in my bed. You, Lyssa. You believe me, don't you?'

His expression was absolutely sincere and he'd never lied to her. 'Yes, I believe you.'

He blew out a sigh. 'Thank heaven you're so sensible! I'd hate to think we were going to waste the precious few days you have left in London with you angry with me.'

Though Alyssa smiled, she wanted to say that maybe she wasn't so sensible. Not that she was angry—how could she be, when she'd given him permission to do whatever he wished?

*You don't want anyone else now...but what of later?* The words clawed at her throat, wanting escape. Before she could decide whether or not to release them, the coach rolled to a stop before their town house.

'Would you like some wine before we go up?' he asked after they'd mounted the steps and given the butler their wraps. When she shook her head, he said, 'Good. I'm ready to retire now.'

He took her arm and led her up to her chamber, leaving briefly for Molly to relieve her of her elaborate ball gown while Russell helped him out of his evening clothes. Just as Molly began brushing out her hair, he strode back in.

Taking the brush from the maid, he said, 'I'll finish that. Go along to bed.'

For long minutes after the maid departed, there was no sound but the crackle of the fire and the rasp of the brush through her hair.

*Time is short...don't waste it*, she told herself as she let the soothing sensations wash away her tension, distress and uncertainty. She wouldn't worry about later. Ben was hers *now* and she would enjoy that to the fullest.

So when he put down the brush and bent to kiss her, she met his lips with all the ardency within her, delving into his mouth, teasing and tantalising his tongue with hers, until he groaned and picked her up and carried her to the bed.

And then there was nothing but him, and her, and bliss.

Alyssa woke in the greyness before dawn, barely enough daylight in the chamber for her to make out the outlines of the furniture—and Ben, sleeping beside her.

Tenderly she touched his cheek. He murmured and stirred, but didn't waken.

No wonder. Perhaps he'd been thinking about her leaving and wanted to make each moment memorable, or perhaps their talk about Lady Darlington had unsettled him, too, for their first lovemaking had been fast, and hard, almost desperate. And then slow, gentle, exquisitely tender, as he touched and caressed the areas experience had taught him brought her the greatest pleasure, until she was almost weeping with the intensity and beauty of it.

As she lay wrapped in his arms afterward, he told her quietly how proud he was of her talent, how much joy she'd brought to his life and how much he was going to miss her.

The temptation swept through her to bring up the matter of her promise to him, confess that she'd reconsidered the matter, and, if he didn't mind too much, would like to rescind it. And then she would remember again how faithfully he'd kept all his promises to her and hesitate.

It hadn't been a wise promise to make. But, caught up in the euphoria of finally being able to pursue her art, to travel freely whenever and wherever she wished, how was she to have guessed how much Ben Tawny would come to possess her mind and thoughts and soul, as well as her body?

*Giving yourself up to passion needn't rob you of anything*, he'd told her as she lay in his arms that first night in Devon. *It could make complete something you didn't even realise you were missing.*

It had certainly done the latter. But though it hadn't entirely robbed her of her desire to devote herself to painting and exploring, it had certainly muted it.

If she asked Ben to reconsider and he agreed to change the terms between them, she would be removing the last barrier, forcing her to be cautious and hold on to herself as an independent woman. Without that, it would be all too easy to lose herself in him—and who would she be then?

Before she took such a step, she needed to think over all the implications very carefully. And to consider the question dispassionately, she needed to get away from Ben's mesmerising presence.

Her provisions and her art supplies were already packed. There was no reason she couldn't leave immediately. And so many reasons why lingering any longer would be dangerous.

Silently Alyssa slipped from bed, took pen and paper from her desk and wrote Ben a note of farewell. Then, gathering her travelling clothes from the wardrobe, she tiptoed out of the chamber into her dressing room, and rang the bell pull to summon her maid. As soon as she was dressed, she'd roust out the grooms and the coachman.

And set out for the coast before the longings of her heart prompted her to stay.

## *Chapter Seventeen*

Three days later, Ben sat at his desk in the fading light of early evening. The previous day, Giles had sent all the Hellions a note cancelling their scheduled meeting, along with the joyful news that his wife was increasing, but not feeling well. He'd promised to contact them again soon to arrange another meeting, to continue their planning—and help him celebrate.

Which must be why, Ben thought, looking down as the note in his hand, the upcoming meeting had been set for tonight, in their old room at the Quill and Gavel rather than at Giles and Maggie's town house. The taproom was nearby to assist in the celebrations, and an ailing Maggie wouldn't have to play hostess.

Even so, Ben had mixed feelings about returning there. On the one hand, until Giles and Maggie married and the group availed themselves of the hospitality of her home, the public house had been their normal meeting place, where the Hellions had hammered out details of the Reform Bill—an achievement Ben recalled with great pride and satisfaction. But it was also the site of that infamous gathering where Denbry had proposed his wager to ruin Alyssa, setting in motion events that had taken control of his life out of Ben's hands and changed it for ever.

Though he'd expected to feel satisfaction that he'd heeded the voice of honour and married Alyssa, he'd also expected to feel some anger and irritation at no longer being able to openly pursue whatever—or whomever—he chose. The wedding, the journey after and his absorption in getting to know and seduce his bride had put those feelings on hold—he'd thought. But his encounter with Lady Darlington the other night confirmed what he'd already known on some unconscious level: he really wasn't interested in pursuing other women. Not now, at any rate.

With Alyssa such a sumptuous lover, he didn't need or want any other woman in his bed. Nor could he imagine that another woman could amuse, stimulate and encourage him as well as Alyssa.

Sighing, he glanced at the note she'd left after her sudden departure. At first, he'd been surprised and alarmed that she'd departed without a goodbye. But after she'd detailed her reasons, he couldn't help but agree. Leaving became more difficult the longer she put it off, she wrote; she dreaded bidding him farewell and, with all in readiness, found it easier just to go. After all, during that last night together they had expressed everything that needed to be said without words.

She was right. If she'd waited to see him, he'd just have been tempted to tease her to linger and she had sketches to complete. He should occupy himself in the interim in hunting up that agent he volunteered to find, someone who could enthusiastically represent the great work she had undertaken. Few other individuals, he thought with pride, possessed the talent to accomplish what she was doing.

Besides, the sooner she left, the sooner she would be back again.

On that cheering note, he rose and headed to his chamber. He'd don greatcoat and hat and proceed to the public house. The meeting wouldn't begin for some time yet, but arriving early would allow him to organise his thoughts—and get him out of a place where everything reminded him of Alyssa.

Amazing how quickly her scent and presence had come to permeate the very bricks of that Queen Street town house.

A short time later, a full mug of ale on the table before him, Ben sat in the upper chamber at the Quill and Gavel. Somewhat to his surprise, none of the other Hellions had arrived yet. He was beginning to suspect he'd misread the time—Giles's assistant must have penned the note, for the handwriting was unfamiliar to him—but unfortunately, he hadn't brought it with him.

He'd about decided to go hunt up Christopher when the door opened. Rather than one of his friends, a scantily clad young female waltzed in.

'There you are, darlin',' she said, coming to him with a smile. 'Didn't mean to leave you waitin' so long.'

Ben rose and gave her a polite smile in return. 'Sorry, miss, but you must have the wrong chamber. We're about to convene a political meeting here.'

'It that what they're calling it now? If the other gents are as handsome as you, luv, doing "politics" will be a rare pleasure.'

Before Ben could imagine what she intended, the

harlot pushed him back into his chair and hopped on to his lap, her skirts hiking up as she straddled him. Grabbing his head with both hands in a surprisingly strong grip, she pressed her lips to his.

More amused than concerned, Ben put his hands on hers, turning his head away from her kiss while he tried to work her fingers loose without hurting her. 'I appreciate your ardour, miss, but it's—'

Before he could complete the sentence, the door burst open. A bevy of gentleman ran in, laughing, trailed by a man with a pen and sketchbook—and Lord Denbry.

'Ben Tawny, back to his old pursuits!' the Earl said with a sneer. 'Guess the shine has worn off the wedding ring already.'

'You arranged this,' Ben said, trying to control an immediate flare of anger—and a tiny niggle of panic. Alyssa had been quite sensible about disregarding Lady Darlington's advances—but a further incident might shake her confidence in him. 'Very well, you've had your fun. Take the girl and go.'

'In good time. But not before we get an image to immortalise the scene.' He gestured to the man leaning against the door frame, tracing in his sketchbook. 'Ralph Winsted. One of the best broadside artists around. What shall we title this one, Ralph? How about "Newly Wed Member of Parliament Cavorting With a Tart"? That should amuse your friends in the Commons. It will make quite an impression in the district of Launton, too, don't you think?'

He snapped his fingers. With a whispered, 'Sorry, sir', the girl clambered off Ben's lap and hurried out of the room.

Ben recognised Denbry's associates, most of them very drunk, as they slapped each other on the back, shook hands, or tippled from the bottles they carried.

'Good one, Denbry!' one cried.

'That'll make up for Dornton,' another said.

While Rossiter added, 'Can't wait to see it posted all over London. You took the dowry that should have been mine; now Denbry will take care of your reputation.'

'Yes, that should even the score for Dornton—and Devon,' the Earl said, the gaze he fixed on Ben a mingling of loathing and triumph. 'I promised you'd be sorry, didn't I?'

His mind working furiously to sort out all the implications, Ben met Denbry's gaze with one just as hard, until Denbry looked away first.

'All right, lads, time to move on to the next amusement,' the Earl said, herding his followers out of the room. 'Though nothing will top the satisfaction of this. I think we can agree I'm the final winner of *this* wager, eh, Tawny?' he said, turning back to Ben. 'Or should I refer to you as the *former* Member of Parliament from Launton?'

Chuckling, he strolled out.

For several long minutes, Ben didn't even move, as he struggled to suppress the anger and turn his energy to deciding how to limit the damage.

Four viewpoints would be better than one.

No wonder he hadn't recognised the handwriting on the note. But although Giles had evidently not called a meeting, Ben was about to convene one for perhaps the most important strategy session they'd ever conducted. With his political future, and perhaps his marriage, hanging in the balance.

* * *

After dispatching Russell to Upper Brook Street to warn Giles of the impending arrival of the Hellions, Ben spent two hours tracking Davie down at a family party and extracting Christopher from the arms of his current lovely. Finally, three hours after Denbry had sprung his trap, Ben and his friends were gathered in Giles's library, Ben pacing as he related the lurid details.

Holding up a hand to silence the curses that erupted when Ben finished, Giles said, 'Let's dispense with commenting on the vileness of Denbry's character, a point on which we all agree, and proceed to assess how best to counter this assault on Ben.'

'Any chance of buying off the artist or publisher?' Christopher asked.

'Probably not,' Ben said. 'With the public's insatiable appetite for scandal, the publisher knows he'll be able to sell out a large print run. Nor are they worried about being hit with a suit for slander; Denbry was clever there. I may have been set up, but I can't claim the image is false; half-a-dozen witnesses can testify they saw it happen.'

'We'll need to go to the party leaders first thing tomorrow, before they can print and distribute the broadside,' Davie said. 'By then, we'll have thought of something they can reply to any enquiries they get.'

'Probably best that they make no comment at all, since the facts can't be disputed,' Giles said.

'You're right, they will probably decide to wait and see how much uproar this causes,' Davie agreed.

'To see whether I've become too much of a liability to continue to support,' Ben added bitterly. 'Damn and blast, it was bad enough to be thought a despoiler of innocents. But to be seen publically cavorting with harlots within a month of my wedding—how could any rational man not doubt my claims to value the worth and dignity of all, when I seem to display such poor taste and bad judgement?'

'Any chance of getting the girl to testify she was paid—or coerced—into doing this?' Davie asked.

'How do you find one tart among so many in the London underworld?' Ben said. 'Besides, the girl would probably refuse, fearing retribution from Denbry—or from the man who manages her, whom Denbry paid to have her do it.'

Christopher straightened, his eyes alight with sudden enthusiasm. 'Maybe it's not so impossible. You all remember my mother's friend, Ellie Parmenter? Long-time mistress of old Lord Summerville, who passed away this fall? Left her well enough situated, my mother said, that she's not looking for a new protector. Instead, to Mama's great amusement, she is quietly assisting girls who want to leave the life. Knows her way around the pleasure districts of London. If there is a chance of finding the girl, Ellie might be able to do it.'

'Would she do it?' Giles asked. 'Ben is right; the girl would be reluctant to speak, knowing the consequences. If Ellie persuades her, offering to protect her if she testifies, she could make herself some unpleasant enemies.'

Christopher shrugged. 'I've known her since before I went to Oxford. As I vaguely recollect, there was something off in how Summerville came to claim her to begin with—she was the daughter of gentleman who hadn't funds to pay a debt and he took her instead, or something. Which might explain her current occupation. If she were a victim of injustice herself, she'd be even more interested in righting the wrong done to Ben.'

'It's certainly worth exploring. But I also think—Maggie, my dear, what are you doing awake?' Giles said, jumping up to meet the lady who'd just entered the study.

'I heard voices,' she said, leaning into her husband's embrace.

'So sorry to have disturbed you, Maggie,' Davie said. 'Please accept our congratulations on your splendid news!'

'Thank you,' she said, pinking with pleasure as Ben and Christopher added their good wishes. 'We're both delighted. Although I'm not pleased to appear such a poor honey, my husband feels compelled to cancel meetings. But such serious expressions! What's amiss?'

'I admit, we would all appreciate your advice on a rather delicate problem. Are you sure you feel well enough to remain?' Giles asked anxiously.

'I think I can promise not to lose my dinner—as long as you don't wave wine fumes under my nose,' she added, pushing away the glass Christopher was about to offer. 'I will take your armchair, though.'

After Maggie had seated herself and tartly told her husband to stop fussing, Ben proceeded to relate his present difficulties.

'Infamous!' Maggie declared. 'How I should like to give Denbry back some of his own! Ben, isn't your father acquainted with Denbry's father? I shall have to ask Papa. But for the near term—you need to visit your district, Ben. Preferably before the broadsheets can be distributed.'

'I was about to recommend the same thing,' Giles said.

'If I weren't feeling so poorly, I would go with you.

Although,' she said, looking back at Ben, 'my presence wouldn't help much; the people of your district don't know me. The female you need beside you, strongly refuting the image in the broadside, is your wife.'

The idea both cheered—and saddened—Ben. 'I'd love to have her beside me, but that's not possible. For one, she's already left London on a sketching expedition to finish the drawings essential to meeting the publisher's deadline. If she misses that, he can pull out on his offer to publish the book. Nor would I wish to embroil her in so tawdry a scandal. Besides, she's been clear from the beginning that she had no desire to play the politician's wife.' He gave Maggie an apologetic look. 'I more or less promised her that you would take on any political hostess duties I needed.'

'Under ordinary circumstances, I would be happy to. But nothing could do more to counter the impression created by the broadside than having your wife go with you to tour Launton. The party leaders will be watching, too, you can be assured.'

If he lost the confidence of the leadership…if they considered his support a detriment to the reform cause, he'd be pushed out of any chance to make his voice heard, to make a difference. In that case, he might as well not stand for re-election, regardless of what the electors of his district thought.

What would he do then? Slink away to the acres his father had promised? If, after the scandal, the Viscount still supported him. But what of the work that had occupied his heart and his life for almost ten years?

For the first time, he fully understood why Alyssa had been ready to throw away her reputation and any chance of marriage, if it meant she could do the work she felt she'd been born for.

'You know where she will be and when?' Maggie's voice recalled him.

'Yes,' Ben admitted.

'Then write to her! Surely she can spare a few weeks, when it might mean rescuing your career!'

'At the cost of hers?'

'You could at least write and ask her,' Maggie countered.

'It's my career. My problem. My scandal,' Ben said, unable to put into words why he felt so strongly about not pulling Alyssa away from her endeavour. 'I agree, it would be wisest for me to set out for Launton without delay and speak to as many voters as possible before the broadsides appear. I've represented these people for seven years. By now, they should trust my word and my promises. If they don't believe me…' He shrugged. 'Maybe I shouldn't be their representative.'

Maggie shook her head. 'I think you're being foolishly stubborn.'

Giles put a restraining hand on his wife's arm. 'It is his problem, though, Maggie love. We can offer advice, but Ben must do what he feels is best for him. So, off to Launton then, as soon as you can get away?'

'Yes. Tomorrow, if I can manage it.'

'I'll talk with Ellie,' Christopher said. 'Even if she can find the girl, it won't be soon enough to stop the presses. But we might be able to get a retraction—or have the publisher issue a follow-on broadside. "Dissolute Marquess's Son Hires Prostitute to Discredit Respectable Member of Parliament."'

'That ought to appeal to the publisher,' Davie observed. 'He could reissue the first, sell them in pairs and double his profit.'

'You'll at least think about writing to Alyssa?' Maggie asked. 'She's your wife. She would want to know.'

'I'll think about it,' he promised. 'Now, if I'm to be off to Launton tomorrow, I'd better start making preparations. Thanks to all of you for gathering on short notice and offering your advice.'

Giles waved off his gratitude. 'We Hellions always guard each other's backs.'

Giving Ben's shoulder a pat, his friends bid their host and hostess good night and left the study.

'If you think of anything else we can do, you'll let us know?' Davie asked as they paused on the street outside the town house.

'Of course.'

'Then best of luck.'

With that, the men set off in different directions, Ben walking slowly back towards Queen Street.

Later, as he packed his belongings and sent Russell off to arrange for a coach, Ben considered again Maggie's plea that he write Alyssa. He felt more discouraged than he'd wanted to admit to the Hellions, and knew he'd feel better with his wife beside him. It shocked him a little to realise that despite *their* support and encouragement, he felt so keenly the lack of Alyssa's.

Because her heart and soul were more closely in tune with his—even closer than the men who'd been as dear as family to him for fifteen years?

Because he loved her?

Taking a long, slow breath, he let himself explore the idea that he might be in love with his wife. Somehow, facing the potential ruin of his career, the possibility that he might have made himself vulnerable by falling in love no longer seemed so threatening.

Why had he been holding back, keeping his heart close, hesitant to make that final commitment? This was Alyssa, not some aristocrat who would abandon him for title and position, leaving him bereft. Loving her placed him in no danger—no more danger than anyone who loves and can be devastated by loss.

If he were honest, he'd probably lost his heart long ago, somewhere on the road to Cornwall and back, when the engaging, surprising, mischievous woman chance had led him to marry had shown him depth of her passion and the power of her understanding.

Did she love him? She was fond of him and admired him, he knew. The urge to ask her at the next opportunity bubbled up and he repressed it. Like passion, if love had come to her, he would have to let her find that truth and admit it in her own time, as he had. She was at heart an artist, who needed to be independent to do her work, who would feel threatened if he tried to force her into admitting affection—or fitting into the role of a politician's wife.

Asking her to travel back from the coast and accompany him on a tour through his district would consume weeks. Quite probably, the rare migrant birds the publisher insisted must be included in her work would have left their winter grounds by then. She'd lose her chance to get her collection published.

He couldn't ask her to do that.

No matter how much he missed her. No matter how helpful it would be to have her in Launton. No matter how much he yearned to have her affirm, not just admiration, but love.

If he wanted her love, he would have to prove his own, by giving her what she'd wanted most when she agreed to marry him—the freedom to pursue her art.

And if he could not surmount the scandal, lost his seat and his influence, could Alyssa love a man who'd failed to achieve *his* purpose?

Damping down despair at the thought of forfeiting her esteem for ever, Ben set his jaw and strapped up his trunk.

Despite Maggie's advice, he would not write to Alyssa.

# Chapter Eighteen

A week later, hat in hand while the assistant she'd hired carried her art supplies, Alyssa returned to the inn in the village near Liverpool she'd made her base for this series of sketches along the coast. Though they normally wintered further to the north, she'd hoped to find some Bernacles, Brent Geese, or Wild Swan, the swan being one bird particularly desired by the publisher.

No luck so far on the swan, but she had been delighted to find a flock of Sea Crows on her excursion today. If she could find one or two more of these visitors from the far north of Europe, she'd be content to return to London. Many of the other winter travellers could be found in the environs of the capital, which would allow her to complete all the sketches she needed—without having to deprive herself of Ben's company.

What would he doing now? she wondered. Probably with the other Hellions, perfecting their strategy for winning over any recalcitrant members of the House, so they might get their bill passed in the next session. How proud and happy they would be to see the culmination of all their years of hard work.

How proud she was of Ben. Smiling, she recalled the intensity of his expression as he explained to her and her mother the various reforms they hoped to implement—one of them benefiting the folk right here in Liverpool. Ridiculous that a city of many thousands had no representation in Parliament!

'Mrs Tawny, a letter for you,' the innkeeper called, halting her as she was about to mount the steps to her room.

News from Ben? The idea of him reaching out to her, even via letter, sent a ripple of pure happiness through her. 'Thank you, Mr Cleveland,' she said as he handed it to her.

To her surprise—and disappointment—the hand that had written her name on the folded missive was feminine. And not her mother's. Wondering who else might want to reach her—and would know how and where to reach her—she hurried up to her chamber.

Instructing the maid to set down her supplies and take some rest, Alyssa shut the door behind her, tossed off gloves and bonnet, and broke the seal. To discover that her correspondent was Lady Lyndlington.

*Forgive me for taking the liberty of contacting you, but a situation has developed of which I think you should be aware and I don't believe Ben will tell you about it.*

Trepidation filling her, Alyssa took a seat, rapidly reading as Maggie described Ben's entrapment by Denbry at the Quill and Gavel. Anguish and fury filling her, she paused to look sightlessly out the window.

Would her reckless desire to confront that man never stop wreaking havoc with Ben's career? She read on.

> *Having his wife support him as he tours his district is perhaps the most effective response he can make to the negative image the broadside will portray. If he cannot overcome that and loses the confidence of his electors—or of the party leaders—it could cripple a career filled with so much promise.*
>
> *It is presumptuous of me to write you something that should more properly have come from Ben. But he feels so keenly your need to complete your own work that he did not want you to know, lest you feel obligated to support him at the expense of your own project. However, I feel that as an independent woman it should be* your *choice whether you stay to complete your work, or go to assist him.*
>
> *You may protest that you do not know politics, aren't clever at polite conversation with strangers and don't think your presence would be much help. Let me assure you, the best way to refute the vile rumours is for electors to see a wife standing beside her husband, the obvious affection between them impossible to deny.*
>
> *I hope you will forgive my interference and know that all the Hellions will support you, whatever you decide.*

Alyssa read the note through again before putting on the table with trembling hands.

Dear Ben, who took his promise not to impede her

work so seriously, he would protect her by refusing to tell her about this threat to his own. But Maggie was right. It should be *her* choice.

How could she make it? Miss this final deadline and the publisher was under no further obligation to her. The portfolio of sketches she'd been so painstakingly accumulating, that Ben's generosity in turning over her aunt's bequest and his understanding in allowing her to travel and work at will, would remain nothing more than that—a portfolio of sketches relegated to a cabinet, never to be brought out as a published manuscript that would illuminate British birds in colour, as Audubon had highlighted the birds of America.

And yet, if she did not go to Ben's side, he might lose the power to influence and shape government in new directions, the goal that had fired him heart and soul for the last ten years.

If she lost for ever her chance to be an independent artist, valued for work done in her own right… who would she be? Like most women, just a helpmate to a husband's career and ambitions?

Anguished, she put her head in her hands, impossibly torn.

But then, as she forbade herself to give way to tears, she heard a still, small voice telling her not to be a fool. Why was she trying to deceive herself? She shouldn't hide the truth behind platitudes about the contribution he could make to government being of so much greater importance to the nation than publishing her smattering of sketches.

In her heart, she'd known at least from that last morning in London that her choice had already been made. Much as she'd counselled herself to hold back and not cede all of her heart to Ben, she'd lost it anyway. The sharpness of the pain she felt at imagining him stripped of his power and his dream were proof of that.

A strong, independent woman could choose to put her own dreams on hold, to safeguard the future of the man she loved. And when had she come to think that her entire identity as an artist must be wrapped up in the publication of this one book? Was that not vainglory, wanting the pride of knowing she had done what few women had achieved, rather than joy in the work itself?

Nothing could take away her ability to draw and sketch, or make her subsume it in being only a wife. Surely there were other avenues in which she might express her artistic soul besides producing a limited edition of expensive prints. She had only to put her mind to considering how.

She should be the bold, independent woman Maggie called her to be. A woman unafraid to admit her love for Ben, to demand that the terms of their agreement be changed and to embrace the joy and companionship he offered, even if he never offered love.

She' always thought she'd loved Will, but compared to the vastness of the emotion now filling her, she realised it had been more gratitude for his recognition of her work and the excitement of a man's admiration.

Never had he touched her as Ben had…and would.

Which meant, she thought, excitement filling her as she imagined being with him again, she'd better start packing for the journey to Hampshire.

Three days later, a discouraged Ben stood outside the Hasty Farmer in the village of Ailnthorpe, trying to hold on to his temper as he endured a tongue-lashing from the wife of one of the town's electors. 'Disgraceful, that's what it is!' she ranted, a copy of Denbry's infamous broadside clutched in her plump fist. 'Promising us all manner of things, telling us how hard you'll be working in Parliament, then spending your time in London cavorting with harlots!'

'Let me say again, Mr and Mrs Winstead,' he said, dredging up the patience to repeat the speech he'd made times out of mind the last six days—with varying degrees of success. 'That broadside was created to discredit me. Have I not worked hard for you in Parliament? Are we not standing on the cusp of creating a new era of representation, demolishing the old rotten boroughs and giving a fair voice to all the people? I ask that you hold fast to the trust you placed in me, the trust I feel seven years of work have earned, and look beyond this crude attempt to blacken my reputation.'

The reaction had been worse than he'd anticipated, once the broadside had made its way on to print-shop windows throughout the borough of Launton. So negative, if it weren't for the important work he burned to continue—and his fury at having a reprobate like Denbry determine his fate—he might have given it up as a lost cause.

He intended to persevere, though. Even if some of the voters remained dubious about the truth of the broadside, if enough men believed him, he could remain in Parliament. Eventually time and newer scandals would relegate the allegations to the rubbish heap of old political disgraces.

No matter how much it sickened him to have such calumny attached to his name.

Pulled out of his grim reflections by a hand clasping his arm, he almost brushed it off, thinking at first it was Mrs Winstead, moving closer to reinforce her point. Until the fresh scent and the immediate tingling of his skin under her touch told him the woman who'd slipped beside was, unbelievably—Alyssa?

Tucking her arm tightly in his, she said, 'I couldn't help but overhear, ma'am, and I most earnestly ask you to reconsider! Why should you believe this vicious image, rather than trust in the hard work my husband has been doing these last seven years? Is it more logical to believe he would have shown one face to you in Launton and been an entirely different man in London—or to believe that opponents of the legislation he has worked so hard to bring about would take any means, no matter how vile, to discredit him—and halt the tide of change he wants to bring about?'

While Ben tried to get his mind around the incredible idea that, somehow, the wife he'd thought to be sketching rare birds on the western coast was standing here beside him, defending him to a voter's outraged spouse, Mrs Winstead's eyes widened. 'You're his *wife*, you say?'

'Yes, ma'am, Alyssa Tawny, and pleased to make your acquaintance,' Alyssa said, shaking the hand of the suspicious woman. 'As you well know, ma'am, we women have little power—at least, until some session hence, when my husband lobbies to extend us the vote,' she added, giving Ben a brilliant smile. 'Many times, the only way we can express our pain or outrage is to stay home and do nothing. Even if I were a meek, obedient wife—which my husband would assure you I am *not*—do you really think I would come out and openly support a man who would humiliate me by entertaining harlots barely a month after our wedding?'

'*I'd* be hiding my head in shame, were such a man *my* husband,' Mrs Winstead declared, giving Ben a baleful glance.

'Exactly!' Alyssa replied. 'If it were true, why would Mr Tawny come here and face you, opening himself to criticism and condemnation? It would be smarter to remain in London and wait for the scandal to blow over.'

Appearing struck by that insight, Mr Winstead nodded. 'Yes, that would make sense.'

'Why is it that those who are evil cannot stand to see those who work for good succeed? That somehow, to justify their own petty meanness, they must seek to pull everyone down to their tawdry level? It near breaks my heart that a man as honourable and compassionate as my dear husband has been targeted like this! I am sure, Mrs Winstead, that *you* never put credence in idle gossip, nor pass on malicious rumours. I am sure you and your husband are just as outraged as I am by this slander and will do all you can to refute it. I can count on you, can I not?' she asked, looking up at the Winsteads imploringly.

Ben had never been able to withstand a plea from those magnificent brown eyes. Apparently Mr Winstead wasn't proof against them, either.

'Bless you, little lady, for coming to support your husband,' Winstead said. 'Of course we will tell everyone you've come to help Mr Tawny confront and deny the story in the broadsheet. Won't we, Mrs W.?'

Though his wife seemed made of stronger stuff, eventually she gave Alyssa a stiff nod. 'Hate to see a wife embarrassed by her husband's behaviour,' she allowed, still giving Ben a suspicious look. 'Aye, I'll be happy to tell everyone you are here, defending him.'

'Thank you, Mrs Winstead. That's all I ask—that you give him a fair hearing and make your own decision. I do appreciate you taking the time to talk with us.'

'My pleasure, Mrs Tawny,' Winstead said. 'Right eloquent little wife you've got yourself there, Mr Tawny,' he added to Ben before tipping his hat to Alyssa.

'She is a treasure,' Ben said with heartfelt emphasis.

With that, the couple nodded and continued down the street.

As soon as they turned the corner, Ben seized Alyssa in a hug. Oblivious to the gawking patrons in the Hasty Farmer and the passers-by on the street, he drew her close and kissed her with all the passion, longing, despair and frustration built up in their ten days apart.

'That's the way to support your man,' one of the patrons called from within the public house.

'Someone oughta sketch that picture and put it on a broadside,' another remarked.

Laughing, Ben linked his arm with Alyssa's and led her away to the barkeep's observation that he'd got himself a proper good politician's wife.

Once they were a good ways down the street, out of hearing of anyone in the Hasty Farmer, Ben stopped. 'Where? How?'

Alyssa chuckled. 'I've settled my entourage at the Royal Crown, at the other end of the village. Let's go to my chamber and I'll explain everything.'

Ben might be filled with elation, gratitude and puzzlement, but once in a chamber alone with Alyssa, there was only one thing he needed as much as breathing.

'Explanations later,' he said as soon as they'd closed

the door behind them. Branding her with a kiss, he picked her up and carried her to the bed.

A long, satisfying interval later, Ben reclined against the pillows, a naked Alyssa in his arms. After giving her a sip from the glass of wine he'd poured them, he said, 'Now, tell me how you got here and why.'

'Maggie wrote me what had happened. She thought I should get to decide whether to leave Liverpool and come assist you. Much as I esteem you for not wanting to force me into making a choice, she was right.'

'I can't tell you how much your support means to me. What it felt like to hear you so valiantly defending me.' *For a man who'd grown up so often hearing himself maligned.* 'You saw yourself how effective it was in swaying a hostile voter. And you say you have no political instincts?'

'I had no strategy,' she said, snuggling into him. 'I just spoke the truth.'

'But what about your sketches? The deadline? If you lose the opportunity to publish your work, I shall feel terrible, knowing I am responsible.'

'If you want to debate responsibility, then in truth, it is mine. Had I not been determined to teach Denbry a lesson back at Dornton, your career would never have been threatened—*twice.* If the publisher holds fast to that deadline and I cannot meet it, so be it,' she said with a shrug. 'What you are doing is immensely important to the future of the country.'

'It may not shape the future of the electorate, but great art is important, too, to delight the eyes, soothe the spirit and elevate the mind,' he countered. 'Few are gifted with the talent you have to create such magnificent images. You need to publish that volume.'

'Perhaps. But while pondering the consequences of leaving Liverpool, I thought about what it means to me to be an artist. And I decided I'd been putting too much emphasis on that one work. Yes, it was a thrill, a dream that's inspired me for years, to think of having my drawings compared to Audubon's. But do I really want my work to reach only the rich, who will file away the volume in their libraries, where only a handful will ever see it? The impact of that scurrilous broadside has made me think that I'd rather reach a much broader audience, like Bewick did with his book. And do it under my own name, not masquerading as a man to please a publisher.' She chuckled. 'Just think—the wife of a Member of Parliament *selling* drawings under her own name? How shocking! I wouldn't, of course, until this current scandal has been put to rest.'

'Whether it is or not, I still win. With you at my side, anything is possible. Nor do I ever want you to sacrifice who you are to support me. Watching you on the street today, taking on that strident woman…'

Now that the moment was here, a lifetime of caution tempted him to hold back. Fighting it, Ben made himself continue. 'I…I love you, Alyssa. I guess I've known it for a long time and was too afraid to admit it. I can't imagine having anyone else in my bed or in my life. I will do all I can to support and cherish you for the rest of yours.'

Tears sheened Alyssa's eyes as she looked up at him. 'Oh, Ben. How do you think I had the courage to risk my dream and come here? I love you, too, as frightening as it is to admit it.'

Scarcely daring to hope he'd heard her aright, Ben said, 'I guess, together, we can work through those fears.'

She nodded. 'You told me once I didn't need to be afraid to give myself to passion, that it wouldn't rob me of anything, but rather complete something I didn't even know I was missing. Love is that way, too. What I felt for Will is nothing compared to the height and depth and fullness of what I feel for you. My life is richer for walking beside you, having two dreams to fight for—yours as well as mine.'

The truth of her words resonated through him, filling the dark and lonely places where the mocked child had cowered, driving out the doubts of the young man who had set his face against love. 'Brilliant, as always, my darling,' Ben said, giving her another kiss. 'My life is richer with you beside me, fighting for both our dreams. And so we will continue to battle on, together.'

She smiled up at him. 'Together for ever,' she said and drew his head down for another kiss.

# *Epilogue*

Three weeks later, after a stay in Taunton that succeeded in convincing the majority of the voters that the broadside was a slander, Ben returned with Alyssa to London. Leaving her the first morning to complete some important business of his own, he returned to discover from the butler that his father had come calling.

For the first time in his life, warmth and anticipation, rather than anger and resentment, filled him at that news. Smiling, he stroke into the parlour where Alyssa was pouring tea.

And stopped short, seeing the black armband on his father's sleeve.

'Lady Chilton?'

His father nodded. 'Yes. A week ago.'

'I'm sorry, sir. A great loss.'

'She was as good a wife as she could be. The great sorrow of her life was her failure to give me a son. I never told her, but I didn't mind, for I already had a son. One who meant more to me than the title and estate that should have been my brother's. Now that she is beyond being hurt by it, I hope to see much more of that son.'

'That would please me, too...Father.'

'That was only part of the news that brought me here today,' Lord Chilton continued. 'I have other information that should please you both. Lady Lyndlington's father informed me of this nasty business with the broadside. One of her husband's friends *was* able to locate the girl involved, who is ready to testify to the truth of the incident. Since I was better acquainted with Denbry's father, Lord Barkley, I volunteered to inform him that unless Denbry commissioned a broadside retracting the slander, Lyndlington would sponsor one accusing his son of attempting to ruin Ben's reputation—and naming names. Appalled at the idea of having his family dragged through the mud to the amusement of the London rabble, he agreed to have the retraction printed. He also promised to send his son to supervise a remote estate in Scotland for a year, where he could set his hand to honest work and ponder his mistakes.' The Viscount chuckled. 'Up early, watching sheep, might make a man of him yet.'

'That is excellent news!' Alyssa cried.

The Viscount looked over at Ben and held his gaze. 'There's nothing I wouldn't do for my son.' After a moment, he continued, 'There was one other thing I wanted to...ask, however.'

To Ben, the Viscount had always been calm, controlled, commanding. He'd never seen him look so tentative and uncertain. Curious, he said, 'What is it?'

'I'll wait a decent interval—I owe that to Cecily and the girls. But after... I would like to call on your mother. I haven't seen her since before you were born. She might well slam the door in my face,' he observed wryly. 'But one faint hope has endured all these years—that some day I might have the chance to make her my wife.' He looked back at Ben. 'It can't make up for the years of scorn and isolation. And I wouldn't do it until the girls are settled. But I've never loved anyone else. If you don't object, I'd like to try.'

To become…a family of sorts. The very notion seemed odd, but like his rapprochement with his father, pleasing. 'I would not object.' Recalling what his mother had confided when he last saw her, he added, 'I don't think she'll slam the door in your face.'

Ben's father smiled. 'I hope not. And thank you. I'm off to the lawyers—all the tedious details in the wake of Cecily's death. But I think you can count on that business of the broadside being laid to rest and carry on with your plans in Parliament.'

Bowing to Alyssa, the Viscount walked out. Ben accompanied him to the door before returning to the parlour.

To his delight, Alyssa ran over to give him a hug. 'How wonderful to have that nasty business behind us! And to know that your father had a hand makes it even better!'

'You might save a bit of that approbation for your husband,' Ben said loftily.

'I thought I might demonstrate that…later,' Alyssa replied, rubbing against him.

Stifling a groan, amazed anew at how powerfully his body responded to her, he said, 'Continue that and I'll forget about the exciting news I have to convey.'

She stilled in his arms, as if contemplating the advantages and disadvantages. 'Very well, I'll stop…for now. Only because you've made me so curious. Oh, Ben!' she cried, her face lighting. 'Now that your name will be cleared, have you been tapped for some important governmental post?'

'Even better,' he replied, leading her back to the couch. 'You'll recall that I promised to find an agent to approach Waterman on your behalf. I decided to go myself. I called on him this morning.'

Her hands tightened on his. 'And?'

'I told him the deadline for submitting sketches would have to be extended, which shouldn't be a problem. Audubon continues to bring out a new folio every five or six months. There's no need to rush to begin a complementary line of British birds.'

'To which he replied?'

'At first, he was angry and irritated, saying he'd waited long enough to receive the project, he wasn't sure he still wished to take on so costly an endeavour and he intended to let the contract terminate on the agreed date. I told him that was fine and thanked him for his time.'

Alyssa grabbed his arm. 'You did what?'

'Thanked him. Because, I said, there were other publishers who would be prepared to offer more time and better terms. Whereupon, I gathered my hat and cane and started to walk out.'

'Other publishers?' she echoed. 'Had you contacted any—?'

'No,' Ben admitted. 'Not yet, anyway. Waterman caught me, begged me to take a chair and said perhaps we should reconsider. After all, he was the one who'd first taken interest and it was only fair he be allowed to continue. We had a nice little chat, the end result being he will take the sketches whenever you have them ready and earn twice the previous royalty.'

'Falsehoods again!' She shook her head wonderingly. 'You *know* there are no other publishers involved.'

'But there could be. I didn't lie, I just...worded my statement very carefully. After all, your drawings are wonderful. The project is bound to be a success. If, after I presented Waterman with "A" and "B"—'

'He erroneously arrived at "C", that's not your fault,' she quoted his explanation of his subterfuge in Dornton Village. Breaking into a peal of laughter, she seized him in a hug. 'How did I exist for so many years without you, Ben Tawny?'

'It's a mystery,' he said, kissing the top of her head. 'But you won't have to live without me ever again.'

She pushed him away, her eyes lighting. 'No! With the deadline extended, I can accompany you on your work and concentrate on finishing the sketches after Parliament adjourns. We can travel together, like we did to Cornwall.' Her eyes grew misty. 'Pursuing both our dreams, together.'

He'd been hoping she would want to arrange things that way, but would never have asked for it. A surge of joy and excitement swept through him as he imagined what a rich, full life they would have together. Could he ever get enough of this passionate, determined, talented lady?

'There is one other thing.' At her raised eyebrows, he continued, 'I told him the artist was my wife, Lady Alyssa Tawny. And that the book would be published under her name, or not at all. He sputtered a bit, until I reminded him what a scandal that would be, an earl's daughter being paid to publish a book—and how everyone in the *ton* would want a copy. Then he agreed to that, too.'

'To be recognised for my work—under my own name? Oh, Ben, what a wonderful rascal you are,' she whispered, tears gathering at the corners of her eyes. 'That demands a reward that cannot wait.'

'I was hoping you would say that,' he murmured. Clasping her hand, he led her up to their chamber.

* * * * *

*If you enjoyed this story, you won't want to miss the first two books in the* HADLEY'S HELLIONS *quartet from Julia Justiss*

*FORBIDDEN NIGHTS WITH THE VISCOUNT*

*STOLEN ENCOUNTERS WITH THE DUCHESS*

*The Earl of Penford knows his passion for Lorene Summerfield is scandalous, but when he's accused of her husband's murder, he must clear his name—and win her hand!*

*Read on for a sneak preview of* ***BOUND BY THEIR SECRET PASSION,*** *the final book in* **Diane Gaston***'s dazzling quartet* ***THE SCANDALOUS SUMMERFIELDS.***

Her old romantic dreams burst forth. Why hold back? Dell's kiss was even more than she could have imagined. Why not give herself to it?

She pulled off her bonnet and threw her arms around his neck, answering the press of his lips with eagerness. He urged her mouth open and she readily complied, surprised and delighted that his warm tongue touched hers.

He tasted wonderful.

She plunged her fingers into his hair, loving its softness and its curls. She liked his hair best when it looked tousled by a breeze. Or mussed by her hands.

He pressed her body against his and the thrill intensified. How marvelous to feel his muscles so firm against her. And more. One hand slid down from his hair to his arm to his hip. How wanton was that?

But she was a widow, was she not? Was not everyone telling her she had license to do as she pleased? It pleased her to touch him. Although she was not quite brazen enough to touch that hard part of him that thrilled her most of all.

"Lorene," he groaned as his hands pressed against her derriere, intensifying the sensations in all sorts of ways. "We should stop."

She did not want to stop. "Why?" She kissed his neck. "I am a widow. Are not widows permitted?"

"Do not tempt me," he said, though his hands caressed her.

She moved away, just enough that he could see her face. "If you do not want this, then, yes, we should stop, but I do desire it, Dell."

For a long time, she realized. Since she'd first met him. He was the man she had dreamed about in her youth, a good man, kind, honorable, handsome. But something more, something that made her want to bed him.





HHEXP0417

# Love the Harlequin book you just read?

Your opinion matters.

Review this book on your favorite book site, review site, blog or your own social media properties and share your opinion with other readers!